DIOR OR DIE

LAURA E. AKERS

ISBN 979-8-98532221-0-1 (eBook)

ISBN 979-8-98553221-1-8 or 979-8-98553221-5-6 (Paperback)

ISBN 979-8-9853221-2-5 (Hardback)

ISBN 979-8-9853321-4-9 (Large Print)

*For those who strive
to make the world a better place*

*Never interrupt your enemy
when he is making a mistake
- Sun Tzu, The Art of War*

*I hate when women wear
the wrong foundation color.
It might be the worst thing on the planet
- Kim Kardashian*

1

Four men shot at me with automatic rifles.

I sat in a chair blindfolded, arms bound behind me with duct tape, and a gag stuffed in my mouth. The relentless gunfire battered my senses.

Control the mind-game, Davia.

Forcing my hands into tight balls, I leaned forward and arched my back, preparing to free myself. In response, a bullet cracked one of my chair's legs, and I almost crashed to the ground.

This ordeal was a boys' club welcome to the first woman assigned to the most elite covert paramilitary team in existence. Of course, the team wouldn't greet me with candy and flowers, but *this*?

My face grew hot from suppressed fury as the rounds whizzed past unabated. I slowed my breathing. Four breaths in, four out. Again.

Finally, there was silence.

The malignant perfume of gunfire burned my nostrils. I listened for the click of empty magazines dropped and replaced. Instead, booming laughter and the dull thud of men slapping each other's backs echoed through the space.

"Let's give Glenn some time to sit in her messed drawers." It was

James Warden, my team's leader. When we met this morning at our training base in Virginia, he radiated Apex Alpha. Now, I amended it to Apex Asshat.

"We can tell the colonel we didn't hit the hostage," said another.

More guffaws.

After their voices drifted away, I renewed my efforts to break the bindings. Within minutes, I was loose. I spat the gag from my mouth and tore the blindfold from my eyes, temples throbbing. How long would it take my shattered hearing to return in full?

My location was a plywood shoot house with movable walls. Dummy targets riddled with bullet holes surrounded me, and spent brass casings blanketed the floor like a golden carpet. Crouching, I snuck to the door, flattened myself against the wall, and peeked out.

Another teammate, Savant, sat at a distant table under a canvas shade, headphones atop his mop of fair hair. Hunched over a laptop, he bopped in time to an unheard beat. Gunfire began at a nearby range.

The group had moved on.

Bending, I lifted the combat knife strapped to my right calf and noticed a bullet hole had pierced a cargo pocket. The round missed my leg by a fraction of an inch.

I was almost a victim of high-speed lead poisoning.

Jaw set, I crept forward and thrust the knife under Savant's chin in case he wanted to continue the hazing. Complex surveillance images streamed across his laptop's screen as heavy metal blared from the headphones I tugged off.

"Don't move," I hissed.

"Oh, hey, Davia." He pointed toward the distant gunfire. "Have fun."

He never looked up.

Dropping Savant's headphones into his lap, I put my knife back in its sheath. At the weapons table, I selected a submachine gun. Popping in filtered ear protection, I stalked out to the range.

Let's find the hyenas.

Four battle-hardened men turned in sync when I approached,

their expressions ranging from surprised to annoyed at my unexpected appearance.

"Sorry, I'm late." My voice was saccharine sweet, like I was tardy for a Sunday picnic.

"We wasn't 'specting you at all," said Hodge, our burly Texan medic. "You're tougher than a one-eared alley cat."

Most worked to hide smiles, but Warden scowled. "Careful with that gun," he said. "I'll show you how to use it in a sec."

Show me? I trained for years on every weapon they used, and some they didn't. Not pausing, I discharged all my ammo, disintegrating the bullseye of the target.

When I finished, teammate Ned tugged at his scruffy beard and said, "We should nickname you Bombshell, and not because you're blonde."

The men all laughed, except Warden.

FIREARMS PRACTICE CONCLUDED, we entered the primary building of the complex. Our boss, Colonel Streeter, kept an office in a nearby wing.

"Why isn't Savant coming with us?" I asked Ned.

"He operates on a different plane than us mere mortals." Besides his unkempt beard, Ned wore his brown hair in a hipster bun. Grooming rules did not apply to this unit.

A female aide who worked with Colonel Streeter beckoned to another team member, K. He put up a hand in acknowledgment. K resembled Idris Elba, but younger and buffer. They moved away down a side hall.

The rest of us turned into a room with a mat-lined floor. On one wall, racks held fighting sticks, knives of various sizes, and boxing gloves.

"Ned, you and H pair up. I'll take on Bombshell," Warden drawled, emphasis on the B. Ned and Hodge pulled on boxing gloves.

Warden handed me two twenty-eight-inch sticks, took two himself, and we faced off. At six-three, he had me by six inches.

It was Davia versus Goliath.

"Ready?" Warden's full lips curled into a sneer.

"Ready to lay you out."

He came at me and didn't hold back, hitting with the power of a rhinoceros in a charge. Stepping fast to keep him from knocking me over, I blocked blow after blow. I pictured Batman bubbles over our heads: *Bam! Pow! Krunch!*

Warden made the men on the cover of *Muscle & Fitness* magazine look like featherweights. He was one hundred pounds heavier than me and sported gallon jug biceps. Our weapons were a mere blur until a searing thwack landed on my upper arm, and I cringed away.

"Give up?" Warden asked, driving me toward a corner.

"You. First." I gasped, sucking wind.

Back up-Duck-Back up.

At the edge of the mat, our sticks clanged. Cornered, I did a quick roll and slammed one of my bars against the back of Warden's knees. He crashed to the floor.

Timber!

A giant hand caught my right ankle and jerked.

I fell hard on my face.

Kicking free, I sprang up, but Warden did the same. Rivulets of sweat coursed from his close-cropped, dark hair and down his face. We circled each other, and I grinned as he also fought to catch his breath.

"Let's go weaponless," he grunted.

"Fine." We tossed our sticks aside.

We went at each other in an all-out grappling fight, working through an entire catalog of wrestling, martial arts, and street fighting tactics. Kyle Kavanagh, my South Dakota neighbor, and his myriad of deadly friends, had drilled me relentlessly through the years. I remembered their admonition: *The bigger they are, the harder they—*

Warden latched onto my shoulder and tossed me to the ground.

His reinforced steel body landed on top of me, and the air blasted from my lungs.

Before he could trap my arms against the mats, I thrust a hand past his groin and wrapped my arm around his upper thigh. He went still for a split-second, hyper-aware I was a woman near his most prized and vulnerable possessions.

To make up for his momentary pause, he grabbed for my hair, but it was too short. He rolled over in an instant, clamped an arm around my chest, and spoke close to my ear. "You don't belong here."

"Says you." I walloped him in the midsection with an elbow, leaped sideways, and broke away.

We jumped to our feet, circling again, checking for weaknesses.

My stamina hit the edge of empty. If I didn't do something soon, this fight would be over. Warden lunged for me, and I caught his forearm. Using the last of my strength, I flipped him to the ground and trapped one of his knees with my legs.

"Call it quits?" I drove his joint to an unnatural angle, grinding my hips against his bulk.

Warden growled with frustration but didn't give up. He bucked against me like a fly trapped in a spider's web fighting for its life. After an age, he tapped out. I released him, falling back on the mat, drained. He untangled himself and got to his feet.

"Here." He reached down to help me up. I took his hand, and he yanked me within inches of his face. Our eyes locked.

He held me much longer than necessary, then let go.

"Welcome to the team," he said and walked away.

2

"How'd it go?" Kyle Kavanagh asked when I called from my quarters, ice packs on my shoulders and one knee.

"About as we expected. But worse."

"Worse than launching a nuclear bomb into a cave?" I pictured my friend's sparkling blue eyes and smiled.

"Well, comparable," I conceded. "Colonel Streeter introduced me and left. The second he was gone, the group crowded in and threw me to the ground. I was bound and dragged off for a target practice initiation."

Kyle gave a short laugh. "Sounds about right. How'd you handle it?"

"I stayed calm in the chaos as you taught me."

Kyle Kavanagh was a former Delta Force operator sidelined because he lost a leg in combat. When I was eleven, I delivered him a "welcome to the neighborhood" cake from my mom, and the course of both our lives changed that day.

"Who's in charge of your team?"

"A guy named James Warden."

"And?"

"And what?"

"Neanderthal?" Kyle guessed.

"Nah. More Cro-Magnon."

"You boosted him that far up the evolutionary chain?"

"You don't get to lead the finest team around if you're not a hotrod. Having the first woman ever in his unit probably doesn't sit well, especially after I beat him in unarmed combat."

A lengthy silence on the other end made me wonder if the call had disconnected. Kyle finally said, "There's something I didn't tell you."

He sounded hesitant.

"What?"

"He signed off on it."

My mouth fell open. "No way."

"I got the info from a friend but promised I wouldn't say anything. You beat out the other competitors and were approved by Captain America there himself."

"Huh. Could've fooled me."

"You in person might have proven different than his expectations. You look better than the mug shot in your file."

We had discussed the effects a woman would have on an all-male, testosterone-fueled unit. The buzz cut helped minimize my femininity, but Kyle still teased me. "You can't do much about those baby blues. Men will get lost in them."

Was Warden's hostility because I was new to the team or a woman —or both? Newbies got hassled, sometimes for years.

"And how did Mean Streets react to you?"

"Who?"

"Sam Streeter. That was his nickname before he moved up the ranks and became a colonel. He's small in stature but has the energy of a Jack Russell terrier after a fox. He could drink most of us under the table and still kill you six ways from Sunday."

"Huh. Well, he's all official now. Polite, but direct."

"Next time we cross paths, I'll tweak him about getting old and sedate. What about the rest of the bunch?"

"They're all different, but the same at their core, deadly super-achievers."

"Just like you, at your ripe old age of twenty-four, and don't you forget it," Kyle said, pride in his voice.

His praise triggered a memory.

I'm twelve, a sniper rifle propped on a stand in front of me. Kyle hadn't allowed me around such a weapon before. A centered target on a stack of hay bales sat a distance away.

Kyle: Study the wind.

A soft breeze from the east rolled across the surrounding wheat fields and ruffled my hair. I estimated the effect it would have on the bullet's trajectory.

Kyle: Here's what I want you to do. First, exhale. Count one, two, and then squeeze the trigger. Continue the squeeze to the back, then release.

Shouldering into my weapon, I cautiously let out my breath and pulled the trigger in a long, slow movement.

My shot hit the center mark at 200 yards, and joy flooded through me.

Later, 1000 yards.

A sudden emptiness tugged at me.

"How are my parents?" I asked. Kyle was one of their closest friends.

"Ate dinner with them tonight, so I'm stuffed." The sound of him patting his belly carried through the phone.

Memories of fried chicken, mashed potatoes, green beans, and homemade pie filled me with unexpected melancholy. I pictured my dad, seated at the head of our oak dining table. His upper forehead was lighter than the rest of his face from wearing a ball cap working long, hard days in the sun, tending to his crops. My mom would fret about whether she made enough food while Kyle regaled them with stories.

"I miss being home." I longed to walk up the front steps, sit on the covered porch, and breathe in the smell of the countryside. How long since I was last there? A year?

"Maybe you'll get a chance to take a break soon."

"Doubtful since I just got here."

"True. Tomorrow, I'm on the road to talk about suicide prevention at a veterans' conference. It might be hard to reach me. Do you think you can handle the initiation?"

"Yes."

"I want you to take time to decide about this job you've worked so hard to get. Sometimes the reality isn't what you expected."

"I'll keep that in mind."

"Okay. Remember, the easy way is what?"

"Always mined," I finished.

We said farewell, and I lifted the ice off my knee, wincing. Duct tape residue stuck to my wrists, and I picked at it, replaying the day.

What would come next?

Wait. Reframe that.

It didn't matter what came next.

My mind gave the middle finger to pain, fatigue, and the games of little boys. No matter what gut-wrenching, excruciating challenges were on the horizon, I was ready.

THE DARK ROAD STRETCHED AHEAD. Two miles into my morning run, the region's heat and mugginess tucked around me like an electric blanket set on high.

A presence behind me closed the distance between us fast. A white-toothed smile gleamed and was gone. Warden moved at the speed of a cheetah, shirtless in black shorts. The sun peeked over the horizon, illuminating his shining muscles like his own personal gaffer.

Couldn't he have picked a different route? Was he determined to show me up?

I raced after him, squinting into the bright morning. At the five-mile mark, I slowed my pace and checked my watch. Under forty minutes. *Fine.* He could run faster.

One for him and one for me.

Following the looping road back, I settled into a light jog before breaking into a brisk walk. Closer to the compound, other team members nodded in greeting as they began their runs.

Cooled down and stretched, I entered the team's co-ed locker room just as James Warden emerged from the showers—nude, head down, running a towel through his wet hair.

Holy crap and hallelujah!

I spun around, but not before noting that below his defined pecs and washboard abs, everything about him was in perfect proportion.

"Any hot water left?" I asked, wondering what to do. I thought I was prepared for all aspects of team life, but becoming inured to this reality would take time.

"Haven't seen a man naked before?" Warden mocked.

Not like you.

There was no right way to answer, so I faced him. He leisurely dried his body and I pursed my lips, keeping my gaze neck-up.

"We're doing shooting drills at 0800." He reached for clothes from a nearby locker. Mine was three down from his, so there was nothing for it but to strip.

Warden's dispassionate eyes raked over me.

"No tattoos?" he observed as he dressed.

"I've got commitment issues. You?"

Warden's body was also unmarred by ink.

"I don't need to improve on perfection."

Fighting off an eye roll, I went to shower.

3

The language instructor fired questions at us in Farsi, following up on a previous hour spent speaking Arabic. My brain wanted to explode. Never one for conversation; K was the surprise star of the show. His voice was deep and silky, like a DJ on smooth jazz radio.

Most eyes were riveted to the ticking of the second hand on the wall clock, counting down the torture. The moment the clock read 1700 hours, Warden spoke, "We're done."

We stood, chairs scraping. Hodge stretched his shoulders. Although he was taller and broader than Warden, he moved like a lithe man half his size.

"Anybody up for dinner?" Warden asked, stifling a yawn.

Hodge and K declined, both heading home to families. Savant muttered something we couldn't hear and wandered out. During my three years on the team, he never joined us in the outside world, preferring his own company and routines. We had grown to know and accept each other's idiosyncrasies. Come mission-time, we worked like an ATM on payday, seamless and precise.

Aubrey Elliot and Luke Upton, aides to Colonel Streeter, walked towards us as we went into the hall.

"We're heading to the tavern. Want to join us?" Ned, always the friendliest in our group, invited.

Luke agreed in an instant. Aubrey and I shared a smile. Luke wanted on the team so badly he would eat a jar of spiders every day to earn himself a spot.

Falling into step with Aubrey, I asked, "How're things?"

"Oh, fine." She tucked an errant strand of her blonde, bobbed hair behind an ear. We were both twenty-seven and often commiserated about being women surrounded by alpha men.

"Are you coming?" I nodded at the backs of the group leaving the building.

"Not tonight. I'm taking advantage of the weight room while everyone's gone."

"Need me to spot you?" Weight-lifting was something we did together whenever time allowed for her. It was a daily activity for the team.

"No." Her hazel eyes were weary. "I need to decompress and think. I'll be fine."

Team logistics could be draining, which I understood. "Have a good evening."

Outside, we headed for our separate vehicles. I was tired but decided to join the dinner crew, not wanting to cook. People from the complex, wearing a mix of business and military attire, swarmed toward their cars.

Ned pulled up beside me in his blue and white Ford Mustang, driver's window down. "Wanna race?"

"Really? Are you going to let me extend my winning record?" I scoffed, picking up the helmet from my Ducati motorcycle.

"If you can catch up." He accelerated, tires squealing.

"Cheater," I muttered, fastened the strap, and threw a leg over my bike. I zoomed after him, blazing out the gates.

Executing some illegal traffic maneuvers, I screeched to a halt outside the restaurant, a hair ahead of Ned. I parked, pulled off my helmet, and gave him a triumphant grin. He got out and grabbed me from behind, lifting me into the air for a second before setting me down.

"Next time," he said.

"Are you two goofballs at it again?" Luke asked, wanting in on the camaraderie.

"Who you calling a goofball?" Ned glowered, and Luke paled.

Ned could turn from playful to a predator in a heartbeat.

"I, uh, I," Luke stammered. Ned cuffed him on the shoulder.

"No worries, wannabe. Maybe you'll get to play with the big dogs someday."

Luke gave him a weak smile.

We went inside, joining Warden at a back table in the Brew and Chew Café.

"You won again, eh?" Warden stated as I pulled out the chair next to him.

"How'd you know?"

"You can't quite suppress that cat-eating grin," he said.

"I don't think cat-eating's the correct term."

"Well, don't want to swear in front of the youngsters." He nodded in the direction of Luke, who listened to a story Ned told with rapt attention.

"But why pick on cats?" I persisted, sitting. "What'd they ever do to you?"

"Well, I found a kitten once while hiking."

"A kitten?"

"Yes. I was maybe, I think, nine or ten. Something like that. We lived near Rocky Mountain National Park in Colorado, and I convinced my older brother Richard to drop me off to hike up to West Creek Falls. He worked in Estes Park, and I hitched a ride. So, I'm out about a mile, and a little orange and white kitten comes charging at me from behind a tree, mewling its head off. I knelt, and it came right up yowling like it was lecturing me about something."

"What did you do?"

"I checked around but found nothing, finally concluding some asshole dumped it."

I shook my head, disgusted at the thought.

"And that's how I wound up with Roscoe. He was my best buddy for a long time." He smiled to himself at the memory.

"I pictured you as a Labrador Retriever kind of guy."

"Oh, we owned dogs, but Roscoe was the boss and my constant companion. Did you have pets?"

"Two cats, but they liked to hunt mice in the barn where I kept my horse."

"Did you have fun growing up?"

"Yeah. I was an only child."

"I can't imagine. I got stuck with four brothers, so my childhood—ha! *and* adulthood —was never-ending tussles."

"And I can't imagine that."

"What did you like to do?"

"Read books, drive tractors, and ride." *Plus, train with our super-soldier neighbor.*

Our server arrived to take our orders. We spent the rest of the time chowing down and engaged in general conversation, never talking about our jobs outside of our work space. My gaze drifted to Warden's profile. During the constant stress of our training and high-pressure missions, he was either hyper-focused or blowing off steam by clowning around. This added dimension piqued my interest, and I firmly reminded myself not to be too intrigued given the no fraternization rules.

He's gorgeous and off-limits. I repeated in my mind for the billionth time, pushing away the familiar, forbidden thoughts.

"You awake over there?" Ned asked me just as I put a fork of pasta in my mouth.

"Mm," I replied.

"Don't you have anything to say to Davia, Luke?" Warden's tone was innocent.

"Uh, I," he faltered, caught out for avoiding speaking to me.

"She thinks she's a badass." Warden gave me side-eye.

"And I'm still ahead of you." Our game of one-upmanship

continued unabated. I was ahead by one point, not that I kept track or anything.

"You're ahead of *Warden*?" Luke was astonished. "In what?"

"Everything, including pronouncing big words," I said.

Warden shot me a stern look. "Har-har. And that's two syllables, by the way."

After our meal, the group exited into the brisk night air. Warden and I walked together to his black Jeep near my bike. As I picked up my helmet, he said, "You know, Glenn—that was nice."

"It was," I responded, cautious about further exploration of my team leader's softer side. His long-lashed green eyes, sometimes the color of grass or darker, incredible body, and keen intellect were already tough to ignore.

And he knew it.

"See you tomorrow." He drove away.

I watched until his taillights grew distant.

My phone buzzed.

Warden's brake lights came on.

What had happened?

My heart raced at the unexpected recall to work.

We gathered in a conference room, curious. When Colonel Streeter entered, his jaw was tight. We exchanged concerned glances.

"I just received some distressing news and wanted you to hear it from me, not mainstream media. About an hour ago, there was a failed operation to rescue nearly one hundred human trafficking hostages, most children. Five ACE operators died," he pronounced, face somber. ACE stood for Army Compartmented Elements, the updated term for Delta Force.

Disbelief shot through the group.

"How, Sir?" Warden asked.

"Hidden IEDs and a well-armed militia."

IEDs are improvised explosive devices, often tricky to spot. We trained to watch for them, but the variables during a mission made it challenging. That five special forces soldiers died was difficult to process.

"You met most of that ACE team when we did a joint mission with them against the same target who we code-named Badger," Streeter continued.

Badger was in his late-forties and originally from Syria. He ran a vast terrorist network funded by illicit money made through human trafficking or donated by anonymous contacts. Badger only came on our radar after he staged pre-recorded charity junkets released later online. He and his men went to villages in vulnerable locations and handed out money and food to engender trust. His crew would later abduct people to traffic—primarily children— and they were gone before someone found the location.

No one spoke as we digested the news. The faces of the deceased operators entered my mind, along with memories of their personalities and high-level skills. It reminded me why we trained as hard as we did and why it sometimes couldn't save us.

After a time, K asked, "Are we going to retaliate, Sir?"

Streeter looked much older than before. "Right now, we're working to locate any warehouses where Badger stores weapons to carry out terrorist attacks. As you know, the mission you had with ACE only took out a minor location. There's intel he plans to blow up a U.S. military installation in Iraq, but it's unclear if that's true or misinformation."

"But what about targeting Badger himself?" Hodge asked.

"We don't have a solid lead on his location, which we understand he frequently changes," Streeter replied. "Recall how long it took to locate Bin Laden? Of course, now this has occurred, we'll make finding him a priority."

No one asked anything else. There was no point peppering Streeter with questions he couldn't answer.

After Streeter left the room, we talked amongst ourselves about the lost men. The thought it could easily have been us was a stark reality. We dispersed with heavy hearts, hoping the day we would find and finish Badger arrived soon.

4

We rubbed shoulders in the helicopter, the steady *whoomph-whoomph* of its blades our background music. Savant, Hodge, and K were asleep, catching some shut-eye before the action. Warden sat across from me, his long legs stretched out. He tapped the underside of my boot with his foot, and I gave him a half-smile. Ned chatted with the pilot, and I muted the conversation in my earpiece.

We would finally get a chance to retaliate for our fallen brothers in arms. The objective of our mission was to destroy Badger's primary weapons storage warehouse in a remote village on the continent of Africa, further specifics classified.

After an easy landing on a ship, we headed for land through the wet door on our two-person driver propulsion vehicles. We wore diving equipment, and the buoyant, motorized hulls carried our gear. We landed and changed clothes, stowed our rides, and prepared to advance through a dry creek bed.

Night blanketed us.

Wee-yayayayaya!

The sharp howl echoed, sliding from a high shriek to a deep tremor. We stopped. Our night vision goggles tinted everything an eerie green, making the landscape weird enough without the Halloween soundtrack.

Wee-yayayayaya! Wee-yayayayaya!

Two lean jackals crouched near a pool of water. They resembled coyotes but with oversized ears and darker backs. When we resumed walking, machine guns at the ready, they bolted. We paused at the edge of the water to double-check our equipment.

"If them ki-yotes bailed any faster, they'd catch up to yesterday," Hodge said.

"I don't get your meaning." Savant frowned.

"H's talkin' his Texas thing again, Sav," Ned told him. "None of us understand him."

Satisfied we were ready for action; we renewed our trek across the shifting sands. Near the outskirts of the rural village containing our target, Warden spread us out. Rusty metal panels and acacia trees bordered the town. Several dogs barked, but we didn't see any people. It was the middle of the night, and I hoped everyone slept.

Warden gestured for me to go with him, pointing toward a warehouse in the distance.

The six of us moved forward, stepping carefully across the rough terrain like a choreographed ballet in Mad Max gear. We got within fifty feet of an entrance when all hell broke loose. A crowd of Badger-Believers holding automatic weapons jumped over the fenced enclosure, caterwauling.

A gunfight began.

Sharp, staccato rounds whizzed past us and thudded into the ground. We returned fire, muzzle flashes lighting the night.

Listening to the tempo of the shots coming at us told me we faced enthusiastic but inexperienced shooters. Our responsive fire was steady and precise.

The enemy began to fall.

To my left, there was a sudden volley of gunfire. Ned went down. Hodge drag-carried him behind the rusted carcass of a car while the rest of us held off the attackers. New enemies flooded out of the village, streaming at us in a never-ending line, like a kicked-over ant hill. The disparity in numbers might make this our swan song. Black ops of this nature meant complete deniability, so if we died, the government would inform our families but provide them no details.

Thinking fast, I pulled a stick of C4 out of my rucksack and wrapped it around a small beano grenade. I launched my improvised bomb toward a group of enemies firing at K and Savant. The explosion killed or knocked down everyone in its vicinity. Grenades and gunfire deployed by my teammates supplemented the impact and put a dent in the opposition's numbers and tenacity.

The dust settled, and the only movement was a gust of sand. After waiting for a beat, Warden radioed that the mission was a go and said, "Bombshell, you're with me."

We didn't hesitate. Savant and K shadowed us as we ran toward the dilapidated warehouse, now unguarded. We slipped in through an unlocked door and surveyed crates of unexploded ordnance and weapons packing the space.

Moonlight shone through the high windows, so I pushed up my NVG's and reached into a sack from K containing more C4. Warden began rigging wiring, and I hustled to catch up, working as fast as possible in the decrepit building.

"Ready to blow this joint?" Warden asked.

We set five minutes on the timer, slammed our goggles down, and exited. Halfway to safety from the coming explosion, a handful of men surrounded us. Perhaps the earlier runaways found renewed courage and thought they were ready to take on the world.

The world is easier to take on than us.

We backed away toward safety just as the warehouse blew, throwing debris and enemies right at us.

Another opportunity to die.

CHAOS REIGNED. I avoided a section of falling metal siding while a committed combatant tried to slice me with a machete. The piece of siding crushed him.

Warden and I fought our way out, back-to-back. We got separated from Savant and K, but we always have a backup plan. Hodge and Ned had already retreated, so we made like the jackals and ran.

"Where are the others?" I kept my gun in the ready position.

"Coming our way. H and Ned are almost back to our extraction point."

After putting miles between the explosion and us, we paused and drank warm, plastic-tasting water from our CamelBaks. I splashed some on my dirty face. My hair contained five pounds of sand and itched.

Please don't let it be lice.

"Time to pop smoke," Warden said. He put what seemed like a mile between us before I stood. I ran to catch up but tripped and fell face-first into the creek bed, my heavy pack slamming me into the ground.

Warden glanced back, unconcerned. I spat out sand and struggled to my feet. Dull pain filled my sweat-soaked body from carrying the load of body armor and weapons, but I sprinted after him once more.

At our exit point, we yanked off our NVG's. Hodge and Ned's underwater vehicles were gone, and I was relieved, knowing Ned would get some expert medical care back on the ship.

"What a mess." I brushed grime from my face.

"It's not my fault." Warden bumped his shoulder hard into mine, like roughhousing on a school playground.

"What's not?"

"You can't keep up with me," he taunted.

I raised a fist to give him a solid thump in the chest, but Warden caught my chin in one hand and kissed me.

What?

The reality of his tongue in my mouth brought me out of my momentary shock. I shoved him away and stepped back.

"What'd you do that for?" I asked, stunned. If he wanted to win a round in our "who's better" game, this was an unfair and unacceptable way to do it.

"Are you kidding? I've wanted to kiss you for ages."

"And you chose now because of what?" I stretched out my arms to indicate our desolate surroundings. "The ambiance?"

"We made it out alive."

"We've made it out of worse. Are you trying to prove something?"

"Davia, I just, um, think you're so—" He put up his hands, unable to find words to explain what must be a brain lapse.

"And you're hot. So what, Warden? We're not allowed to like each other!"

Warden gave me a lop-sided grin. "You think I'm hot?"

I bent to pack my gear. "I don't know what this is, but we can't—"

"We can't what?" Warden put a hand on my arm.

I pulled away. "This is a—"

Bad idea. Bad idea.

Our competitive relationship had tipped over in an unexpected direction. *Why now? And now what?* I couldn't continue to work with him without violating the no-fraternizing rules. I knew I would wish to replicate our kiss—minus the dirt.

"Hey, guys." It was Savant. "K tweaked his ankle, but he'll be here in a sec."

When K limped up, we retrieved our underwater vehicles, stowed our gear, and prepared to leave. We worked in silence. My brain raged, but I shut down my thoughts. It was time to focus on our preparations. Sorting out what happened on the mission could wait until we reached a safe destination. The same held for my recent kiss from Warden.

The sound of rotors made us turn.

A helicopter came straight at us. A man holding a machine gun with a hundred-round belt of ammo hung from a side door. Opposite, another aimed an assault rifle.

They opened up.

Trapped without cover, we returned fire. K reached for an anti-tank, shoulder-launched weapon, effective against bunkers, concrete, brick walls, and light armor. We often used it to introduce ourselves, but never against a helicopter.

Rounds from the enemy sprayed the ground.

As I aimed for the pilot, a bullet grazed my left arm, and another struck full force into my outer left thigh. Lightning hot pain exploded through my leg, and I screamed. Gritting my teeth, I kept pulling the trigger while my blood darkened the sand.

A loud noise concussed the air.

An instant later, the helicopter exploded.

Warden ran to my side and fell to his knees, face drawn. "You got hit."

"You're supposed to keep your eyes on the hostiles, not me."

He slapped a pressure bandage on my leg wound. The pain, exhaustion, and blood loss made the surroundings grow hazy.

Was this the end?

I surrendered to darkness.

5

The trip back to the ship was a blur. Random memories of wound assessment and further transport back to our operations base were all I had when I woke in a private room with utilitarian decor. A nurse bustled in and checked my vitals.

"Here." He handed me antibiotics and a small paper cup filled with water. I sat up and gulped down the pills.

"Can you tell me the extent—"

"The doctor will give you the details." He took the cup and tossed it, made some notes on my chart, and left.

I ran my hand with care across the gauze covering my heavily bandaged left leg. The pain wasn't horrible, but I didn't know how many painkillers were in my system. Probably not a lot, since I was awake. Stretching out my left arm, I examined the bandage around my bicep. Was the injury superficial? I rubbed my eyes, straining to remember.

"You're awake," a doctor said as she entered. "How do you feel?"

"Fine, I guess."

"You were lucky. The round in your leg was high-velocity and could have been fatal if it struck a major artery. That said, you lost a lot of blood. You were fortunate your teammate applied both pressure bandages and a tourniquet."

Memories surfaced of Warden's pale face, his brow furrowed in concentration as he knelt beside me.

"I—" I stopped, unable to remember.

"You likely don't recall a lot due to the morphine." The doctor was abrupt. She was middle-aged, gray peeking through her dark hair. "I've treated enough of you 'special' types to shoot straight. Forgive the pun."

I nodded.

"The bullet in your leg caused a deep cavitation or groove in plain language. Fortunately, it didn't spin or fragment, which could have left a debris field or impacted your bones. We won't know about nerve damage until you are up and around. During the initial suturing, I checked but didn't find any obvious nerve impingement. It could take a while for effects to manifest."

Slipping my hand under the sheet, I pressed down hard on the wound.

"Feels fine to me."

The doctor gave a humorless laugh. "If your leg hurt like hell, you wouldn't tell me. You might have some pain when you get up and move around. I don't recommend it. You need to rest."

"For how long?"

"This is a significant injury. I recommend at least two weeks and, if you do walk, use crutches." She pointed at a pair propped nearby. "Be cautious, and allow yourself time to heal. Also, getting shot can be mentally traumatic, so—"

"Can we skip the lecture about emotional trauma?"

"Let me guess," the doctor said. "Your injury is typical for the work you do, and you'll be fine. You're not dead, you're not bleeding, and you could kill me at a moment's notice." It sounded like she recited what numerous operatives had told her.

She picked up my chart, made some notes, and left. Her disapproval trailed in a wake behind her.

Still filthy, except for my bandaged wounds, bathing became my priority. I couldn't wet my injured arm and leg but would play a game of Twister for some shampoo and soap. Sitting up, I swiveled my legs off the side of the bed, pulled the IV drip out of my arm, and tried to stand.

Ouch. Ouch. Ouch.

Hopping to the bathroom, I grabbed the sink to steady myself. The mirror reflected an image of me as Wile E. Coyote after being blown up by the Roadrunner. Blood mixed with dirt and conceal-ment paint decorated my face and hair. My mind went back to the battlefield and Warden. He kissed *this*? He couldn't have been in his right mind. I flushed, remembering his lips on mine.

Closing my eyes, I stopped the memory.

I can't desire more of what I'm not allowed to have.

The grit brushed out of my teeth; I turned on the shower, standing with care to relish the hot water. I poured an insane amount of shampoo on my head, lathering, rinsing, and repeating. On the third lather, an extra pair of hands covered mine. Warden towered over me, wearing camouflage pants and a tight black t-shirt he didn't seem to mind getting soaked.

"Warden! What are you doing—"

He stopped my words with a kiss. "Much better this time, Dav," he murmured against my lips,

"Funny." Pushing away my conflicting thoughts, I slipped my hand under the back of his damp shirt and pulled him closer, tracing the defined muscles.

With a mischievous grin, Warden picked up a bar of soap and lathered his hands.

"I think you need some help getting clean." He caressed my face, clearing away the grime with tender strokes before moving to my breasts. My nipples went rigid at his touch, and a shudder ran through my body. I wrapped my uninjured arm around his neck, pulling him into a deep, fervent kiss.

A booming voice stopped us cold.

"Glenn! Glenn!"

Colonel William Streeter. The one person in the world we couldn't ignore. We were so screwed, but not like we intended.

I turned off the water, and Warden got me a towel. He pulled on his boots, lifted me with no effort, and carried me back into the room to lay me on the bed. Streeter said nothing. He was of average height, with salt-and-pepper hair and bushy eyebrows.

"How's your leg?" he finally asked.

"The doctor briefed me. She hopes I won't need more than a few weeks to recover."

"That's good news. Ned's was a through-and-through of his side that missed anything important. He'll be fine," Streeter said.

We tried to gauge the colonel's mood, knowing better than to offer explanations.

"The AAR's at 1330. I'll expect you both. Oh, and a message came for you, Glenn." Streeter handed me an envelope then went to the door, where he paused. "Warden, you might want to change." He left, face unreadable.

Warden retrieved another towel and dried himself off. "Want to see what's in your note?" he asked. Neither of us wanted to talk about the coming fallout, so I scanned its contents.

My mom's only sibling, Lilah Latham, had died.

Ding-dong, the witch is dead.

Reading further, I was flabbergasted.

I was the sole heir to her fortune.

"What's wrong? You're white as a ghost," Warden said.

"This note says my aunt died and left me most of her estate. She was mega-rich."

Warden whistled. "An heiress to a fortune? Are you kidding?"

I handed him the note. "It's ridiculous but true." Nothing made sense. To call my relationship with my aunt strained was diplomatic.

After graduating from high school, Aunt Lilah married a wealthy businessman, moved to New York City, and honed her control-freak ways. Her much older husband died a decade ago, and she never had children. She had demanded I move in with her once I reached debutante age, but I begged mom to say no, and she ultimately refused to send me. The dispute led to a rift between them for years.

Warden finished reading. "Does this mean you're leaving?"

"I don't know what to think. I just got shot, I'm on morphine, and Colonel Streeter caught us fraternizing. It's not like my head's in a good place."

"When is it?"

I tossed my pillow at him, and he caught it. Warden returned my improvised weapon, then sat on the edge of the bed.

"But, seriously. What would happen if you accepted the inheritance?"

"If the money's as substantial as I suspect, I'd be able to stop operating and help my parents. They've struggled to keep the farm going, and now they're getting older."

Warden's face clouded over. "I can't believe you'd value money more than what we do."

"That's not fair."

Warden looked down.

"Sorry, I shouldn't have said that."

"I think we're both shaken up, and rightly so. This is a mammoth decision on a good day. I'll need to spend some time exploring my options but, after what happened, maybe leaving for a while would be best."

"Does the *after what happened* mean you getting hurt or us?"

"If there's an 'us,' you know it'll be a problem. I'm the first woman, the test case. At least this inheritance, coupled with my injury, gives Streeter plausible deniability about why I might leave, even if it's temporary," I said.

"We should still try to convince him to keep the status quo. I shouldn't have kissed you. We can promise it won't happen again."

"He wouldn't believe us. Besides, I'm equally guilty, since I didn't stop you."

Warden stood, face bleak. "I don't want to think about our team without you. I can't explain why I kissed you. It was just—"

"Just what?"

An impulse? A game? Something he regretted?

I braced myself.

He took my hand. "Davia, beyond you being one of the best operatives ever, I've been fighting this attraction to you for ages. Probably since I saw your blue eyes looking ready to kill me that first day."

At his words, I reminded myself to let out the breath I held.

"Well, if I'm honest, I've struggled with my feelings for you as well," I said.

After our admissions, the tension left. We bent forward to touch our lips together, staying that way for a satisfying time.

"I don't want you to go," Warden said, pulling me against him. "Let's talk to Streeter together."

Colonel Streeter made some exceptions to rules, but I bet he wouldn't be lenient in this case. He lectured me about the perils of fraternization when I arrived, and Warden and the whole team likely received the same admonishment.

I sat back. "At best, he'll transfer me to a different team."

"Maybe. I don't know. I'm so, so sorry for screwing this up."

"I should ask Streeter to rotate *you* out. That would solve the problem."

Warden's eyes narrowed until he realized I was kidding. "This is quite the conundrum. I don't think you should rush any decisions," he said.

"You're right. I have a lot to consider."

"I should've thought this through a lot more as well," Warden admitted.

"Since when do men think?"

He lunged for my towel, and I mock-struggled to keep it.

"We'd better get ready for the meeting." I knew what would occur if the towel dropped.

"I'd rather blockade the door." Warden checked his watch. "Damn! We have to be at the debriefing in ten minutes."

He kissed me on the forehead, and hurried out.

I forced myself up to search for clean clothes. Putting my injured leg into the stiff khaki pants and pulling on my boots was rough. I ran a hand through my still-wet hair, grabbed the crutches, and hobbled out. Focused on my dilemma instead of the physical pain, I made it down the hall to our meeting place without remembering the journey.

Craig Kilburn appeared, using his imposing six-foot-four height to loom over me. He held the meeting room's door open with one scarred hand and grinned at me like Jack Nicholson in *The Shining*. Kilburn was an operative who worked solo. He was responsible for umpteen clandestine assassinations of high-value targets and slipped in and out of war-ravaged countries to gather intelligence. Some said Kilburn had lived on the edge so long he took up permanent residence there. I hadn't seen him in over a year and wondered at his presence.

"Miss me?" He leered, bald head gleaming.

"I'm a better shot than that," I retorted and moved past him.

Once in the conference room, I sat as far away from Kilburn as possible, choosing an empty spot between Ned and Savant. Ned gave me a nod, and neither of us inquired about the other's injuries. Warden sat at the front of the room, now in dry clothing. My heart thudded as I stared at his broad shoulders.

Colonel Streeter came in, flanked by Luke and Aubrey. He walked to the front and sat at the head of the table. Aubrey and I exchanged brief smiles. Luke kept his focus on Streeter, still hopeful his faithfulness would lead to a promotion.

The after-action review began, each of us recounting the mission while Savant projected photos and surveillance data. Colonel Streeter requested our conclusions, but a laugh rang out.

Kilburn slapped a manila folder against his leg.

"Be afwaid, be vewy, vewy afwaid," he said in his best imitation of Elmer Fudd. Then, he spilled the folder's contents in front of Streeter, who bolted straight up.

"Where did these come from?" he demanded.

"While you guys were making a mess of it in Africa, I was in *(classified)* and got these off the dead body of an affiliate of Badger," Kilburn answered, satisfaction in his pale blue eyes.

Photos of each team member with detailed information about our training lay in front of us. We held the highest security level clearance, but I didn't want to be privy to this knowledge.

A red circle and an X marked our faces.

Another reason to take the damned inheritance.

6

The meeting concluded, Warden was the first out the door. Once the team reached the hall, he signaled for us to follow him. We crammed into a nearby room.

"Who's the rat?" Ned's eyes blazed.

"I think you mean mole, after all—" Savant began.

"I'm confident we can agree the leak isn't from any of us," Warden cut in.

"How do you know?" Savant challenged.

"Ridiculous. We've saved each other's hides too many times," Hodge said, and K nodded in agreement. Footsteps echoed in the hall, and I closed the door.

"Two of us got shot," I said. "The leak nearly got us killed."

"Maybe to take suspicion off those who were wounded," Savant said.

"This isn't the movies," Ned scoffed. "We don't get shot just to be ruled out as traitors."

"Right," K agreed.

In truth, Savant playing devil's advocate didn't upset us. We relied on his mind working through all the parameters. He sucked at interpreting or showing emotions, but his analytical mind was one of our greatest resources.

"I went through the docs," Warden said. "They only have our photos, and some of the info on tactics is from last year. We've upped our game since."

"But they were waiting for us," Ned said. "Badger knew we were coming."

"The news gets worse," Warden said. "Kilburn told Streeter he got intel we killed Badger's only son, a teenager, during that joint mission with ACE."

"I don't remember anything coming up in an AAR." Ned looked baffled.

Warden said, "As you know, sometimes, the collateral damage of an op isn't obvious. We're suffering the blowback now."

Savant began muttering about an intelligence failure, waves of frustration rolling off him.

"Badger has horns holding up his halo," Hodge said. "What else do you think he has planned?"

"He has trained killers on his payroll, "K said. "Do you think we're targets in the real world? I'm concerned for our families."

"I think we need to assume if he comes after us, they're vulnerable as well," Warden replied. "He might have a scorched earth policy."

"So, what should we do?" I asked. *Were my parents at risk?*

"You're all stove up," Hodge said. "You can't get back out there for a bit."

Inhaling, I tried to calm the disquiet churning my stomach. The team's crisis made thoughts of leaving even more difficult.

Warden changed the subject. "The news blindsided Streeter. He'll have the best intel people hunting for who leaked the info. We need to increase our vigilance."

Everyone's faces were set in stone, focused on the problem of battling an unpredictable enemy.

"I'll try to find out anything else Kilburn might have," Savant said.

Everyone left, leaving me alone with Warden.

"Our lives were already complicated," I said.

"That's an understatement."

"I'll talk to Streeter. He'll be in a state, but I need to get things sorted."

"I'll come with you."

Would having Warden there make things easier or more difficult?

"No. I need to feel him out. I'll approach him from the inheritance angle and see what he thinks."

"You sure?"

"Yes."

Warden placed his back against the door and kissed me. We put years of pent-up desire into the embrace, knowing we might not get a chance to be together for a long time.

"Good luck in there," he said and let me into the hall.

COLONEL STREETER WAS in his office on the phone. Aubrey was also on her phone, as was Luke. The search to find the leak was already in full gear. I sat, relaxing into the buzz of activity.

"You can go in now," I heard Aubrey say and sat up with a start. I must have drifted off. Leaving the crutches, I walked into Streeter's office, ignoring the pain.

"Close the door, Glenn," Streeter said. "And have a seat. You're putting a brave face on your injury, but now's not the time."

"Thank you, Sir. I wanted to discuss my situation." There was no point skirting around the issue.

"And quite a situation it is," he said. "At this point, fraternization has landed at the bottom of the pile."

"Warden and I both realize our actions affect the future of us together on a team."

"Now's too soon for a decision, but moving one of you would be best."

My heart sank.

"Maybe I should quit operating for a while. I inherited some money from a relative, a wealthy woman. I need time to recuperate, so leaving might not be a bad idea."

"An inheritance? The timing's impeccable, considering everything. I'm extremely disturbed about the breach and the proof provided by Kilburn. With what happened to ACE and on your last mission, we can't know what's to come."

"Indeed."

Kilburn's news was the icing on a shitstorm cake.

"Are you considering a leave of absence or a permanent transfer to a new team?" Streeter asked.

The decision was difficult. I didn't answer, staring at the floor.

"Let me make a suggestion," he said. "You take leave for a year. You're a key asset, Glenn, and we don't want to lose your talents. That will give me time to sort both these issues, or at least I hope."

"Thank you, Sir."

Streeter told me Aubrey would make travel arrangements to any destination I desired. I spoke to her then went toward my room to retrieve my few meager possessions. Head down, preoccupied. I ran into Savant.

"Hey, Dav, better hurry. We're heading out from Tarmac Two in ten minutes. Kilburn's coming along." He kept going without a backward glance.

I found myself alone in the hall. Overwhelmed, I covered my face, then dropped my hands back to my crutches.

Suck it up, Buttercup.

Time to take my first steps toward a new life.

7

Aunt Lilah's lawyer, Mr. Morgenstern, arranged for a limo to meet me at La Guardia airport. A white-haired man held a sign with my name and introduced himself as Frederick. He took my worn green duffel bag like it was personalized Louis Vuitton and placed it in the trunk of a black town car, then held the rear door. He helped me situate my crutches inside, saying nothing. He and K were kindred spirits.

Mr. Morgenstern reserved a suite at the Four Seasons in Manhattan because of its proximity to his offices. He told me he could provide me with the keys to Aunt Lilah's penthouse on the Upper West Side, but I refused. At age six, the only time I visited her there, the place had seemed like a palace. The residence featured high ceilings, marble floors, and a spectacular view of the city. I ran to press my hands flat against one of the picture windows, gazing out in wonder. Aunt Lilah never let me forget the mess wrought by my sticky fingerprints, even as years rolled past.

The limo pulled away from the curb, flowing into a stream of traffic. I sank back into the leather seats, spending the time it took to reach the hotel ignoring New York City, filled with regret. Was this the right decision? I ran possible solutions through my mind but still came up with nothing.

Preoccupied, it startled me when the limo halted.

Marble columns and an abstract print carpet graced the entrance to the Four Seasons. I slouched across the spacious entry like an intruder. A personal attendant swept me away to a suite with unending views of Central Park and the skyline, followed by a bellhop with my bag. She chattered about the amenities, instructing me to ring the concierge if I needed anything.

How about James Warden?

The heavy door shut, leaving me in solitude. I took in the king-sized bed, plasma screen TV, walk-in closet, and marble soaking tub with shower. After years of faded green or beige paint, paired with second-hand furniture, the opulent surroundings were too much. I threw down my crutches, sank onto the edge of the bed, and phoned my mom.

"How was your trip?" she asked.

"Good. I put the stuff from my apartment in storage until I learn more about Aunt Lilah's legacy." The only item of real value was my bike.

My parents knew I worked for the government in some secret capacity, but I never gave them details. They wouldn't forgive their now dear friend Kyle Kavanagh if they found out he got me into something so dangerous. He promised me he would tell them enemies from *his* past were targeting him. Some of his veteran buddies volunteered to help keep a lookout, giving me some relief and time to focus on sorting out Aunt Lilah's inheritance.

"Aren't you happy about having a break?" Mom asked.

"I don't trust Aunt Lilah."

"You're right, but we don't know what she left you." Mom resembled her sister, both tall and thin with high cheekbones. The difference to me was Mom possessed a soul.

"I bet she paid someone to put a hex on the will."

Mom laughed. "She loved to control people. She often said, "Mary, this will be so much fun!" The activity always turned out to be something she liked, not me. You don't need to accept anything, you know."

"I know."

"Still, I do miss her," Mom said, voice breaking. "We were never close, but she was my only sibling. I never thought pneumonia would take her at this age. Our parents are gone, and now her. I'm devastated."

"I'm sorry, Mom. I'll check if she made any plans for a funeral."

"Thank you." She blew her nose. "How's work been going?"

"My recent assignment was challenging. How's Dad?"

Mom went straight for the diversion. "Oh, he's already gone to bed. He finished harvesting, and he's worried the market's bad."

Farming in South Dakota, like farming anywhere, was unpredictable.

"You guys won't need to worry anymore."

"Davia, we don't need anything. I have my steady paycheck as a school nurse, and it always works out."

"You don't *need* anything, but I can at least hire some help, buy some new equipment."

"Let me think about it."

Stubborn, independent—the apple didn't fall far from the tree.

We chatted a while more, and I promised to tell her about my visit to Mr. Morgenstern. After the call, I took a folded piece of paper out of my pocket. Warden somehow slipped a note into my personal belongings in the hospital room.

Dav—You'll be away from the team, but you'll be with me in my heart. W

My first relationship was my senior year of high school with a guy named Bobby. We went out long enough to attend the prom and provide me with some boy-girl experience. He dumped me because I didn't need his help, lean on him enough, or some other stupid reason I didn't care enough to remember. In college, I dated, but not a lot. I focused on training and studying, which left little time for a relationship. During my years as an operative, flirtations in far-flung cities were my only brushes with romance.

Now, memories of Warden were my most cherished possession. Here we were, at the beginning of a relationship, when we should be learning each other's likes and dislikes and savoring the early, sweet days.

Our wills and fates do so contrary run.

Shakespeare's words from a long-ago class, but so applicable now. I read the note once more, running my fingers over the paper and thinking I might never see Warden again.

Where was he? What if Badger ordered hits on us? What if the team's future missions went wrong without me there to help? Not being with them ached more than my physical injury.

The weight of everything crashed down, and tears stung my eyes.

I took a deep breath.

Operatives don't cry.

~

"Please read that again," I said to Mr. Morgenstern.

My aunt's high-priced lawyer sat at a polished desk. Behind him, an immense window offered a spectacular view of Manhattan. Though young, he wore all the accoutrements of a successful man, a designer suit, gold cuff links, and the calm demeanor of someone used to the idiosyncrasies of the rich.

"You are to receive the bulk of Mrs. Lilah Latham's estate, with certain sums left to charities," he read in his quiet, well-modulated voice. "The total amount is eighty-five million dollars with the following restrictions: To retain this inheritance, the beneficiary must:

1) Purchase a home in one of the five most expensive zip codes in the United States;

2) Serve on the board of a non-profit organization;

3) Be featured in the society pages of the local newspapers or magazines and/or their social media websites at least three times per year;

4) Date one man per quarter with an annual net income of one million dollars or more until you marry, and;

5) The inheritance is forfeited if you don't meet the conditions, and the money goes to other specified causes."

Eighty-five million! Who needed that much money?

"Can't I just give most of it away?"

"Not until you live with the restrictions for twenty years, after which you'll have unfettered access to the full amount. Until that date, you'll receive twenty percent per year and full use of the penthouse."

"What about the dating requirement? Does it have to be a different man every time?"

"No. The only requirement is their net worth."

The will tightened a noose around my neck, the knots tied by a dead person. I clenched my jaw until it hurt.

Mr. Morgenstern had already read the conditions. The first time, I spit out, "You're joking, right?" Most people would jump for joy or give up their firstborn for this much money. Picturing the door to a cell slamming shut, I almost got up and left.

"Tell me more about serving on a non-profit board." What could I do for any organization except steal all their secrets? Mr. Morgenstern believed the cover story about me being a glorified personal assistant who often traveled with her company CEO on business.

"Ms. Glenn, you're now an affluent woman. You'll be a desirable asset to any community," he said.

"I understand people might want me for my money, but how do I get on a non-profit board?"

Mr. Morgenstern made a face at my characterization of wealth. "There are numerous non-profits. Their officers consist of people who love doing charitable work. For example, a garden club, a philanthropic society, an organization fund-raising for abused children, and the like."

"Do the officers get paid?"

Mr. Morgenstern laughed. "No. The people on these boards

volunteer to be on them for two reasons: either they want to help their communities or attempt to control them."

His blunt assessment surprised me.

"Where are the most expensive zip codes? I guess they're places like Beverly Hills or Manhattan?"

Another chortle. I should charge for being so funny.

"No. Those aren't exclusive enough." He handed me a folder with slick inserts containing descriptions of five cities whose names I didn't recognize. I guessed the rich like their privacy to the point of keeping their locations secret from the rest of humanity.

After flipping through the choices, I narrowed my options to New York or California but ruled out New York because I didn't want to be on Aunt Lilah's former turf. Four locations in California remained. Two were near San Francisco, which I nixed because of the fog and cold.

If I must do this, Southern California was my choice.

One of the two available locations was on the coast, the other a short drive inland. I recalled a vacation at the beach and sensed an immediate problem: lots of people and traffic. Solitude is preferable if you're on a hit list.

"Do you need some advice?" Mr. Morgenstern was polite, but I bet my casual attire of jeans, t-shirt, and leather jacket, coupled with a bad haircut, made him rank me with the person who emptied his waste can.

"What I require is a defensible location."

"Do you mean a gated community?"

"No." Since Badger might be after me, I wouldn't trust my safety to some mope working for minimum wage.

"You can always hire a bodyguard."

Now I was the one to laugh.

Regaining my composure, I handed a brochure to Mr. Morgenstern. "Tell me about this one."

A broad smile stretched across his face as he settled back in his chair. "Rancho Suprema is one of the best places in the country to live, Ms. Glenn. An excellent choice."

He acted like we ordered a fine wine instead of choosing a location with astronomical property prices.

"Rancho Suprema is an exclusive community with strict rules on the types of homes built, each on a minimum of two acres. Founders developed the restrictions in the early part of the last century, and the association has maintained the standards. It features a top-rated golf course, tennis club, fine restaurants, and luxury shops. Although most of the residents are somewhat older than you, the area is secluded and first-rate. You won't want to go anywhere else."

To mingle with the unclean?

"I can recommend several competent real estate agents to assist in locating an estate to meet your needs," he continued.

"Thank you ."

"May I be frank?"

"Yes."

"You're an attractive young lady. If you make certain modifications to your wardrobe and style, you can easily meet all the requirements."

I translated this to *You resemble what the cat dragged in, but you might be acceptable if you spend your money on a complete makeover.*

"Challenges are nothing new to me, Mr. Morgenstern. I can do this."

Could I? Did I want to?

"Yes, and if you don't, the fortune goes to a wonderful cause."

"Which is?"

"Continuing the lobbying efforts to stop the rich from being taxed."

"You're not serious."

"Of course I am."

Scarcely able to contain my anger, I got up, pleased to tower over him despite the lifts in his shoes. The polite, helpful Mr. Morgenstern would never speak to me again if I lost the fortune.

"Oh, I almost forgot." He reached into his desk and brought out a sealed envelope. It was heavy, cream-colored stationery, my name emblazoned across the front in Aunt Lilah's distinctive handwriting.

"What's this?" I took it.

"For your eyes only."

Now what?

I decided to wait until I was alone to read it and slipped the envelope into my jacket pocket.

"What will happen to the belongings in Aunt Lilah's penthouse?"

"What do you want to happen?"

Call a priest to do an exorcism of the space? Set her clothes on fire?

"Leave it." Maybe my mom would have some ideas.

My aunt had left instructions for a quiet cremation and interment next to her deceased husband, which already took place. Mom would be sad she didn't get to hold a formal service for her only sibling, but the arrangements were consistent with my aunt's thoughtless nature.

"Thank you for coming, Ms. Glenn," Morgenstern said. "Please don't hesitate to get in touch if you have the slightest question."

He provided a notebook containing information about bank accounts, investments, rental properties, and more. He didn't want to lose me as a client because people like me paid for his expensive view.

"One more question. How do I prove I'm dating?"

Even saying those words made me nauseous. What would I tell Warden?

"Email me the name of your companion and the place you went."

"I could make it up."

"Don't worry; your aunt retained a private investigator."

Bitch.

BACK IN MY ROOM, I tossed the documents on a table, despite being tempted to chuck everything in the waste bin and leave. I limped around the suite, madder than a box of frogs as Hodge would say, whatever that meant.

Wearing my anger down to a simmer, I sat. The sound of paper crinkling reminded me of Aunt Lilah's note. Tearing the expensive envelope in a jagged line brought a small amount of satisfaction. Inside was a heavy card, with *Lilah Latham* engraved in gold at the top.

Well, la-dee-da.

Fuming, I pulled the card out and read.

My Dear Niece:

I have contacts and know the truth of what you do for a living. I won't share how I feel about that because it doesn't matter now. However, I believe you need time to consider your job's long-term consequences and see a different side of life. I'm sure you feel angry, but my will's conditions are because I want what's best for your future. You'll meet a new class of people and enjoy what your current lifestyle hasn't offered.

Love,

Aunt Lilah

A swear word escaped my lips. My current lifestyle? What did that even mean?

I fought the urge to rip her card to pieces.

My whole life, Aunt Lilah refused to recognize my interests. She sent me a fortune in clothes unsuitable for living in a small town in South Dakota, dolls I never played with, and subscriptions to fashion magazines I never read.

Her infrequent visits were like dropping a lion into a room full of babies. Mom cleaned for days while my dad made himself scarce. Her arrival was worse for me than the most strenuous training from Kyle.

Aunt Lilah's husband, Uncle Edwin, resembled a walrus. He came along once on a visit, waddling in. He held his elbows bent and hands flat like he stood in a pool, touching the top of the water. His sentences began with a disapproving harumph from deep in his throat.

Harumph, quaint place.

Harumph, small towns are so charming.

I recalled my aunt standing in our guest room, silver-blonde hair cut in the latest style, clad in designer duds. She left on her oversized, dark sunglasses indoors, her mouth set in a tight, disapproving line as she took in the antique brass bed and homemade quilt. She spun around, catching me in the doorway.

Where did you get that sweater?

I love how you just wear anything.

I admire how you don't care about your appearance.

On and on, the edged words flew. After their visit, my whole family waited until their car disappeared from view, and a bit longer to ensure they didn't return.

Walking away from my whole identity, the job I fought so hard to achieve, Warden, and my team, was tough enough. Despite the endearments and loving sentiment in the note, Aunt Lilah kept trying to turn me into someone I could never be, even after she was dead.

Time to make some decisions.

8

Attacking the will's terms like they were a mission, I set a one-week deadline to find a home in Rancho Suprema. By staying focused, I hoped to stave off the enduring ache of loss inside me.

I checked into the five-star resort Morgenstern recommended, the cost per night an unspeakable amount. Each morning, staff delivered freshly-squeezed orange juice and a newspaper to my door. There were options for an attendant to draw a bath and add essential oils, or I could book a private massage on the room's garden patio. Used to a spartan lifestyle, all I could do was laugh at my sumptuous surroundings.

After a round of viewing properties, I called Mom.

"What's Rancho Suprema like?" My parents refused to accompany me, saying they were confident in my abilities. The truth was, they preferred their rural lifestyle and associated California with jam-packed freeways, earthquakes, and celebrities running wild.

"The community is like being on a movie set. Everything's too perfect."

The downtown area of Rancho Suprema consisted of Spanish-style white stucco buildings roofed with terra cotta tiles. Well-tended trees and flowers lined the streets. Residents chatted, dressed in casual clothes costing thousands. Some walked pedigreed dogs, stopping to let them drink bottled water poured into bowls left outside by businesses catering to their needs. I saw a hint of gold, the flash of diamonds , leopard-patterned mules, and checkered pants on men.

Rancho Suprema screamed exclusive until its throat grew hoarse.

"Have you looked for a place to live?" Mom asked.

"Yes, I toured three already. These estates are unimaginable! The freezers in their kitchens could contain wild animals. There are three-thousand-bottle wine cellars and even helicopter pads in case you don't want to drive."

"It sounds right up Lilah's alley. Nothing was ever too expensive or over-the-top for her."

During my short time in town, real estate agents taught me a new vocabulary: book-matched marble, Circadian rhythm lighting, Bulthaup appliances, wellness center, and atrium, to name a few. I never knew they existed nor even cared. I still didn't.

"These estates contain so many features they need manuals," I continued. "At first, I was overwhelmed by the extravagance. Now, I want my house search to be *over*."

"Remember what we discussed. Try it. If you can't take living out there, you don't need to."

"Well, one property featured a swimmer's pool. I'm tempted," I said.

Mom paused. "What other kinds of pools are there?"

"Exactly."

We tittered over the absurdity and said goodbye.

After a shower, I stared at my reflection. My fair skin, blonde hair, and blue eyes resembled Mom and Aunt Lilah, but scars caused by knives, hot lead, and other deadly encounters marred my skin like a map of near-fatal exploits. My recent wound was a red, six-inch sutured gash on my thigh. I carefully changed the bandage each day, praying the injury would heal with no complications.

My mind went to Warden's muscular body, where a dark scar ran across his side from an assailant attempting to gut him with a combat knife. Our wounds, both physical and mental, came with the job.

I thought about Aunt Lilah's note and how she wanted to expose me to a different world.

Which world? This false fantasyland?

Drawing on a robe provided by the resort, I returned to the goals I set. I would do this to help my parents. If, after one year, I hated this make-believe place as much as I did now, I would return to my operative life.

I PARKED my 3-series BMW rental next to the Tesla driven by my *realtor du jour*, Christa Matthews. I got out, acknowledging her without enthusiasm. She wore a fitted dark pantsuit and pumps. I still kicked about in casual attire, unwilling to think about a new wardrobe.

"Good morning, Ms. Glenn," Christa said in false, bright tones, setting my teeth on edge. She tried to hurry me into the house, but I didn't move.

A marble fountain gurgled next to the motor court where we parked. Centered in a sculpted stone circle was a Grecian statue of a nude male, water pouring out in an indecent arc from his erect penis.

I refused to budge, waiting for Christa to explain. She ran a hand over her sleek mane of hair and played with a dangling bracelet at her wrist. Still not making eye contact, she said, "A contractor can remove it."

"What would I do about the gaping hole in the driveway?"

She reverted to full sales mode. "I can give you a list of consultants to assist you."

"I don't want consultants," I muttered, trying to picture the type of person who commissioned the monstrosity in the first place.

"I called the owner to tell him we'd be dropping by but didn't get an answer. I'm sure he won't mind." She unlocked the door while I waited with most of my weight slumped over my crutches.

We stepped inside. A design inlaid in the foyer simulated frolicking nude cupids, and I sensed an unfortunate theme.

"Ahead is the living room," Christa announced, in a flight-attendant, tray-tables-up-please voice.

Oh no, not another agent who points out the obvious!

Aunt Lilah's manipulations, coupled with being on Badger's hit list without backup, gave me frayed nerves and a short fuse.

"I'm going to explore on my own." I sped down a long hallway before saying something I might regret.

Christa didn't follow. Some agents never got the hint. They trailed along, pointing out everything. *(Ceiling! Floor! Wall!)*

"I'll be in the kitchen!" she called.

At the end of the corridor, two doors led to a master bedroom suite whose furnishings were straight out of an old west bordello. Patterned red velvet wallpaper and a sign announcing *Get Naked!* completed the distasteful decor. As I tried to wrap my head around this, Christa let forth an ear-splitting screech.

There must not be granite countertops in the kitchen.

Her cries took on a hysterical quality. Alarmed, I traced the sound and found Christa.

Her mouth was open, the color gone from her face.

A body lay at her feet.

Christa screamed again, building to a level out-pitching the best alarm system. I scoped the perimeter for possible assailants, looked around two islands and up at the ceiling. A clever way to avoid detection is to hide above the line of vision as most people don't look up. A cast iron cook's rack with copper pots gleamed overhead.

What did I expect to find? Ninjas?

Satisfied, I returned my focus to the body of an older white male. I put fingers to his wrist. He was ice cold.

"He's gone," I said.

Christa grew paler, and I imagined her emitting an *eep, eep, eep* distress signal. I recalled the first time I saw a dead person and the disquiet and shock that hit me.

"Let's go outside." We left the residence and went to a short wall near our cars. Instructing Christa to sit, put her head between her knees and take deep breaths, I dialed 911 and provided the relevant information.

"Help's on its way. I'm going back in," I said, driven by curiosity.

Inside, my faltering footsteps rang in the silence as I passed arched windows overlooking a garden of colorful blooms. A hummingbird sipped from a lilac, a stark contrast to what the kitchen contained.

The deceased lay near the sink, holding one rinsed cup drying in a steel dish rack. The tidy room featured a copper teapot on the stove, a box of decorative, homemade tea bags, and the usual appliances. Nothing indicated a struggle.

Who was this guy?

He might have been considered good-looking in life, with a dark tan and thick head of brown hair. He wore a robe over pajamas. A sizable diamond ring graced his right hand, paired with one of those gold chain necklaces favored in the past century. I concluded he was the owner of the house.

Careful not to touch anything, I left the kitchen and went through a door on the opposite side leading into a formal dining room. On the table, a crystal bowl was framed by candlesticks of entwined nudes. A passage led to the garage, and I eased inside. Light from high windows shone on a king-sized, oval bed centered below a ceiling mirror, its sheets in a tangle.

Yuck.

On my way out, I took note of a nude male light cover. The switch was his private parts.

I must hurry and buy this place. Can't let that little feature get away.

When I went back outside, a police officer talked with Christa. I introduced myself to a second, more senior officer.

"I'm David Sterling with Rancho Private Security. We were the closest unit available."

Officer Sterling's demeanor baffled me since I never expected law enforcement to be pleasant and forthcoming at a potential homicide scene. Perhaps the residents of Rancho Suprema demanded deference from their force.

We went back inside to the body. Officer Sterling conducted a cursory probe for a pulse. "Mr. Weston will be missed."

"Oh?" I had thought of him as the local Lothario, one who made the women, or men, scurry for cover.

"He served in the Rotary Club and the Ladies' League."

I looked confused.

"The Ladies' League is a charitable organization open to members of both sexes, founded over a century ago by the women of this community."

"Oh. How old was he?"

Officer Sterling glanced down. "Fifties?"

"Did you know him?"

"Only to wave at or converse about the weather. Mr. Weston was friendly, but I was usually on patrol and headed somewhere else. His photo was often in the local paper. He was a real man about town, a fixture."

The paramedics arrived, did a quick assessment, and left. Officer Sterling and I went back out into the sunshine to await the homicide team. I took a seat on the wall beside Christa while Sterling spoke into his radio, relaying additional info to dispatch.

"How're you doing?" I asked Christa.

She began to sob again, and I patted her back in an ineffectual attempt to placate her. After a time, she attempted to wipe away the black runny mess left by her mascara with the back of her hand. Officer Sterling handed her a handkerchief.

The homicide team arrived. I repeated my observations to a female detective, thinking I would never have foreseen discussing a potential crime while an indecent statue peed behind me.

An hour later, I left.

Hungry, I drove to downtown Rancho Suprema to buy some groceries, unaffected by Mr. Weston's death. I held a master's degree in compartmentalization, practiced through much of my life. Some of my mental chambers contained such grim memories; I welded them shut and wrapped them in chains.

At the Suprema Market, I headed straight for the produce department to peruse their wide array of offerings. *What was dragon fruit anyway?* A man sidled up, and I moved a few inches away out of habit. He was mid-forties, his lank brown hair and droopy mustache paired with Bermuda shorts and a worn t-shirt. A diamond-and-ruby studded Rolex counterbalanced the laid-back attire.

"Are you new here?" He ogled me.

"I'm only visiting." I picked up some organic bananas.

"Allow me." He put his hand over mine, took the fruit, and put it in the bag I held.

I counted to ten.

"If you'll excuse—" I began.

"Here." He provided me with his business card. "Let's have dinner sometime. You should call me."

Call you what?

Various unpleasant names suggested themselves.

As suddenly as he appeared, he left the store.

Weird day.

I checked the mystery man's card, printed on the finest quality paper.

Kenneth Clayton, CEO, VRMF Corporation.

Even I knew if Kenneth Clayton sneezed, stock markets crashed worldwide. I almost tossed it in a nearby waste bin, but the will's diabolical dating requirements stayed my hand. I wished I could talk to Warden about this nonsense.

What would he say? Would he care? Why hadn't he called or texted?

Although I hadn't even been gone a week, not hearing from him triggered unexpected insecurities and doubts I refused to dwell on.

Focus on the mission.

⁓

BACK AT MY suite at the Hacienda Verde resort, a mega-hot shower burned off the slimy residue from the Weston house and Suprema Market. Afterward, I sat in one of the garden veranda's overstuffed chairs to eat my lunch and decided to phone Kyle.

He supported my leave, disturbed by both my compromised identity and injury. "There's danger, then there's *danger*," he'd said when I first phoned to report the Badger news. "You get out of there, missy."

Having him concur with my decision helped.

"Hey, Kyle."

"What's happening?"

"I can't take much more of this. I need someone I can whine to."

"Most people would slap you for saying that."

"I bet they would."

"I told you this would be difficult. Fitting into the civilian world is different, and I speak from experience," he said.

"I had no clue everything would feel so, well, meaningless. I don't have a purpose anymore."

"You have a *different* purpose. Give it time."

"The only purpose I have now is dancing to Aunt Lilah's tune."

"Well, at least she's not shooting at you."

I gave a small laugh. "True."

"Heard anything from anyone on your team?"

"No."

A pause.

"Don't overthink. They're probably in the ass-end of nowhere and can't reach out."

"Probably."

"How's your leg?"

"Better, I think. I'll be off the crutches soon."

"And the house search?"

I told him about my recent experience, and he laughed at my description of the décor, but not as much about the dead Mr. Weston.

"You can't escape the dark side of life, eh?"

"Nope."

"Well, after you purchase a home, and Badger isn't snooping around after your parents, I'll come out for a round of golf. My prosthetic needs the challenge of a championship course like the one in your new community."

"Don't you have enough frustration in life without golf?"

"Beats the hell out of farming."

"Has anyone suspicious come around?"

"No."

"Are you telling me the truth?"

"Of course. The only excitement was a new combine at the John Deere store."

"Thanks for keeping an eye out."

"You're welcome. Can you get your mom out there?"

"Not until I find a place to live."

"Maybe you could make some women friends? Us men have monopolized enough of your time."

"The only women I've met have been realtors, and they're interested in me to make a sale, nothing more. Finding somewhere to live is taking *way* longer than I thought. Who knew I would be picky about which multi-million-dollar property to buy? Our whole farm would fit into one of these place's bathrooms."

"Well, you either buy something or chuck the inheritance."

"I wish, but Mom thought I should at least try. The money would make their lives easier, and yours."

"Your parents and I are doing fine. We've made it this far, and we'll keep making it. I do agree with your mom, though. Take a break from being a warrior. You might find something you enjoy out there."

Not a chance in hell.

"I'll try."

After we said farewell, I thought about Kyle's words. He was right. I didn't have any close girlfriends, but my chosen career path made making friends difficult. Aubrey Elliot and I worked out together but never did anything outside of the office except share meals as a group. My college roommate liked to party, and we had gone to fraternity or sorority functions. I'd melt into the crowd and huddle against a wall, a drink in my hand. At the earliest opportunity, I would vanish into the night like a prisoner escaping confinement. Making small talk terrified me.

Now, the will's mandates dictated my priorities skew toward stereotypical female impulses, like socializing, makeup, and fashion. Was this what Aunt Lilah eluded to when referring to my "current lifestyle" and how I should broaden my horizons? I kept up with the most ruthless men on the planet. Hadn't Aunt Lilah heard about shattering the glass ceiling?

I stared down at the banana peel in my hand.

Tomorrow was Sunday, the day for open houses. I resolved to head out first thing.

9

Mid-morning the next day, I swung my crutches down the palm-tree-lined path toward the parking lot. Staff was everywhere. Housekeepers pushed carts, bellhops pulled trolleys spilling with luggage, and waiters delivered room service orders. A fair-haired man wearing a resort uniform watched me from a nearby cabana.

Warning bells clanged in my head. I reached for the loaded handgun stashed in a hidden compartment of my purse. I didn't have a concealed weapons permit in California yet but didn't care. Safety came first.

When I looked up, the man had disappeared.

Nearing my car, I began to touch the remote unlock to stash my crutches, but hesitated.

What if someone rigged my car to explode?

Expensive cars packed the lot. A brick wall at its end provided me convenient cover, and I ducked down. Fingers crossed everyone kept up on their insurance payments.

I touched the unlock button.

No boom.

After a walk-around of the car, I straightened my injured leg and got down to ground level. Underneath, no duct tape, wires, finger smudges, or other tell-tale signs were visible. I would be fine unless someone put in a delay switch.

Seated inside, I hesitated before pushing the starter.

I needed to get a hold on my overactive imagination.

The engine rumbled as usual.

GPS navigation brought me to a location high on a valley ridge. The estate boasted two separate entrances guarded by massive gates. The home was Spanish-style, with vines growing on the white stucco walls. A tiered fountain framed the front door, water cascading into a basin paved with colorful Mexican Talavera tiles.

A handsome man in his sixties met me at the door. "I'm Bob Brooks." He provided me a spec sheet and I perused the details: 6,500 square feet, five bedrooms, guest house, four-car attached garage, three acres, pool, pool house, gym, home theater, citrus orchards, barn, and riding arena.

"This property permits three horses, but there's only one here now," Bob said, adjusting his spectacles. "The owner is interested in selling the horse because they're moving to a condo. Or you can convert the arena to a tennis court and the barn into another guest house."

"I don't want to remodel."

"I don't blame you. This is a constantly changing community. The tear-downs and re-builds wear on everyone."

"I bet. How long have you been an agent?"

"Oh, since I retired a few years ago. I grew up here in Rancho Suprema and decided a second career selling homes and meeting new people would be fun."

"What did you retire from?"

"I was an investment banker, successful enough to keep an older home here, nothing like these recently built McMansions. I also play golf and enjoy our championship course."

"Would you give me a tour of the house?" I said, surprising myself.

"I don't walk too fast these days." He pointed to a cane propped nearby.

"No worries. Neither do I!" I held up a crutch.

"What happened?" he asked.

"Tore a muscle running. Nothing major," I said. "Would you fill me in on what this community's about?"

"What can I tell you?"

"I'm interested in serving on a non-profit board."

A total lie.

We moved along a hall with slate floors glistening in rustic gold-brown hues. "I think the best thing would be the Ladies' League. They're the oldest and could use an infusion of some young blood. The members are mostly old-timers like me, long-term residents. They put on an annual gala to raise money for charity. The event is the happening of the year."

"Sounds interesting." Interesting translated to *never in a million years would I want to be involved.*

We turned into a master suite with high ceilings. It featured both his-and-hers walk-in closets and separate bathrooms. Bob didn't ask who would use *his* side, and I liked him even more.

"They need someone to replace the gala chair, Willie Weston. A realtor found his body in his home."

I spoke without thinking. "I was there."

"Oh, no. You must have been shocked!"

"No. I mean, Christa found him."

"Christa Matthews?"

"Yes. Do you know her?"

"We've crossed paths at realtor caravans, the one day each week we can tour properties coming on the market. I don't think she's been a realtor long, but she's ambitious."

"Did you know Mr. Weston?" No way could I say Willie with a straight face.

"How could I not? He was all over town, at every event. His first wife was heiress to a substantial fortune but passed away. After she died, he donated a lot of her money to charity but asked the organizations to feature both their names."

"What do you mean?"

"The Sarah and William Weston wing, the Sarah and William Weston pavilion. Come to think of it, I have it backward. His name always went first."

Of course.

"For the past several years, he and Amelia Meadows dated," Bob continued. "She comes from old money. I think her great-grandfather was part of the Carnegie and Rockefeller crowd, making a fortune investing in the early industries of this country."

"At least Mr. Weston stayed consistent."

"I agree," Bob replied. "But they broke up recently."

"Why was he selling his house if he was a fixture here?"

"He wasn't leaving. I hear he was in escrow on a newer, bigger place Christa Matthews found for him."

I wondered if he would've taken that wretched statue with him but decided not to bring it up.

"Getting back to our discussion about a non-profit, Willie's death leaves the Ladies' League in a lurch, so they'll welcome any help you could offer. I'll give you the contact info of their president."

"Thank you."

We finished the tour of the home and went out to inspect the grounds. A Saltillo tile path led to a four-stall barn. A tack room and office were on one side, with living quarters opposite. A tall black gelding with kind, intelligent eyes put its head into the alleyway through a slot in the stall's upper door.

"What's his name?" I let the horse nibble my hand.

"They told me, but I can't remember. I'm not a horse person."

As a child, I owned a fat brown pony named Sonny. I loved to ride him bareback through the fields, racing along so fast my hair blew back. Whenever my life became troubled, I threw my arms around his neck and breathed into his coat. This horse toted a pudgy hay belly but gave me a friendly nudge when I rubbed his neck.

"Considering the price of this place, they might throw him in for free," Bob said.

A well-muscled, mid-twenties Latino man came out from the barn's living quarters. He reached for a pitchfork hung on a wall rack.

"Senor Brooks," the man greeted. "*Como esta?*"

"*Bien, gracias,* Jose," Bob returned.

Jose went out toward the pasture.

"Does he live here?"

"Yes, but you needn't employ him, although he's a hard worker."

"Is anyone else living here?"

"No one except the horse. Upkeep on a property this size is difficult without help, so on-site staff is common."

One reliable person was better than itinerant crews going in and out. I made a note to get Jose's full name and run a background check. Bob talked about the arena and pasture on our return to the house while I considered where to place an external alarm system.

"I want to put in an offer on this place," I said.

Bob unlocked the front door. "I think the horse sealed the deal."

Negotiations on price didn't take long, and escrow would close in record time. I purchased the horse, Ace, and his tack. Having a place to live lessened the angst but didn't fill the emptiness. I was at the end of my second week since leaving my team, and Warden remained radio silent. The only path forward was to plot out security for my new home and stay busy.

I left a message for the Ladies' League president, Mrs. Beatrice Gibbs, about joining their organization and serving on their board. Next, I decided to shop for a new wardrobe, one more acceptable to Rancho Suprema's residents. I could've stayed in jeans and t-shirts forever.

Boxes of flowers placed along the downtown streets bloomed in a riot of colors on yet another sunny day. A breeze rustled tree leaves, casting patterns on the sidewalk. I ditched the crutches, overjoyed that the days of wrestling with them were over.

A trellis of sweet-scented jasmine vines covered a path to Bryce's Boutique. A silver-haired woman browsed through a sidewalk-sale rack outside the front door. She exuded an invisible barrier proclaiming she disapproved of anyone outside her social class, and brought Aunt Lilah to mind. While I was preoccupied evicting my dreaded relative from my head, the woman removed a blouse off a hanger and slipped it into her purse.

Should I do something? Did I want to engage a thrill-seeking petty thief?

"Excuse me," I said, stepping inside her exclusive personal bubble.

"Yes?" Her sharp eyes sized me up, then attempted befuddlement.

"You need to put back what you just stole."

The woman drew herself up to her full height of around five-four.

"Don't you know who I am? I'm Beatrice Gibbs," she declared. "I'm President of the Ladies' League. Who are you?"

Beatrice Gibbs? Oh, holy beep.

"I recognized you from your picture in the society pages," I improvised. "I'm Davia Glenn. I left you a message about joining the Ladies' League."

Beatrice Gibbs's face was disdainful.

"I'm demonstrating my observation skills," I continued, giving her a conspiratorial wink. "They'll be useful at your gala since Mr. Weston isn't around to help anymore."

Recognizing a way out, she chose to play along. " I understand you bought the Lafferty estate. A fine place."

"Yes, thank you. Now that I'm a resident of Rancho Suprema, I want to get involved in the community, and have heard your organization is the best."

Mrs. Gibbs preened at the flattery. "We're having a meeting about the annual gala two days from now. You can fill out your membership application and pay the dues."

Confirming the time and location of the meeting, she air-kissed me farewell and tottered away.

My attention returned to my quest for a new wardrobe. Squaring my shoulders, I stepped inside the shop, ready to face the Battle of the Browse.

Merchandise filled every conceivable space in the small store. Shelves stacked full of folded blouses and pants seemed ready to topple. Two customers gave me a quick, disapproving once-over.

"*Bonjour, bonjour!*" A male in his mid-twenties called. He wore dark jeans and a shirt sporting a designer logo on his pale, lean frame, his dark hair styled in a short, razored cut. He zipped around to grab outfits and hold them up for the two other customers' consideration.

One woman, a tan brunette with super-size-me implants, wore a dress so short she flashed the world each time she bent over. "I need something *amazing* for Monaco, Bryce. Alex is competing again. I hate that we go every year!" she whined.

"Now, Kelly, he pays for the lifestyle by driving." Bryce whirled around her, snapping his eyes between his other customer and me, like a Tasmanian devil on crack.

"Yes, but all Formula One drivers and their crews *do* is talk about *cars*," Kelly pouted.

"How much money did you receive this time, *Cheri?*" Bryce asked.

"Oh, one hundred."

One hundred? That would pay for the collar of a blouse in here. Maybe.

"Hmm, enough for the whole trip *and* about twenty to lose at the casino." Bryce began to pull together outfits like bunnies out of a hat.

One hundred *thousand* dollars for a shopping spree? I almost threw up in my mouth.

The door chimed as the other customer left, and Bryce trapped Kelly in a fitting room. Edging around a stack of shoeboxes, I wound up in a corner, next to a display of scarves. As I peeked into an orange box labeled Hermes, a multicolored scarf launched itself to freedom and slid to the floor.

Bryce picked it up, a light sheen of sweat on his face.

"*Mon Dieu,* she is a consumer of time." He jerked his head at Kelly's dressing room. "Apologies! What did you need?"

"I moved here recently. My current wardrobe consists of the type of clothes I'm wearing, so I need everything."

Bryce glanced at my figure.

"Five-foot-nine, size six, size seven-and-a-half shoe, size 34C bra," he summed up.

"Uh, I'm not a C."

"No? You wear the wrong size." He tossed me a lacy bra. "Try this one."

Tiny pearls adorned the delicate, pale pink cups, making me cringe. I wore sports bras, not flimsy, impractical undergarments.

"Catch!" Bryce snapped a matching thong my way. It was so small it would fit in a thimble and have room left over. "Come on," he urged, garments appearing in his arms as if by magic. "Once we figure out your wardrobe, we can talk about your hair."

I ran a hand over my short locks. *What was wrong with my hair?* It had grown to three inches, longer than it had been in years.

Inside the changing room, I put the bra and panty on a chair, determined to ignore them. A white lace mini skirt, sheer blouse, and coordinating chunky belt caught my attention. I stuck my head out of the room. "Excuse me?"

Bryce paused, carrying a pile of clothes for Ms. Hates Monaco.

"Yes, Mademoiselle?"

"Uh, I can't wear miniskirts."

"Why not? Your legs are like the giraffe. Show them off!"

"There's a scar on my thigh."

"I'm so sorry," Bryce said, stricken.

Kelly came out of her dressing room. "Br-*eye*-ce, I want something dazzling, not this!" She tossed a belt at him, the rejected item able to blind you at twenty paces. She might as well strap a flashing neon sign to her waist.

I gritted my teeth and went back to considering the clothes, all costing so much money my head began to throb. *This is ridiculous.*

Until I got used to spending thousands per piece– which would never happen– I decided to buy the minimum.

Bryce returned, knocking. "How's it going?"

"I can't decide what to try on."

Bryce flung the door open and made a face. "Those are your underwear?" he cried at the sight of my gray cotton Jockeys.

"Please stop, Bryce." I put up a hand. "I don't know what I'm doing, so this shopping excursion is difficult enough."

"Try this one." He plucked out a red knit sleeveless dress and stayed while I slipped it on.

"What do you think?" I asked, feeling like an alien on a foreign planet.

"*Belle!* Another," he commanded and left to ring up Kelly's selections. Her clothing pile almost reached the ceiling, giving me time to return to being unnerved and overwhelmed.

After Bryce returned, we went through the rest together. He put approvals on the door and rejects on the chair. The stack of clothing on the door grew. Slacks, tops, jackets, dresses—*Keep breathing.*

When we finished, I said, "I'll need a gown I can wear to the Ladies' League gala."

"Be right back." He returned carrying a long garment bag. "This is a couture gown by a designer from South Africa who only does custom work." He spoke in a hushed, reverent whisper. "I acquired this from a woman in New York who gained too much weight."

Bryce drew out a brilliant blue evening gown. Iridescent flowers in peacock-tail colors streamed from the waist down, growing gradually denser until they reached the hem. I couldn't believe something this exquisite existed, but wondered why it appealed to me. Bryce helped me into it. My breasts were lifted by the laced bodice, and the dress's shimmering blues highlighted my eyes.

I touched the embroidery. Why did I desired to purchase it? Was it to compensate for never playing dress-up as a child? Was a princess trapped inside me, ready to catapult out of her tower?

"You can have it on one condition. New lingerie," Bryce said, interrupting my bewildered thoughts.

After further contemplation, I agreed, and Bryce looked triumphant. While he rang up my purchases and bagged my clothes, he delivered a lecture about my hair. "Long hair, l-o-n-g, *Cheri.* The extensions must happen!" He gave me a *fabulous* male hair stylist's information. To distract from the colossal total cost of my purchases, I wondered if they were sleeping together.

I left the store carrying bags and boxes of clothes, shoes, purses, jewelry, and scarves. My packages began to slip as I neared the parking lot, and I moved to catch them.

Tires screeched, and an engine roared.

An *accelerating* engine.

Someone shoved me backward, causing my packages to scatter across the sidewalk as I fell. The same person landed on top of me.

A speeding car had nearly run me over.

10

My Good Samaritan raised himself off me, and his features came into view. He was cover-model hot with high-cheekbones, a strong jawline, and fine eyes surveying me with concern. If this were a romantic movie, the scene would be our meet-cute moment. Instead, I gripped Mr. Magnificent by the shoulders and tossed him aside.

"Hey!" he cried, rolling across the pavement.

Jumping to my feet, I sprinted forward to chase the car. Two steps in, searing pain and numbness shot through my injured leg. A yelp of surprise escaped my lips before I crashed face-first to the hot asphalt.

The car disappeared from view.

My guardian angel rushed to me, kneeling.

"Are you okay?"

What was his accent? British?

"I'm fine," I lied, attempting to massage some feeling back into my leg. The nerve damage lecture the doctor gave me rushed back.

Oh no.

"Here, let me help you." He put down a hand, which I took. My leg couldn't bear weight, so I clutched his arm, embarrassed.

"I strained my leg a few weeks ago and think I got too optimistic."

"Let's go sit down." He wrapped an arm under mine, and my brain moved past mortified to register his exotic spice fragrance.

He smells as delicious as he looks.

The thought was followed by immediate guilt for noticing.

After depositing me on a nearby bench, he snagged his fallen sunglasses off the sidewalk. In his early thirties, he stood at six feet with a swimmer's toned body and broad shoulders. His sandy brown hair was longer and more tousled than I expected for someone clad in a tailored suit.

"I'm sorry I—" I began.

"Tossed me arse over tit to the sidewalk? Cheeky," he said with a smile.

"I wanted to catch the driver." My explanation sounded lame.

He brushed at the dust on his suit. "It was probably some git on their cell phone."

As I continued to rub my leg, my attention turned to my scattered clothes. Only one bag spilled open, the one containing the lingerie. *Of course.* The pink, violet, blue, and black embroidery glittered in the light. The man raised an eyebrow at me, but Bryce ran up holding a forgotten garment bag before I could speak.

"What did you do?" he screeched at me, staring at the strewn packages. When he observed the man at my side, his attitude of high indignation melted.

"Mr. Monroe, forgive me!" He spoke with deference like this guy was the pope.

"No worries, Bryce. And please stop being so formal. Call me Adair."

"Thank you, Mr. Mon—Adair."

Adair Monroe cast me a face full of regret. "I'm late for a meeting. Do you think you can manage?"

"Yes. Thank you again."

"Cheers."

When he disappeared from view, Bryce said, "Don't you know who that was?"

"No."

Bryce stared at me in disbelief. "You don't know?"

"No."

"How can you not? He's one of the most eligible bachelors in the world!"

"So what?" Sensation returned to my leg, and I stretched it.

"So what? So *what*? What happened? Did you bump into him?"

"No, he pushed me out of the way of a speeding car."

"Monsieur Monroe *saved* you?"

"I guess."

Would my leg hold weight? I stood and tested it with care while Bryce continued. "He owns homes all around the world, a fleet of jets, a collection of supercars—"

"Around here, those are requirements," I interrupted, my impatience growing. I needed to get away and think. Was someone trying to kill me, or was it a distracted driver?

"Ah, but he is so, how you say, mysterious? He sends women to my shop—"

"What's their shopping allowance?"

Bryce shuffled his feet, gaze downcast.

"Unlimited."

"Oh, I understand now." I picked up some of the boxes. "You love him because he lets his string of bimbettes spend a fortune at your store."

"*Non,* Mademoiselle." Bryce helped pick up the scattered packages. "Besides being *magnifique* in appearance, he's also charitable."

"Whatever." I was in no mood to listen and limped toward my car. Bryce took the keys from me and began to hit the trunk unlock button.

"Don't! I need to check something first."

"*Check?* Check what?"

"I can't explain." I did a slow, walk-around inspection.

"You're worried about scratches?" Bryce wore a puzzled expression.

"Something like that."

Satisfied, I popped the trunk, and Bryce helped me load the bags.

"Thank you for the help." I put a hand against the car's rear panel to take the weight off my still-unsteady leg.

"*Pas de probleme. Au revoir.*" He wiggled his fingers at me and runway-walked back to his store.

Anxiety filled me as I got in the driver's side and used trembling hands to lift my aching leg into the cab. Being helpless in the face of a potential enemy was unfathomable and unacceptable.

People speed through parking lots. Don't overanalyze things.

Believing that taking action in a different form might help, I touched the steering wheel's phone button.

"Morgenstern and Ludwig, may I help you?" the firm's receptionist, Mrs. Fritz, answered.

"May I speak with Mr. Morgenstern, please?"

"May I say who's calling?"

I almost said no, but Mrs. Fritz recognized my voice by now. "Davia Glenn."

Did she sigh? "One moment, please."

Mr. Morgenstern answered. "Ms. Glenn. What can I do for you today?"

"I'm changing hotels."

"Do you need a recommendation?"

"No."

"Then why did you call?"

Was that exasperation in his voice?

"I need a car. How much can I spend?"

"I gave you the financials."

I never lived anywhere long enough to balance a checkbook, much less interpret complex financial data. My only actual purchases were travel costs, the property, and my new wardrobe. How much of my annual money was left? The name of the financial advisor escaped me.

"Remind me again why I'm paying you?" I used haughty Beatrice Gibbs tones.

A pause. "Unless you plan to buy a car for each day of the year, I think you'll be fine. You're not planning to do that, are you?"

"I'm thinking about getting a Maserati." The old Joe Walsh tune my dad liked now played in my head.

"Your investments are doing well, and you don't need to worry about finances. Do you need anything else?"

"No, and thank you."

Shifting into gear, I headed back to the resort and checked out, deciding to up my safety measures. A bellhop wedged my duffel bag into the trunk with my recent purchases. I tipped him and left to search for a more anonymous motel. The move to my new home was in a few days, and I planned to remain firmly under the radar until I could be in control of my security.

Before trying to find a motel, I stopped for lunch. An outstanding feature of living in Southern California was the Mexican food. Sitting with my back to the wall, I assessed each patron while enjoying my carne asada burrito. Satisfied the customers were day-laborers, I made a to-do list in my iPhone notes.

1. *Supplies for a security system. (5 asterisks to emphasize importance)*

2. *Furniture, unless you want to sleep on the treadmill.*

3. *Take the concealed weapon test.*

4. *Run a background on Jose.*

5. *Make a hair appointment. (Sad emoji.)*

6. *New car. Anything you want. (Smile emoji.)*

7. *Riding boots- the thigh-high Dior boots from Bryce won't work!*

8. *Call Mr. VRMF for a date. (Vomiting emoji.)*

Making a doctor's appointment about my leg didn't make the list. The limb felt back to normal now, and I put the collapse down as a one-off, shoving my anxieties into a distant corner of my mental closet.

A helpful salesperson at a nearby furniture store provided me with much-needed guidance. I picked out a bedroom and living room set and a kitchen table with chairs and arranged for their delivery. Leaving, I put my head down on the steering wheel. I still didn't own dishes, glasses, sheets. Would this ever end?

Focus on the mission.

Checking into a chain motel within ten minutes of Rancho

Suprema, I situated my belongings in the closet and then dialed Aubrey at Colonel Streeter's office.

"Davia? I can't believe I'm hearing from you! Are you coming back?" Aubrey gushed.

"No, I need a background check. I didn't know who else to ask."

"Is it for someone you're dating?" She sounded amused.

"Dating? No." I let out a laugh at the complete absurdity of the thought. "It's for a potential tenant at a property I bought in Rancho Suprema. His name is Jose Valenzuela Macias." I supplied his information.

"You're in California now? Bored with the East Coast already?"

"I'm on an extended vacation." I fought the urge to ask whether they found the leak because she couldn't tell me anything.

"Let me run this; it won't take more than a sec." Aubrey typed on her computer, and a door opened and closed. She said, "Hey, Luke," and he grunted a response.

Luke made no secret of his disgust for my work as an operative, wanting the position for himself. Only Colonel Streeter's presence had kept him from jumping up and down when I left the team.

"Why don't you get back to me later?" I suggested.

"Yes, Sir, right away." She refused to give Luke a hint about the person on the other end. I searched in my bag for the business card Bryce gave me, flopped back on the bed, and dialed.

"Salon Divine," a chirpy female answered.

"I'd like to make an appointment with Ramon."

"What did you need?"

"A cut, color, and hair extensions." I recited Bryce's list of necessary improvements.

"The soonest we can fit you in is two months from now, okay?"

Why would she think a lengthy delay was okay?

"Bryce told me Ramon would get me in immediately," I said.

"Would tomorrow at four o'clock work?"

I smiled, my suspicions about Bryce and the stylist confirmed. "Perfect."

The receptionist took my information and said, "See you tomorrow."

My phone rang again within a minute. "He's clean," Aubrey told me.

"Thanks. I owe you."

Furniture, *Done*. Hair? *Done*. Jose? *Done*. I needed to swing by the house and tell him to stay on and figure out his wages. Next, schedule the concealed-carry test. I pulled up the contact information on Google.

"Sheriff's Department, licenses," a male answered.

"I need to finalize my concealed weapons permit."

He gave me the information on the shooting test's location and made an appointment to finish the paperwork.

"Is there a range near Rancho Suprema where I can practice?"

The man let out a bark of laughter. "Those people would never allow a range anywhere near that place."

"What's the closest?"

"Try United Shooting. Here's their number."

I tapped the information into my phone, resolving to arrive early the following day. If I had to subject myself to sitting at the hairdresser's all afternoon, I needed to shoot something first.

11

____

s I stowed my gear in the trunk of the Beemer the next day, my cell phone rang. The ID read _Unknown_.

"Hello?"

"Ms. Glenn?" asked an unfamiliar man's voice.

"Yes?"

"This is Detective Montoya from Sheriff's Homicide. I need to speak to you about the William Weston case."

"What did you need to know?"

"I'd like to go over your statement and ask you a few more questions.

I tried to place him, only recalling a uniformed, young Caucasian patrol officer and a female detective.

"You left before I arrived," he said, reading my mind. "Would you be able to come in this morning, or did I catch you at a bad time?"

"I'm on my way to an appointment."

"How about this afternoon?"

"Is Mr. Weston's death being considered a homicide?"

"I can't comment."

"I have an appointment at four p.m."

When did my calendar fill up?

"Can you come by at 1:30? This won't take long."

I took down the address. Was Weston murdered? The only evidence of a crime I observed was his taste in decorating.

Four other vehicles were in the parking lot of United Shooting. A well-dressed man unloaded aluminum cases out of the immaculate trunk of a luxury vehicle. Next to him, a pile of disheveled people sat in the cab and bed of a rusty pickup. One of their many bumper stickers read *Honk if you've never seen a gun fired from a vehicle.*

Two minutes before the place opened, I popped the trunk, took out my bag, and made for the front door.

Tell me again why I didn't use a military range?

"We offer an introductory class for women on Wednesday night," a clean-cut young employee said as I completed the necessary paperwork and paid their fee. My pieces were new, so he assumed I was a novice. I declined through gritted teeth. "We have indoor and outdoor ranges. What's your preference?" he continued.

"The least busy location."

"Well, I can't make any guarantees, but our outdoor range is for farther than twenty-five yards and doesn't get as much use."

"What's the concealed weapons course standard?"

"Farthest point is ten yards outdoors."

"Fine, outdoors."

"Do you need any targets, ear/eye protection, or ammo?"

"No." A local contact of Colonel Streeter supplied me with everything upon my arrival.

"You can use whatever space is unoccupied."

The outdoor range included a covered roof but didn't cause much of a dip in the balmy temperature. I stapled a target to a wooden frame with a bulls-eye in each corner and the center and fitted it in a ground slot at the fifteen-yard mark. I laid out my equipment and ammo, popped in my ear protection, and left on my sunglasses.

The backwoods bumpkins headed toward me while I loaded the .45. They all carried muskets.

"Ya'll go right ahead, now," said the oldest man. "We'll wait."

They didn't wear ear protection; their hearing loss, not mine. I put in a magazine, trying not to think about the various stains in the man's beard and down the front of his plaid shirt. I fired all my rounds, the bullets hitting dead-center.

The rustic family used pieces of beat-up cardboard as targets. The seventy-something matriarch was a small woman who looked like she walked in from a wagon train in her lengthy, faded skirt and button-up blouse. The man who spoke to me might be her son. Hard to say. Two young men and one girl, all inbred and odd, hovered behind them. They smiled, revealing stained teeth.

I loaded my 9mm and chose the upper left bulls-eye, firing my rounds in rapid succession. Much to my relief, my aim was perfect.

The youngsters put up targets. Grandma pulled a wad of cloth out of the side of her mouth, stuck a musket ball inside, and inserted it into her ear. She did the same for the other side.

Hillbilly ear protection.

They poured black powder into their muskets, pulled wads of cloth out of their inner cheeks, and used rods to tamp musket balls into the old armaments. Maybe they were civil war reenactors?

"Ready?" I asked, and the group nodded.

With my revolver, only four of my shots hit the mark. I dumped the spent casings and was about to reload when Grandma hoisted her musket and fired off a round— right at me!

A ball flew past my ear.

Grabbing my empty 9mm and a loaded magazine, I hit the ground, slammed it in, and racked a round in one smooth motion. As I raised my arm to fire back, the whole clan pointed with urgency at something behind me.

"He was about to shoot you!" one of the young men exclaimed.

A man carrying a gun ran away.

The assailant wore a ball cap pulled low, obscuring his features. A trail of blood marked his path, but he disappeared behind a storage shed.

Biting my lower lip, I ran. Jabs of knife-like pain spiraled down my leg with each step, but I ignored the agony and kept my gun up and ready.

Reaching the building, I flattened against a wall and checked around the corner. The man scaled a chain-link fence surrounding the range. He vaulted over its razor-wire top and dropped to the ground. I ran forward, hoping to get off a shot, but numerous cars whizzed past as he dashed across a busy street.

Thwarted by innocent bystanders.

He held his left shoulder, blood streaming between his fingers. He got in the driver's seat of a dark sedan and accelerated off, license plate obscured by a paper cover.

When the car was out of sight, I turned back. The younger members of the group rushed up to me.

"Who was that guy?" the oldest boy asked.

"You loaded fast! Are you a superhero or something?" the girl commented.

I shook off their questions and went back to the range.

"I owe you one," I told Grandma. "You got him."

The woman broke into a toothless smile. "Of course, I did. I don't miss."

"A woman after my heart. I'm Davia Glenn."

"Arlene Knecht. This is my boy, Chester."

"Pleased to meet you." Chester turned to spit something on the ground, adding to the nastiness of his beard. "These are my kids: C.J., A.J., and Bobby Jr., named after my wife's father. Bless his soul."

I got why he didn't say B.J.

"What was that about?" A.J. asked.

"That was my ex-boyfriend. He causes problems sometimes."

"Well, I wouldn't mess with you," Bobby Jr. said to laughter.

"Ain'tcha goin' to report this to the police?" Arlene asked.

"No. Too much time and paperwork."

Their faces showed understanding. I bet they didn't involve the police in their disputes, either.

My leg throbbed, and adrenaline gave me a buzz, but there was nothing more I could do about my unknown hitman. This incident confirmed Badger planned to eliminate me, despite me no longer being part of my team. In a way, he was clever. Without my deadly teammates and contending with my current limitations, I would be easier to kill. Setting aside my apprehension for now, I refocused on why I was at the range.

"Let's go practice," I said. "Arlene, I'm firing my .22 high and left. Can you help?"

"Sure thing."

Half an hour later, I fired my .22 with extreme accuracy. My new friends all joined in the coaching, having fun offering advice. Before I left, I gave each ear protection, and their celebratory jubilation was better than Christmas.

Aware of the time, I thanked them and went to my car. After performing a quick check to ensure it wasn't tampered with, I needed to break some speed limits to make my appointment with Detective Montoya.

As I drove, I considered the details of the failed assassination attempt. Was the gunman the same person who tried to run me over near Bryce's Boutique? How had he known I would be at the range? Did he follow me from my previous hotel to the new one? My eyes went to the rearview. Despite the time, I wrenched the wheel, cutting across two traffic lanes.

Horns blared, brakes squealed, and more than one motorist flipped me off.

Once in the slow lane, I allowed cars to speed past. After observing traffic for several miles and spotting no tails, I sped up again. Having an assassin targeting me when I wasn't full strength with no one for backup unnerved me.

If not for that wacky clan, I might be dead.

Parking at the sheriff's department building, I divested myself of all weapons. There were enough problems in my life without lighting up their metal detectors. The three-story tan building's sliding glass doors displayed the sheriff's logo. Passing through security, I approached a front desk staffed by a deputy reading a *Guns & Ammo* magazine and said I was meeting Detective Montoya.

Waiting, I kicked around the lobby, read the elder abuse prevention posters, and pamphlets on domestic violence victim resources. A few minutes later, an elevator dinged. A man in his thirties, with a slim build, dark hair, and Oscar Isaac eyes, stepped out. He was my height and wore tan pants with a white long-sleeved shirt and loosened tie.

"Ms. Glenn? I'm Detective Montoya. Why don't you come upstairs with me?"

Receiving a visitor's badge from the desk deputy, I went with Montoya to the elevator.

He gave me a quick once-over. "Out shooting?"

Who was this guy, Sherlock Holmes?

"Yes."

"You have gun powder on your face."

I stopped myself from trying to wipe off something I couldn't see.

"I was practicing for my concealed weapon permit test."

The elevator doors opened to an office space separated into cubicles. You applied for a CCW?"

"Yes." My superiors provided plausible reasons to obtain a permit, but nothing gave away my past.

Montoya led us to a side room containing a table and two chairs.

"Coffee?" He threw down his notepad.

"I don't drink it."

"A soda?"

"Water would be fine."

He gave me a small bottle.

"Thanks."

We sat, and Montoya spent a minute scrutinizing me. I drank some water, polite interest on my face.

"There's more to you than meets the eye, Ms. Glenn."

"Of course there is, Detective. I'm a woman."

He smiled, took a small machine out of his pocket, and put it on the table. "I'm turning on the recorder now." He recited his name, the date and time, and asked me to say and spell my name.

After the introduction, Montoya began his questions. "Had you met William Weston prior to his death?"

"No."

"Why don't you go through what happened."

I recounted my memories, and he asked a few more questions. Concluding our discussion, Detective Montoya shut off the recorder.

"What killed him?" I was curious.

"Most likely a heart attack, but we interview everyone to be careful." Montoya got up, and so did I. He did a silent assessment of me again.

He's a smart one.

"Didn't you do an autopsy?" I asked.

"Yes."

"And?"

"Thank you for coming in, Ms. Glenn," he said, shutting down further questions.

"Call me Davia."

"I'm Ricardo." He escorted me back to the elevator. "Is the number I have the best way to reach you?"

"Yes. As far as an address, I'm settling into a new residence."

"Where?"

"Rancho Suprema." I gave him the address. "I'm moving in tomorrow. If you need to visit, give me a heads up so I can buzz you in the gate."

"A CCW and security? Sounds like you're a careful lady."

"Shouldn't everyone be?"

"Of course. What did you do to your leg?"

Was I still favoring it?

"Strained it while running," I said, recognizing that today's chase set my healing back once more. Thinking about the injury made the pain intensify.

The elevator arrived, and I got in. Detective Montoya stayed motionless until the doors shut.

Glad I'm not a bad guy. Wouldn't want Super Detective on my tail.

I bet he went straight back to his computer and had my application to carry concealed already pulled up on the screen.

12

———————

Leaving the sheriff's department, I drove through a nearby fast-food place. It was almost three p.m. I wondered how to begin home surveillance measures, plus show up for that stupid hair appointment. Canceling was tempting, but I recalled the Ladies' League meeting was in two days.

When did any of this new reality become important?

As I pulled out of the drive-thru, my phone rang. The screen showed an unknown number request for FaceTime.

"Hello?"

"Dav?"

"*Warden*?" My pulse quickened as his familiar features came on screen. I slid the car into a parking spot.

"I need to make this fast," he said, sounding intense like he did when delivering unexpected bad news at team briefings. "We think Badger's tracked you. Are you in California?"

"Yes."

His expression said he wanted to ask more but didn't have time. "You need to—(*shsssh, crrk.*)"

His image wavered, and a series of colored zig-zag lines cut across his face.

"I'm having problems hearing you. Please repeat."

"Can't help—in-country—" Tired circles rimmed his eyes. A fresh, bloody gash crossed an eyebrow.

Static roared, obliterating his image.

"Warden? *Warden!* Can you hear me?

I kept the line open, hoping the signal would clear. Over a minute later, the connection returned.

"Do what I told you, and don't be reckless," Warden admonished, green eyes boring into me.

"I didn't catch—"

"If anything happens to you, I'll never forgive myself for not being there. I miss you—hope soon—"

Interference blared again for several long minutes before the call abruptly cut off.

I banged my hand hard against the steering wheel. If Warden reached out, the situation was no joke, perhaps worse than my assessment. Why hadn't Streeter's office given me a head's up?

Putting together the fragments of what Warden said, I knew "in-country" meant he was off-grid and couldn't help. The glimpse of him wrenched my heart and I missed him beyond words.

I want to be with you, James Warden.

Would we ever be together? Who was after me? How many?

There were so many questions, but sitting in a parking lot wouldn't provide the answers. I pulled out, shoving fries into my mouth without tasting them. Getting back on the freeway, I hit the fast lane.

JOSE WEED-WHACKED the driveway's edge as I lowered my driver's side window.

"*Hola*, Ms. Glenn. *Como esta?*"

"*Bien, gracias.* Would you like to keep working here?"

Jose nodded, and I decided to tell him the truth, "Jose, there are some bad guys who want to kill me, so I plan to increase the property's security."

"Senorita!" he exclaimed but didn't appear panicked, and any lingering doubts about him eased.

Together, we plotted where to install triggers for alerts. Although I couldn't navigate the uneven terrain well, I pointed and relayed my plan. Jose ran back to the barn and retrieved a shovel.

"I'll be back tomorrow to help!" I promised, racing to my hair appointment.

Salon Divine occupied a space in a shopping complex surrounded by expensive boutiques and restaurants. A young receptionist, her blonde hair pulled into an elegant French Twist, greeted me from behind a polished mahogany desk.

"Hi, I'm Bambi. Ramon is running behind schedule, Ms. Glenn. Would you like something to drink? We have organic tea, sodas, water—"

"Water, please."

"Flat or sparkling?"

"Um, flat?"

Bambi brought me a bottle of chilled water and went back behind her desk. Quiet music played, and a wall fountain gurgled. The serene and chic décor surprised me, but Supercuts was my previous salon of choice. I took a seat facing the windows, careful not to be lulled by the stacks of tabloid magazines waiting to seduce me. Instead, I replayed Warden's call in my mind, searching for any nuance but coming up with nothing new.

Half an hour later, a woman emerged, coiffed to perfection. Behind her was a Black man built like a football player, a series of studs in his right ear. Metal bracelets on his left wrist jingled.

"Ms. Glenn? I'm Ramon."

I shook his outstretched hand. "Nice to meet you."

Ramon focused on my hair. At least he didn't share Bryce's horrified reaction. "Bambi!" he called. "Please tell Bryce I won't be home in time for dinner."

Ramon gave me a sleek black smock to wear, then sat me in his chair.

"Bryce didn't sell you those clothes, did he?"

"I need the Rancho look before I wear the Rancho clothes."

Ramon gave a hearty laugh. "I understand. While you're processing, Annette can give you a manicure and pedicure and wax your eyebrows."

Would the torture never end?

"You won't be surprised to learn this is all new to me."

Ramon stared at my reflection in the mirror. "You're kidding, right?"

"No. The state of my nails and hair didn't matter until I inherited some money."

"You've clearly spent time with a personal trainer," he said, wiping some kind of foul-smelling solution on my hair.

"Nope, no trainers."

"Well, once we get your hair done, you'll rock this town," he said.

The salon experience took three hours, with more steps than some of my most intricate missions. While my nails and toes were French-manicured, I sat under a dryer with my newly colored hair.

"Oh my, you must play a lot of tennis or golf!" the manicurist remarked when she noted the callus in the web of my thumb on my right hand from years of repetitive shooting drills.

"Something like that."

Ramon cut and dried my hair, then retrieved a bundle of lustrous, wavy blonde extensions. "Below the shoulder blades, I think." He put them next to my face, letting the hair drape over me like a cape.

Kyle warned me long hair was convenient for an enemy to hold. Putting in flowing tresses while an assassin trailed me was lunacy. Still, I needed to blend in and throw whoever was trying to kill me off their game.

Why let self-defense get in the way of making a fashion statement? Besides, most of the women in this town were blonde. I guess blondes have more funds.

The final result astounded me. No one would be able to tell the sleek hair drifting down my back wasn't mine. Ramon stood behind me, satisfied. "Now, *please* wear the clothes."

"I promise," I said, thanking him for the transformation. "And tell Bryce hi."

"I will, and also bring home chocolates. I'm *so* late!"

The experience of paying the exorbitant cost of my purchases at Bryce's Boutique came in handy. I couldn't conceive of hair and nail care costing thousands, but everything in this town required what seemed like a zillion zeros.

A full moon shone on a nearly deserted parking lot. I yawned, wiped from the stress of the day's events. Absentminded, I touched the unlock button— and the BMW blew up.

13

The explosion threw me a fair distance, and my bad leg slammed into the sidewalk. A white-hot inferno reached for the sky, and black smoke spewed forth, obscuring the scene. In an instant, I was up with my revolver in hand, ears ringing from the blast. People flooded out of buildings, pointing and taking photos or videos with their phones.

I spun around, checking in all directions for threats.

No one stood out.

Before anyone got me on camera, I tucked the gun into my waistband and let my shirt cover it. Excruciating pain radiated down my leg, and I hoped I could remain standing.

Ramon and Bambi ran up, Bambi murmuring what looked like *"Oh my Gods."* I put a hand to my head, wondering when my hearing would return. If I strained, I could make out faint sounds.

A breeze shifted the smoke to reveal only the passenger side of my car sustained serious damage. The assassin was either beset with Attention Deficit Disorder or flunked his explosives course.

Whatever the reason, he blew it.

The piercing sound of sirens reached me as if from a great distance. Everyone in the complex might have dialed 911 since cars don't explode in Southern California every day. Ramon came to stand beside me, and we viewed the devastation. Bambi didn't move, mouth open and face colorless.

Ramon asked me something.

"Could you speak up? I'm having trouble hearing right now."

"Is that your car?" he asked at a higher volume.

"Yes."

Ramon covered his mouth with a hand, eyes wide. "What do you think happened?"

"Faulty wiring?"

"Were you injured?" He looked me over.

"My hearing's still off, but it's gradually getting better."

"You sure?"

I nodded, and he squeezed my shoulder. "At least your hair is still fine. I need to call Bryce," he said, and Bambi followed him back to the salon.

Emergency vehicles pulled in, and firefighters unrolled hoses to begin spraying. Hyper-alert, my eyes darted around the complex. After a time, I concluded whoever did this was gone. Limping to a bench, I sat to wait until someone needed to talk to me.

A deputy sheriff came towards me, moving with the casual yet alert stride of a seasoned professional. "Miss, did you see anything or anyone?"

Relieved I could hear his question, I said, "The car that exploded was my rental. I didn't see anyone."

"What happened?"

"Faulty wiring?"

The deputy cocked his head. "Why don't I believe that?"

Because only an imbecile would?

I couldn't conjure a better explanation. Almost getting blown to bits spooked me. As I gathered my nerves, Detective Montoya appeared through the spray of the fire hoses. He glanced at me, startled. "Ms. Glenn?"

"Detective."

The deputy nodded to Montoya and went back to his patrol car.

"I'm glad you didn't change clothes since our interview. I would've mistaken you for a model," Montoya said, his hooded eyes showing male appreciation.

I stood. "I never pegged you for a flatterer."

"First, the Weston scene, and now this?" He indicated the smoldering hole behind us. "I don't believe in coincidence."

"I think I got a rental with faulty wiring."

He raised an eyebrow. "That was a forceful explosion."

"It was a connection error—or something."

I needed to shut my mouth.

"Are you an explosives expert?"

Not as much as K, but not too shabby either. "Oh, I caught a TV program about IEDs in the Middle East."

"Ah-huh." Disbelief dripped from him. "I think someone is trying to kill you."

"What? *No!*" I brought my hand to my chest and did my best to appear shocked.

"Can you think of anyone who might want you dead?"

A long list of names scrolled past.

"No."

He studied me. "Tell me what happened."

I did, without elaboration.

"So, you hit the unlock, and it blew up?" he read back from the notes he made on a small pad.

"Yes. Glad I didn't wait to pull the door handle."

"Did you notice anyone suspicious?"

"No."

"And you can't think of any reason someone would target you?"

"No."

"Are you hurt?" Montoya noted I swayed a fraction from the pain of putting full weight on my leg.

"When the blast knocked me over, I think I aggravated that strain."

"Want me to call over the paramedics?"

"I'm fine."

Montoya looked unconvinced, but said, "I need to inform our criminal intelligence unit and get the bomb squad out. Don't leave."

Damn.

"I won't. I'll be in Salon Divine."

Inside, Bambi reclined in a chair, damp cloth on her forehead. Ramon talked on the phone to Bryce, explaining why he ran so late.

"Turn on the TV," Ramon implored.

I went to find a cold water bottle to hold on my leg, then chose a chair in reception. Ramon soon joined me.

"Bryce told me to make a hair and makeup appointment for you on the day of the Ladies' League Gala."

"I don't know the date."

"I do, believe me." Ramon made a notation in his appointment calendar, providing me his business card with the date and time written on it. Bambi didn't move.

Ages later, Detective Montoya entered with the female detective who interviewed me at the Weston scene. Montoya introduced himself and Detective Worth. She took statements from Ramon and Bambi while I forced myself to stand and offer them something to drink.

Gee, I should find a job as a hostess at crime scenes.

Montoya trailed me as I limped into the back, where I got him a soda.

"Is your leg better?"

Other than feeling like someone rammed a hot fireplace poker through it, yes.

"I'm good. Do you think the firemen could pry open the trunk of my car?"

"Need your guns?"

I considered a denial but relented. "I qualify for my CCW in a few days." I didn't mention the piece now returned to my ankle holster.

We went back outside. Remnants of smoke left a haze, accompanied by a strong smell of hot metal, gas, and oil. Montoya asked the firemen to cut the trunk.

"Do you need a ride home?"

"I'm staying at a motel. I can catch an Uber."

"I can drop you on my way back to the office."

"Aren't you done for the night?"

"Nope, my work's only beginning." He sounded weary.

"I'd appreciate it." I retrieved my gun case from a fireman.

We got into Montoya's car, but he didn't start the engine. Instead, he turned in my direction.

"I realize you're in shock, but things aren't adding up for me. I find it difficult to believe you don't have a clue who blew up your car. Doesn't anyone come to mind, like an ex-boyfriend?"

I scrunched up my face with pretend concentration and waited a reasonable amount of time before replying. "Sorry. I can't think of anyone."

Except inept assassins.

Montoya's perceptive brown eyes remained on me, and I did my best to appear overwhelmed. Finally, he started the car and we rode in silence, reaching the motel.

"Do you remember anything else?" he asked, pulling to a stop.

"No. Sorry."

His lips thinned into a line.

Inside my room, I tossed my gear and myself on the bed.

That was close, so close. Twice in one day!

Pulling off my jeans, my hands moved to my injury. Some blood seeped through the bandage, but the overwhelming pain had diminished.

Please don't let this event set back my recovery.

I considered phoning Kyle, but it was late in South Dakota, and he would be on a plane out here first thing to back me up if I told him everything. I didn't want him to stop safeguarding my parents. At least tomorrow, I could move into my new home. For now, I would count my blessings, thank my lucky stars, and get ready for anyone who might come next.

14

My happy fantasies about buying a car now struck me as a chore. I contacted the rental agency to inform them about the explosion and that the sheriff's department had impounded the BMW.

Doing soft movement accompanied by three aspirin, the pain in my leg dwindled to a manageable state.

Hooking up a ride on Uber, I dressed in a gray Burberry pantsuit. When my driver arrived, I put all my belongings in the trunk. She took me to my new home so I could drop everything off.

"Bonita!" Jose said when he saw me. He helped carry all the bags and boxes to the master closet. They took up an eighth of the space, hanging forlornly in a corner. Bryce needed to stay out of my home.

I put on colossal Chanel sunglasses, my automatic in my purse, and Aunt Lilah's ostentatious diamond ring on my right hand. The crutches stayed behind once more in hopes my leg would continue to hold me up.

Inside the Maserati dealership, a smartly-dressed man with an Italian accent said, "Welcome to Exotic Motors, Miss. My name is Anthony. Are you interested in any car in particular?"

"I'm don't know. I need to look around."

Stairs led to an intimate showroom containing four vehicles.

"Let me show you the models. If you like any of them, we can order one in whatever style, color, and interior you would prefer."

Was buying a Maserati like purchasing furniture? "I need one today."

"Well, you can choose from what's in our showroom."

Relieved, I went toward a polished, black car. "I like this two-door." Its aerodynamic, sporty style made it appear to be going 200 mph even while parked.

"The model is our Maserati MC20. It just arrived."

Anthony held the driver's door open for me. I slid in, appreciating the feel of my silky pants against the leather seats. "Can we take this for a drive?"

"I'm not supposed to."

His answer surprised me. "Why not?"

"This car was a special order, and the owner is coming by soon."

Darn it. My luck continued its downward trend.

While I considered what to do, a familiar figure entered. Although he wore casual clothes, you didn't need to be a trained operative to recognize Adair Monroe. His symmetrical features and ripped body would make him stand out anywhere.

"Ah, here's the owner now," Anthony said. "He won't mind letting you drive his car."

"I doubt it."

"Excuse me?"

"Never mind." I climbed out.

Adair wore tight black jeans and a pastel blue v-neck t-shirt, enhanced by his lanky frame. He honored Anthony with a grin, revealing white teeth.

"*Ciao*, Anthony." Noticing me, he said, "How do you like my new —" He broke off. "Have we met?"

I wanted to say no but didn't. "The last time we saw each other was near Bryce's Boutique."

Adair's eyes widened. "Oh my gosh, how are you? How's your leg?" He kissed me on both cheeks like we were best buddies.

"I'm Davia Glenn, by the way."

"Adair Monroe."

I didn't say I knew because that might imply I cared.

"Miss Glenn is interested in purchasing a car like yours," Anthony said.

"Are you copying me?" Adair's tone was flirtatious, dimples appearing as he gave me an impish smile.

Wanting to shut him down, I said, "My car got blown up yesterday, so I need a new one."

"Blown up?"

"Yes."

"Blimey! Was that you? I read about it on Twitter this morning. I'd still be in bed if that happened to me! Was someone trying to kill you?"

"No. I think it was faulty wiring."

"What kind of car?"

I told him.

"I own a few BMWs, but not that model. My mechanic can check them just in case."

I wanted to tell him not to bother but didn't.

Adair put his hand on my arm. "I'm curious, Ms. Glenn. Why does violence follow you around?"

Violence would happen to him if he didn't let go. He was *so* touchy-feely.

"To keep my life interesting, I guess."

Adair tightened his grip. "If you want the car, it's yours."

"*What?*" Confusion spun.

"I mean it. You need something to go your way after what happened." He lifted his hands in a conciliatory gesture. "I can order another one."

I was speechless.

"Thank you?" I said at last.

Warden would've shrugged at the news of the explosion and said something like, "You're still here, aren't you? Go find the idiot who muffed the wiring job." Adair was a near-stranger but acted with kindness and consideration, which gave me pause. I never expected anyone from Rancho Suprema to exhibit those qualities.

He said, "Anthony, why don't you expedite the paperwork for Ms. Glenn?"

Anthony sped to his office, relieved.

"Thank you again. I appreciate it, but please call me Davia."

"Davia? That's an unusual name."

"My parents thought I would be a boy and wanted to name me Dave, after my grandpa. When I was born, they modified it but pronounced it Dah-via to make it sound more feminine."

"At least I'm not the only one who has a wonky first name. I think mine came from some Scottish relative's surname."

Anthony returned to retrieve me to sign documents and pay for the vehicle.

"Thank you again," I said to Adair.

"I do need one more thing." He put a hand on my arm *again*. "Would you give me a ride home? I got dropped off."

The way he asked for a ride with puppy dog eyes made me wonder how anyone turned him down. Of course, being his personal Uber was nothing, considering.

"I'll be happy to."

"Thanks! Do you have time for lunch?"

Did I? He gave up a custom car, so I needed to be gracious.

"Yes, but I'm buying."

I should have offered to dry clean his suit the last time we met.

"We'll see." Adair studied me in a way that made me remember I wasn't wearing a bra.

In less than an hour, we were out of the dealership and headed for downtown La Jolla. Adair turned down Prospect Avenue and into a parking garage under a multi-storied building. He pulled into a spot marked AAM-Reserved.

"I own this building," he said.

Oh.

We took a nearby elevator, emerged into the sunlight, and went past some high-end jewelry and clothing shops. Stairs led to the restaurant's entrance.

"Do you like the ocean?" Adair asked.

Images of late nights wearing scuba gear, swimming into hostile territories went through my mind.

"Sometimes."

"My place in Bali has some spectacular lagoons."

His place?

Adair held the door for me, and we stepped inside.

"Ah, Mr. Monroe," the maître d said. "Welcome!"

"Ernesto, a table for two, please."

"If you'll excuse me for a minute." Ernesto rushed off to expedite the ejection of a couple finishing their meal. He snatched up the check as two waiters pulled back the customers' chairs to usher them out. The staff reset the table so quickly they could qualify for the Guinness Book of World Records.

"I don't remember seeing you before we met at Bryce's. Are you new here?" Adair asked while we waited.

"Yes."

"Your table's ready, sir." Ernesto bowed and swept out an arm.

Adair let me go first. Diners turned to stare at him, dumbstruck, like a tiger sauntered past. They took photos with their phones, but Adair didn't seem to notice.

Ernesto stopped next to a table with the most impressive views, pulled out my chair, and set a cloth napkin in my lap with a flourish.

"Would you like the wine list?" Ernesto asked.

Adair looked at me, inquiring as he sat.

"Iced tea is fine," I said.

Adair ordered iced tea as well, and I turned my attention to the menu. "I like your hair," he said.

"Thank you." The compliment made me blush. I kept my eyes down, pretending to consider the menu.

The waiter returned with our drinks, took our order, and collected the menus.

"Where did you grow up?" Adair asked.

"The Midwest. You?"

"Manchester."

"Oh, Northwest England?"

His face brightened. "Have you been there?"

"No." For once, I honestly hadn't.

"Ah well. But now you know why I don't sound posh."

"Your accent is rather hard to pin down."

"I travel a lot, and I'm like a Mynah bird, picking up accents wherever I go."

We sipped our tea. The people in the restaurant resumed their meals but kept glancing over.

"You get a lot of attention."

Adair put his hands to his face in mock-comic despair. "One of those celebrity magazines put me in a 'world's hottest man' feature. I get recognized now, and sometimes my life is insane."

"How do you handle the scrutiny?"

He bent close to me. "Can I tell you a secret?"

"Yes."

"I play a game to distract myself."

"What kind of game?"

"I come up with backstories for other people, like they're probably doing for you and me. If people see me out with any woman, even my sister, I'm in a new relationship. I hate to tell you, but you and I are secretly engaged."

"You're joking, aren't you?"

"No. It's barmy, but I deal. Want to play my game?"

"Sure."

"I'll go first. Over there, a guy is eating alone. My story is someone stood him up for lunch. He expected the woman he connected with in line at the bank would meet him, but she didn't show. So now he's on the piss to drown his sorrows."

The man wore a dark navy suit, a bulbous nose overwhelming his other features. He took a long drink from a nearly empty glass of red wine.

"Your turn," Adair prompted.

"Same guy. He works for himself because he isn't concerned about the time. He's also not waiting for someone for the same reason. He's around forty-five, likes to run rather than lift weights, and spends a lot of time thinking about how to make more money, even though he's already well-off. Also, he knows you."

"You're skilled at this. I do know him; we've done some business together. How'd you guess?"

"He hasn't paid much attention to you, but his face showed recognition as we came in."

"Wow. You're a real observer and a keen one. Where did you get those skills?"

"I like to people watch." Our classes on body language plus years of practice made reading people second nature.

"I forgot to say these are supposed to be made-up stories rather than the truth."

"Oh."

Our meal arrived to interrupt this line of conversation. Adair expressed surprise at my prime rib and baked potato order, perhaps used to his women ordering one bean sprout with dressing on the side.

We chatted about the weather and La Jolla. I enjoyed watching swimmers and kayakers making the most of a deep, blue water cove not far from our table.

"Were you near your car when it blew up?" Adair asked. The abrupt shift in the conversation startled me.

"Why?"

"You radiate a calmness like nothing ever bothers you."

"Well, you did see me upset when my leg gave out."

"For what? Two seconds?"

"I was shaken for much longer."

"I won't think you're Wonder Woman, then."

"You could think of me as Captain Marvel."

Adair smiled, then turned serious again.

"But are you sure you're fine?" He put his hand on mine and kept his eyes on my face.

"That close call did unnerve me," I confessed.

When was the last time I admitted to being rattled?

"You said you're from the Midwest, but is there anyone out here to support you?"

"Uh, I'm an only child."

"Are you close to your parents?"

"Yes, but they work full time."

"Ah. It can be difficult not to have anyone nearby. My dad died when I was young, and my mum and younger sister are still in England. Business keeps me running place to place."

"What type of business?"

"A teacher got me interested in investment strategies for a math class. I think he tried to keep the Year Eights from going crazy from hormones."

"Year Eight? What age were you?"

"Twelve or thirteen. Anyway, I developed a real knack for seeing patterns, then I parlayed my skills into tech investments and did pretty well."

His modesty suited him. As I listened, his eye color shifted in the light, like sunshine sparkling on a green-blue sea. His face was expressive, and I wondered how he survived in the cut-throat business world.

"Anyway, there's a few Rancho people whose company you might enjoy. I'm thinking of having a small get-together soon, and—"

"Dessert?" The waiter offered us menus, and I was glad of the interruption. I didn't want to attend an intimate gathering of well-to-do people. What would I even say? At the thought of a room full of Aunt Lilahs, I almost shuddered.

"I need to get back. I'm having furniture delivered today," I said.

Adair waved the server away, stood, and pulled back my chair. "Shall we go?"

"What about the bill?"

"I put it on my account."

"This was supposed to be my treat," I protested.

"Next time."

I refused to move from his path. "Swear."

"I wouldn't want to be on your bad side."

"You wouldn't."

Ernesto bowed us out of the restaurant, and we went back to the car.

"Mind if I drive?" I asked.

"Of course not."

Here we were on a glorious day, me driving a high-performance car, a desirable man at my side. He turned on the radio, tuning to a SiriusXM pop-rock station, while I considered what supplies I needed for my security system. No point thinking about Adair. He was like a store of dainty, breakable collectibles. Peruse all you want, but don't touch.

We reached Rancho Suprema as Adair sang along loudly to a Harry Styles hit, moving his arms, hips sliding on the seat. He poked me playfully with a finger in the shoulder, encouraging me to join him.

"You're allowed to have fun," he said.

Hesitant, I launched into the song with him, bobbing my head and tapping the steering wheel in time to the beat. The piece concluded, and we fell back, laughing.

"We should try out for America's Got Talent," he said.

"You're not American."

"Oh, but I have dual citizenship."

"My off-key singing is another reason not to compete."

"You're not bad. Don't be so hard on yourself," Adair said. "Turn here."

We drove next to wrought-iron fencing for several miles, then turned into a gated driveway. He pulled a slim card out of his wallet and hit a button to open the ornate barrier. I drove in along a tree-lined road with a lake on either side.

"How many acres do you own?" I was staggered by the immensity of the property.

"Around thirty-two."

At over a *million* an acre?

We passed a barn the size of a typical house, two arenas, several citrus groves, pastures, and a helicopter pad. His residence was a grand English manor, as vast as many hotels, with ivy growing on its stone walls.

I parked under a portico.

"Would you like to come in?" He opened his door.

"I have a lot to squeeze into the rest of my day. Raincheck?"

"Of course."

Adair bent forward to kiss my cheek and his upper body pressed against my right arm and shoulder. The close contact made my eyes shut as his warm lips lingered on my skin.

"Thanks for the ride," he said, implying provocative possibilities I fought to ignore.

I gripped the steering wheel. "No problem."

Adair straightened and got out, waving goodbye. I worked to order my tumultuous feelings as I drove back toward the gate.

Any woman with a pulse would have the same reaction around that man, Davia.

At Home Depot, I parked my sporty car between two work trucks. Men loaded pipes, lumber, and other home improvement supplies into their beds, giving me incredulous stares. Inside, I tried to locate what I needed for a seismic intrusion device and break-wire system but kept being delayed by offers of assistance. My feet and weak leg killed me after hiking up and down concrete store aisles the size of Canada, searching for parts.

Once home, I shed the designer duds, and pulled on jeans, a t-shirt, and blessedly comfortable boots. Jose and I started installing the seismic system but still needed a few more hours on the tripwires.

The furniture delivery halted our progress.

"I'm Joe, and this is Bill," the man in charge said. "Where do you want this stuff?"

I tried to figure out the best place to put each piece, and they assembled everything. At nine p.m., they prepared to leave. "Excuse me?" I said to Joe.

"Yes?"

"Um, where are the mattresses for the beds?"

"None were on the order form." His brow furrowed.

Did the customer service person forget? Or, more likely, me.

Whatever. Another chore.

I thanked the men and handed them a generous tip. Relief stretched across their faces at not having to answer any more of my stupid questions. Frustration filled me at the thought of purchasing mattresses, sheets, blankets, and pillows, but I refused to spend another night in a motel.

Muttering, I pulled up the location and hours of a Target on my phone, went over, and headed for their camping section. Slinging a sleeping bag into my cart along with a pillow and pillowcases, I also added washcloths and towels.

Returning home, I took a shower, careful to keep my hair dry. Stepping out with wet feet on the slick marble floor, I cursed aloud for not remembering to get a bath mat. Pulling on the black, silk negligee Bryce sold me, I shoved the pillow into a case, laid out the sleeping bag, set the alarm system, and turned out the lights. Once settled, I stared at the elegant ceiling while pondering the irony before falling asleep.

15

My first Ladies' League meeting put me in a near panic.

How should I act? What if an assassin comes for me?

I avoided social situations much of my life, preferring to be alone. Parties or similar gatherings drained me.

"You're an introvert," my dad told me. "The extroverts of the world suck other people's energy, like vampires. Introverts give out their energy to others, so your sense of being drained is your gas tank running low. You have to be alone to refill."

How many vampires would be at this meeting? A lot, I bet.

I chose a pale blue skirt with embroidered flowers paired with a navy blouse, hoop earrings, and *the* ring. As I slipped on some flats, butterflies flew into my stomach, accompanied by a backup hornet of anger at Aunt Lilah.

Remember the mission.

My next concern was my hair. It was a *disaster* as if I stuck a hand-mixer into it during the night. After brushing, swearing, and cajoling for ages, the locks smoothed into place. Grabbing the can of twenty-dollar hair spray Ramon insisted I needed, I sprayed until the fumes choked me. Makeup took two minutes: lip gloss and mascara. I still didn't apply mascara well and dabbed a tissue at the black spots where I missed my lashes and dotted my cheek.

The Ladies' League was near Rancho Suprema's downtown, a Spanish-style building evocative of the centuries-old missions scattered throughout California. A courtyard entrance took me through a garden with a two-tiered fountain at its center. A stream of people entered the interior through two carved wooden doors, chattering to each other.

I hesitated by the fountain, not wanting to go inside. What was my problem?

Underneath the expensive clothes, I'm still a farm girl from South Dakota.

An orange and black koi swam to the surface and stared at me, bulbous eyes telegraphing the clear message that I didn't belong. I knew fish didn't have opinions, but I stayed rooted to the spot. Lifting my eyes to the street, I scanned my surroundings for anyone suspicious but saw nothing.

"Hello," a voice said.

I checked everywhere but right behind me.

An older woman with iron-gray hair and kind blue eyes peered at me through glasses with thick, black frames.

"I'm Mrs. McGregor."

Mrs. McGregor? The Peter Rabbit stories my mom read me as a child came to mind.

"And no, I don't eat rabbits."

"I guess you hear that a lot."

"I do, so I bring the subject up right away. Did you come to learn about the Ladies' League?"

"Yes, I'm Davia Glenn." I held out my hand, and she took it with a firm grip.

"You may call me Lydia. Please come in, and I'll introduce you to people."

"Thank you."

My feet somehow came unstuck as we made small talk. My

mouth was dry, and my hands were clammy, but we reached the front doors.

I scrambled for something to say. "How long have you been a member of the Ladies' League?"

She swelled with pride. "Over forty years. Tradition is important, and I like to be active."

Inside, the entry opened onto a grand room done in warm gold colors. Floor-to-ceiling windows and French doors made up a wall on the opposite side. Sunlight came through the windows and reflected on lush tapestries and paintings adorning the walls. Rows of wooden folding chairs faced a lectern in the center of the space.

About thirty people socialized, the noise from their conversations a happy buzz.

Quit analyzing all the exits.

Beatrice Gibbs held forth to a crowd of women and several men, and we exchanged looks of mutual loathing.

"I should introduce you to our club's president," Mrs. McGregor said, and I followed her like a naughty child called to the principal's office. "Beatrice, I want to introduce you to a young lady interested in joining our organization."

"Yes, I invited her to attend today. She's interested in helping with our gala." Beatrice appeared gracious on the surface, her black aura simmering underneath.

"Wonderful to see you." I fought to keep the sarcastic inflection out of *wonderful.*

The women wore expensive outfits, and I recognized a few garments from Aunt Lilah's favorite designer, Chanel. Their interlocked C logo buttons reflected more warmth than the eyes of their owners. A few gave me fake beauty queen smiles. If the sturdy Mrs.McGregor hadn't been beside me, I might have left.

"You want to work on the gala? I'm so pleased!" Mrs. McGregor remarked, perhaps to fill the silence.

"I don't possess any experience but want to be involved," I said.

"Lydia is the perfect person to explain everything. She's been one of the driving forces behind the club forever," Beatrice said. "Lydia, would you mind showing Davia to the office? She needs to fill out a membership application."

"Of course," Lydia said. "Come with me."

I followed, giving Beatrice points for subtly removing me from her presence. Mrs. McGregor entered a side hall leading to one of the other wings.

"Our office and meeting rooms are on this side, and down the other direction are the kitchen and catering facilities," she narrated as we moved past framed photographs taken through the years. From decades past, women posed holding shovels, standing behind newly-planted rosebushes and other flowers. "The original members took the streets from plain to spectacular with blossoms of color."

"Does the club still do the upkeep around Rancho Suprema?"

"No. The Association has a paid staff of gardeners working full-time to keep the trees, bushes, and flowers trimmed and the trails tidy."

We turned into a well-appointed office, and Lydia retrieved an application and pen from the desk. "Fill this out."

I decided not to ask about completing it online. The organization didn't appear to operate in the current century.

"We've formed committees for the gala," Lydia said while I wrote. "But, we need help with our silent auction."

"What's a silent auction?" I hoped she wouldn't mock me for my ignorance.

"We display the donations, and people write their names and the amount they want to pay on a sheet of paper, with the highest bid winning. We do a live auction of the more expensive donations after dinner. They typically sell for much more than face value, allowing our club to continue its charitable work."

A voluptuous woman with a helmet of black hair entered and came to a stop next to my chair.

"How was South America, Lydia?" she asked.

"Different, but interesting. Amelia, this is Davia Glenn. She's joining our organization and wants to help with the gala."

"Amelia Meadows." The beauty's sharp gaze focused on Aunt Lilah's ring.

"Pleased to meet you." Meeting Amelia was like being introduced to a barracuda with vivid red lips. Recalling she was Willie Weston's former companion, I wondered if he led her to the boudoir garage. *Ew.*

"I need a clipboard," Amelia said. She took one off the desk and swept out again.

Mrs. McGregor made a clucking sound of disapproval.

"You were vacationing?" I asked.

"Yes, I took a trip to South America, a short vacation. I enjoyed expanding my expertise on the rainforest but needed to return in time for the gala. Since Willie died, we're stuck with more work."

I finished the application and returned it along with the membership and gala fees. She reviewed the paperwork.

"You're coming by yourself to the gala? I don't bring anyone either, so you can sit with me if you like. My husband's been gone for over twenty years, and I'm the odd girl out."

"That would be perfect, thank you."

Mrs. McGregor filed the money and papers in a cabinet. "We should go back. I think the meeting's about to start."

We took our seats, and Beatrice Gibbs began the meeting.

"Since this is our fiftieth anniversary, Willie planned some surprises. Since he didn't share his ideas in detail, we'll handle the gala like previous years."

Surprises planned by Willie Weston? Nude women? Men popping out of cakes?

"A sensible plan," Mrs. McGregor commented, and others nodded.

"Let's hear from our decorations chair, Lisa Kane," Beatrice said, and the woman rose and began her report. A discussion about how to decorate the dining tables caught my attention. Suggestions popped into my head.

What was wrong with me?

Committee chairs continued to give reports about the theme,

flowers, catering, and potential bands for the after-dinner dance. After an hour, Beatrice retook control. "I want to introduce everyone to our newest member, Davia Glenn. Tell us about yourself, Davia, and do stand up."

I stood. "I'm a new resident of Rancho Suprema and would like the opportunity to serve on your board."

"On our board?" Mrs. McGregor whispered to me as I sat, relieved. "I'm so pleased."

They must be super short-handed.

The meeting ended, so I poured some punch from a table of refreshments. Two men chatted nearby.

"Sheriff's homicide is investigating Willie's death," said one, catching my attention.

The other gave a dismissive wave of his hand. "He died because of his heart condition, Ted. They're careful because of his high-profile status."

"Careful due to his position, not because someone killed him?" Ted asked. His eyes were gray, and his chin was weak.

"Oh, I doubt somebody murdered him. I mean, who would kill Willie?"

Ted nodded toward Amelia Meadows, standing surrounded by women who appeared every bit as difficult as her.

"They had a nasty break-up, yes," the other man said. "But murder?"

Mrs. McGregor approached with a woman in her wake. In her early thirties, she was thin as a famine victim and wore a fitted green suit with a pair of pearl earrings.

Really, Davia? Now I care about jewelry and clothing?

"This is Francis Downs, head of the auction committee."

"Welcome to our committee." She fiddled with a strand of golden-red, curly hair.

"What do you need help with?"

"What don't I?" She blew out an irritated breath. "This was Willie's committee, and I took over."

"Do you think somebody murdered him?"

Francis took a step back. "Murder? Of course not! Willie had a bad heart, right, Lydia?"

"What did you say, dear? I wasn't attending," Lydia said.

"We were talking about Willie. You don't think it was murder, do you?" Francis said, aghast.

"No. It was heart issues." Lydia said.

Francis look strained, perhaps waiting for me to say something else indiscreet. Relief flooded through me when a couple drew near.

"Davia!" It was Bob Brooks, my realtor. "This is my wife, Alexandra."

"Bob told me so much about you." Alexandra wore her brown hair short. Her hazel eyes and heart-shaped face gave her the appearance of a pixie. I avoided checking out her jewelry.

"Are you moved into your new home?" Bob asked.

"Yes. I love it, but I need more furniture."

"I can recommend a designer," Alexandra and Francis spoke simultaneously.

"I think Kit Malloy is the best," Francis asserted.

"She's brilliant if you want to pay ten thousand for a lamp," Alexandra said.

"Yes, and it's so worth the cost!" Frances responded, indignant.

Alexandra's eyebrows rose. "Are her services really worth $200,000 a room?"

"Let's talk about this later," Bob said. "We're on the decorating committee and need to decide which vases to use for the side-table floral arrangements. We can't agree if they should be Han or Tang Dynasty."

"Oh, Bob." Alexandra slapped him lightly on the arm. "Details are important."

They said goodbye and left. Mrs. McGregor made her excuses, saying she needed to speak with a Diane about the valet parking.

"Lydia's such a dedicated member," Francis said.

"She told me she's been at this for over forty years."

"Yes. The core of the Ladies' League members are from her era. They're all hard workers."

What, and I wouldn't be?

Would my insecurities ever simmer down?

"Tell me about the auction," I said.

"Let's see if we can find the donations." We moved into a side hall, and Francis opened the door to a storage room. It burst with all manner of novelties.

"This is where we keep what we use for our various functions. We store so much I don't know where things are half the time. The donations are supposed to be here somewhere."

I slinked past a stack of boxes ready to topple over. "Do you log in what people donate?"

"No. I have no clue what was donated this year."

I stopped. "What? How can—"

"Oh, it sounds ridiculous, but no one paid attention because Willie's been around forever and took charge."

"Can't the details be recovered from his computer?"

"Computer? Willie?"

Oh well.

The amount and variety of objects crammed into the room could fill the Smithsonian's basement. Francis chewed on a manicured nail as she viewed the space, uncertain.

"Did you run a committee in the past?" Should I find Mrs. McGregor?

"I was on Pat Bell's auction committee a while ago but not in charge. We need to find the donations and wrap everything for display."

Find? More like excavate. "What was your job?"

"I typed up descriptions. I'm one of the few people who use a computer. Most members have their assistants do it."

I commanded my face to stay blank. We checked boxes stacked on shelves containing decorations for every occasion; bows, ribbons, vases, stuffed animals, wreaths, and *much* more. Dust and debris clung to my skirt. Add finding a dry cleaner to the unending to-do list.

After a time, Francis threw up her hands. "I give up! I can't begin to guess where Willie put them. This room is a disaster."

"Why don't I try to locate them?" Compared to my prior career, this was nothing.

"You would?"

"Yes, but I'm not volunteering to help with their display. I'm not the artistic type."

"Others in the club are excellent at devising creative presentations. Well, *some*," she amended. "Most pay their assistants to do it."

What else was new?

"I can start tomorrow."

"How about Thursday? I have a tennis game tomorrow."

"Why don't you give me the key?"

"I can't. They're sacred. Only committee heads have them, and we're required to log ourselves in and out."

"The League is strict about the register but not about keeping track of donations?"

"Oh, it's down-the-rabbit-hole all the time around here."

We nodded in agreement at the understatement of the year.

Francis led the way out as we made plans for our next meeting. She would let me in the building ahead of her massage appointment. Bidding her farewell, I headed for my car, relieved. I recalled my mom telling me most worries never came true, how after we went through something and came out the other side, we looked back and saw the experience wasn't as bad as in our minds had conjured.

Lunch loomed, so I drove to the Suprema Market to fill my empty fridge and pantry. In the fourth aisle, I sensed someone behind me, pivoted, lost my balance and rammed right into Kenneth Clayton.

Did he lurk in grocery stores?

His eyes traveled all over me. "Are you new here?"

"Yes," I said, pulling away from him.

"Are you free for lunch?" Either he didn't remember me, or the hair extensions and wardrobe change made me unrecognizable.

"No. Another time, maybe?"

He took a business card from his front shirt pocket. "I'm free for dinner tomorrow night."

"I'm Davia Glenn, by the way."

He blanched. Perhaps in his world, tits and ass didn't have names.

Curse the conditions of the will!

"Give my secretary your address. I'll pick you up at eight," Kenneth said, not bothering to introduce himself.

Time to unleash a roundhouse kick to his head.

Nope, my skirt was too tight.

He swaggered off, and I made a face at his back.

Finished shopping, I headed for home, itching to remove my restrictive get-up. I needed to put away the groceries, change, and get a mattress delivered.

Today.

16

I woke to the comfort of a pillow top high-performance mattress costing so much it should tell me good morning and make the bed itself.

My dreaded dinner engagement was twelve hours from now. Kenneth Clayton's assistant took my address, revulsion spiraling through the phone. Maybe I should have tried to count my lunch with Adair as a date, but Aunt Lilah's investigator might contact him, and that would be beyond awkward to explain.

Jose and I had finished the security measures, and now I needed to try to get back to one hundred percent. I weight-lifted with music by Disturbed turned up to a pounding volume. My date was bound to be disturbing, so I stuck with the theme. After my workout, I showered and dressed. With reluctance, I asked Siri to search for interior designers. I tapped the first name, not paying attention.

"Kit Malloy Designs," a woman answered.

The ten-grand-per-lamp lady. "Sorry, wrong number."

Not trusting the task of finding a designer to an AI again, I phoned Bob Brooks. He answered on the second ring, much to my relief.

"Davia, what can I do for you?"

"Who's your wife's interior designer?"

"She uses Julia Winters, but Julia's out of the country selecting antiques in Europe."

My team broke down doors to bag terrorists whose houses brimmed with ostentatious European antiques. They had delusions of grandeur while I simply needed something to sit on.

"Any other suggestions?"

"Not my department. Alexandra's in Los Angeles today, visiting our daughter. Would you like her cell number?"

"No, I don't want to bother her. I'll figure something out."

"Did you like the Ladies' League?"

I fished out the one positive aspect. "I liked Mrs. McGregor."

"Lydia can be set in her ways, but she works hard. What's your assignment?"

"I volunteered to find the silent auction donations."

"I don't envy you. Think I'll stick to the discussion about vases."

After our conversation concluded, I consulted the Platinum Pages, an exclusive Rancho Suprema directory left by the previous owner. Ignoring the full page, colorful ads, I scanned the interior designer section for someone with minimal advertising. Sherilyn Silvers Designs only listed a name and phone contact, so I called.

A perky female voice chirped, "Sherilyn Silvers Designs,"

"Yes, I'm interested in making an appointment with Sherilyn Silvers to give me advice on the decor of my new home in Rancho Suprema. Is she available?"

"Speaking."

Perfect. I introduced myself. "When are you available to meet?"

"Within the half-hour."

Details provided, I hung up. "That was easy," I said aloud, not believing it.

Twenty minutes later, my gate buzzer rang. The video footage displayed an enthusiastic cheerleader type, and I buzzed her in. She bounced out of her car in a pair of black slacks, black pumps, and a white button-up shirt, her shoulder-length blonde hair swinging side-to-side. She held an iPad clasped against her chest.

"This is a spectacular home," she proclaimed, rushing forward. "Are those bougainvillea? I love them! They are *sooo* perfect for Spanish-style houses, but sometimes they can be prickly and messy, and they drop their—*ooh!* What an elegant fountain. Those wrought-iron benches look inviting, or are they fiberglass? No, they're wrought iron because this place is, like, *sooo* expensive!"

I sought to halt the torrent. "Let's go in."

She bounded after me, surveying my spacious living room with a sparkling but critical eye. "This is, like, the best place! You need a rug, some plants, and paintings." She made notes on her iPad. At least she didn't say I needed to replace the furniture I had already bought.

"I mean, like, this is a totally great home, but the rooms are so *empty*," she continued. "You'll love what I select! A Persian rug, no, Indian, and I mean Native American Indian, not India like the country. Mother Theresa helped all the lepers and everything, and they do make rugs, but I think the Navajos—"

I tuned her out. If I didn't, my actions wouldn't be pretty.

We went from room to room. Sherilyn assessed my needs at the speed of sound while I bit my tongue almost in half. Once she offered to obtain all the towels, sheets, utensils, kitchen appliances, and other necessities, her personality became more tolerable.

"This is, like, so cool!" she concluded.

I expected her to do a backflip and splits.

"Would you like some water?" Would that stop her from talking?

"Yes, thanks."

After I fetched two water bottles, we sat at my dining room table to finalize our business. Sherilyn provided me with her contract. "$150 an hour?" I questioned.

"Kit Malloy charges, like, $1500 an hour!" she protested.

"Which is why I didn't hire her." I gave Sherilyn a self-assured stare.

"Here." She changed the amount to $50 per hour. If she saved me the headache of doing everything myself, the cost was acceptable.

I gave her a deposit, and she informed me she would start immediately. On the way back to her car, she kept up a running monologue about everything she needed to do the job.

"I can't wait to get started!" She radiated excitement as she got in her car and drove away.

Ah, the blissful silence!

My stomach growled. I needed to eat some lunch and make a post office run. Assembling a turkey and Swiss cheese sandwich and snagging a bottle of peach-flavored iced tea, I went to the back patio and perched on a wall beside the built-in barbecue and fireplace. A distant plane droned above the peaceful view, relaxing me.

Memories of Warden invaded my mind.

We ran an obstacle course carrying dummies while wearing gas masks each morning, and he didn't always win.

We were late getting to our extraction point and chased the departing truck, pumped from success despite the bullets still whizzing past us.

He watched me and I watched him, both aware that we did. Had he lied to himself as I had about why we were hyper-conscious of each other's presence?

Should I leave a message on his cell? Perhaps he reconsidered our brief romantic encounter and now lay naked next to some girl, and —*stop*. When Warden called to warn me about Badger, he was haggard, not happy. I could imagine the chaos on my team's end of things.

He called a few days ago. He hasn't forgotten me and will contact me when he can.

After rinsing my plate, I put it with my breakfast dish in the dishwasher. At this rate, it would be a year before I turned it on.

At the post office, I parked between two luxury autos so new they were without license plates, like mine. Mail delivery was to private boxes at the centrally-located post office as mail carriers would have difficulties bypassing security gates and other impediments. A private company could deliver your mail to your home, but I considered them another security problem.

On my two previous trips to the post office, I completed paperwork, received my keys, and picked up the surveillance mini-cameras and sensors shipment. My parents and Kyle were the only people who knew my address. Oh, the bills. I would change them to online payments.

At the building's entrance, a tall man looked toward the parking lot, head tilted to one side and lips pursed.

"Hey, Frank!" Another man in golf clothes greeted him.

"Heya, Dennis! I can't find my car."

Auto thieves in Rancho?

It took me a few minutes to find my box, a small receptacle on a bottom row in a maze of cul-de-sacs. Junk mail and two magazines I didn't subscribe to, *Opulence* and *Suprema Home and Garden,* filled the small box. Several copies of the local newspaper, *Suprema Gazette,* a handful of advertising pamphlets from local realtors, and bills added to the bulk. I tried not to drop anything.

Leaving, I dodged women in tennis outfits talking on their cell phones and men confident the world moved around them. Frank still stared at the lot. I started to ask if he needed help when he said, "I forgot! I drove the Rolls today."

The world went off-kilter for a moment.

Back home, I culled the unsolicited mail, dumped the stack in the recycle container in the garage, and spread the rest on the kitchen island. A manila envelope addressed in unfamiliar handwriting slid out from between some magazines, causing me an immediate Unabomber jolt of alarm. I jumped backward, putting distance between me and the packet.

When nothing happened, I pressed with care along the edges and surface. Feeling no wires or other objects, I used my pocket knife to slit the envelope down one end. Inside was a flat piece of paper, folded once. It was a picture of me talking to Mrs. McGregor at the Ladies' League.

A red X blotted out my face.

I berated myself for letting my guard down due to nerves over attending a social function. If someone could take zoom-lens photos, I knew what they could do with a sniper rifle.

I phoned Aubrey for more information.

"Colonel Streeter's office."

It was Luke.

"Luke, it's Davia."

A groan on the other end. "You don't work here anymore."

I ignored his comment. "May I speak to Aubrey?"

"She's on vacation."

"Then please put me through to Colonel Streeter."

"He's in a meeting. What can I do for you?"

"I got an interesting photo today."

Silence.

"What can you tell me?" I prodded.

"What are you talking about?"

"I received another red X photo."

"Different than the previous ones?"

"Yes, a recent one of me."

"I'll tell the Colonel right away." Luke hung up.

I put my head in my hands. Did Luke dislike me so much he wanted me taken out and wouldn't pass on a message? That was a stretch, but I wondered if I would ever hear back from him.

Picking up the photo, I analyzed all the angles and continued my self-flagellation over letting this occur. Why was someone sending me a picture and not merely shooting me? Was this a psychological warfare tactic, an attempt to give me the jitters so I would make a mistake? Agent Wills was my handler in California, but he was for emergencies only, and I didn't plan to call and tell him I needed a babysitter.

An hour went by. I passed the time paying bills and realized I needed stamps, which I put on the endless to-do list.

When no one called after several hours, I knew I was on my own.

IT WAS time for my date with doom.

I selected black wide-legged pants, a black stretchy blouse, and a thigh-length beaded jacket.

Kenneth Clayton was forty minutes late. My displeasure increased with each passing minute. If he stood me up, I'd hunt him down in the grocery store and toss him across a pile of vegetables.

The gate buzzed over an hour past our appointed time. The monitor showed Mr. VRMF bouncing his index finger on the steering wheel, eyes straight ahead. I was tempted not to answer but touched the button to let him in.

The doorbell rang, and I picked up my evening bag. Kenneth wore black slacks and a black turtleneck sweater but wouldn't be mistaken for a commando with his toneless form.

"Darlene?" he ventured.

"Davia."

"Ah, yes," he said without enthusiasm. "Are you ready?" He went back toward the courtyard exit without waiting for an answer.

A hissing sound like air escaping from a tire burst from my lips. I calculated whether my aim was accurate enough to hit him in the back of the head with my purse.

Surely assault is justified in this circumstance.

My date sat behind the wheel, tapping his finger again. Yanking open the front passenger door, I got in.

"Do you like my Bugatti?" He revved the motor.

"Your what?"

"My Bugatti," he repeated, annoyed.

"I don't—"

"My *car!*"

"Oh." The car was a low-slung dark something, another exotic auto in a town overrun with them.

"This one cost over a million. I collect the finest supercars in the world, store them in hermetically-sealed garages, and my staff is devoted to their care."

"Mm."

"I keep them at my estates around the globe, something suited to each country's roads. My staff readies a car to meet my jet, or a car and driver are available if I'm tired and don't want to drive."

"Mm." I stared into the night.

"Today, I was on the phone all morning, negotiating a multi-billion dollar takeover. The deal almost fell through, but I saved it. Afterward, I lifted weights with my trainer. Do you work out? No, you don't strike me as the athletic type. Here we are."

Kenneth parked in front of Chateau Rouge, and two facts became evident. First, we would dine at a five-star French restaurant in Rancho Suprema, and second, Kenneth Clayton would talk about himself *all night*. I got out, and Kenneth went around the front of his prized car, placed his hand on my back, and steered me toward the entrance.

An auburn-haired hostess held two menus. "Mr. Clayton, welcome!" Her voice adored him, but her eyes told a different story. "Right this way."

She led us to a table in an alcove, a cozy two-person booth in an intimate dining room full of patrons who snickered upon sighting Kenneth. The conversation soon returned to a faint murmur, and wine glasses clinked. Instrumental music played from hidden speakers, enhancing the candlelit atmosphere.

"So," Kenneth faced me, "what would you like to drink?"

"You've had a long day. Let me choose." I tried to sound sympathetic and sincere.

"Go ahead, doll." He turned to greet a man at a nearby table.

Doll? Grrr.

I perused the wine list, not the names, but rather the cost. What was the most expensive bottle on the menu? *How about a $3,500 bottle of champagne?*

The waiter returned, but Kenneth kept talking to his friend about money, stocks, and other subjects adored by capitalists everywhere. I ordered several bottles of champagne and also some wine. Kenneth didn't introduce me to his buddy, and they kept yakking, leaving me time to figure out the most expensive appetizer, salad, and entrée, plus matching wines. I should order two entrees. If the portion sizes were small, like many French restaurants, I would eat both.

A waiter set fluted glasses next to the wine goblets. Another server carried a bucket full of ice and placed it on a stand next to the table. The bucket held my order of two bottles of champagne. A server uncorked one.

All conversation in the room ceased as three men entered.

One was Adair Monroe.

He wore a black suit with a crisp white shirt and a black, geometric pattern tie, his hair in an intentional disarray. Every woman in the place probably fantasized about how it would feel to run their hands through it, except me. I concentrated on doing the "in plain sight, not seen" ninja trick, wishing I could duck under the tablecloth.

The hostess ushered Adair to a table across from ours. I was relieved when one of his companions chose the chair facing me. Adair sat and smiled up at the hostess, who touched him on the shoulder. I bet women came up with reasons to grope him every day.

Kenneth said something to me.

"I'm sorry, what did you say?" I stopped my scrutiny of Adair. Kenneth's friend had left, so his attention returned to me and the champagne.

"What are we celebrating?" Kenneth raised his glass, and I picked up mine.

"Oh, our first date, of course."

And last.

"Bottoms up!" He clinked his glass against mine and drank all the contents in one gulp. I took a small sip, trying not to grimace. The company made the superb vintage hard to swallow. An efficient server stepped forward to refill Kenneth's empty glass.

"Did Miss decide on wine?" The waiter asked after taking our orders.

"Yes." I ticked off a bottle for every course of the meal, determined to make this cost a fortune just on principle. Kenneth launched into another interminable story about his brilliance and his money.

"Did I ever tell you about the time I outmaneuvered Warren Buffet on a deal?"

"Mm, no?" I sipped my drink and refocused on Adair's table. One of his dinner partners seemed familiar. Why? He was middle-aged but in good shape. Although I couldn't place him, his craggy features made alarm bells clang with the urgent warning of a torpedo about to destroy a ship. The man caught me looking at him and gave me a lazy smile. The other man was younger, perhaps in his early thirties. He had dark hair, and spoke with animation to Adair, leaning forward to emphasize his words.

Our first appetizer course arrived, diverting me.

"Ah, oysters!" Kenneth gave me a wink. "You're a saucy girl, aren't you?"

Mistake! Mistake! Now he thought he would get laid.

More like laid out.

A waiter turned one of the champagne bottles over in the bucket and popped the next. I still nursed my first glass. Kenneth slurped a raw oyster off the shell with one hand and held out his glass for a refill with the other. He began to eye my chest.

"Now, where was I?" Kenneth's mouth was full of another oyster.

"Um." No clue. Again.

"Well, I acquired a company through a hostile takeover—" And he was off to the races again, bravado in the lead and detestability a close second. I returned to studying Adair's companions, but nothing specific came to mind.

Our salads and the first wine course arrived. Now full of liquor, Kenneth's eyes grew unfocused, and his hands began to wander. He groped my thigh, and I removed his hand.

One more time and I'll snap something.

"Excuse me. I need to use the ladies' room," I said.

As I went toward the front of the restaurant, the hostess and I crossed paths.

"Are you enjoying your time with Mr. Clayton?" Sarcasm dripped.

"This is for business," I lied. "Is he a regular?"

"He's come in with so many women, not counting his ex-wives, I've lost track."

A discreet sign designated the location of the restrooms. I reapplied my lipstick, washed my hands, and yawned. A gaggle of women crowded in, necessitating I leave to make room. Straightening my shoulders to face Kenneth, I rounded the corner and ran right into Adair Monroe.

"Davia!" He kissed me on each cheek. His signature cologne was so intoxicating it should be labeled Catnip for Women.

"Adair." I was happy to see him but not.

Please greet me and go.

"Did you just arrive?"

"No, I'm heading back in." I didn't want to say anything else, hoping I could get away without having him notice my dinner date.

Of course, Kenneth chose this moment to stagger over.

"Monroe!" He slammed a hand on Adair's shoulder. "I shee youf met my date."

"Your *date*?" Adair gaped.

"Yesh, Dar-leee-ne, she's a fine gal," Kenneth slurred. "Ah-scuse me. I must use thuth 'lil boys' room."

He wove toward the bathroom.

Adair's dismayed expression didn't change. He stepped closer and spoke in a confiding tone. "Davia, I realize you just moved here, but Kenneth Clayton isn't someone you should be dating. I mean, he's a real womanizer."

"I know."

"You *know*?"

"I'd rather not explain." Not here, not now.

"Do you need money?" he hazarded.

I gave a short laugh. "No. *Having* money is the problem."

"I'm confused—" Adair began, but his companions walked up.

"Adair," the older of the pair called. His strong patrician voice held a Middle Eastern accent. "I didn't know what kept you, but now I see it is a woman. I understand." The man favored me with another smile, one tinged with some fleeting emotion.

"Rashid, this is Davia Glenn," Adair introduced.

"Enchanted." Rashid bent over my hand and kissed it. A webbing of light scars ran across his knuckles.

"A pleasure," I replied, keeping my face impassive. My brain ran visuals of Rashid's face against briefing photos, like a movie on fast forward.

Who are you?

"And I'm Nabil Nasser." The younger man's eyes drifted down my body like a caress.

"If you'll excuse us," Adair said, "we're due at another meeting. We just popped in for an appetizer course. Let's talk more later." He gave me a quick kiss on the cheek, and the men moved to the front door, where Rashid paused.

"It was lovely to make your acquaintance, Ms. Glenn." Something I couldn't name rose to the surface of his eyes, like a killer whale coming up for air then sliding back into the depths.

Think, think, think. Was he affiliated with Badger? How about the other guy?

When I sat back at the table, a server placed my entrée in front of me. Kenneth hadn't returned from the bathroom and, if I were lucky, he would stay awhile. Disquieted by my encounter, my appetite vanished. I speared the halibut with a fork, moving it in circles around my plate, still thinking about Rashid. Nabil acted domineering, inappropriate yet in keeping with his assertive personality. But Rashid—what was it about him that made the hair on the back of my neck rise?

Kenneth returned.

The server placed Kenneth's meal in front of him. "More wine?"

"Of courshe!" Kenneth held out his glass.

We finished our meal, and I declined all other offers of dessert, coffee, tea, and liqueurs, wanting to go home. Kenneth flung down a black American Express to pay the bill. The waiter returned with the total, and he scrawled his signature across the receipt but didn't fill in the tip line.

"You aren't leaving a tip?" I was appalled.

"Wassa point? Thuh service was slow." He got up. "I must use thuh fashilities again." He staggered back to the men's room.

I took the receipt and added a forty-percent tip, bringing the total to a whopping number, then waited by the front door. Kenneth joined me.

"Ah, Dar-leeene." He draped one heavy arm around my shoulders and exhaled liquor breath into my face. "What shay we go to my place?"

As we exited the restaurant, he lost his balance, and I almost let him crash to the ground.

"Where are your keys?"

He leered at me. "Why don't you try to find 'em?"

The patio was deserted. I twisted out from under Kenneth's arm, smashed him face-first into an outdoor table, and reached into his pants pocket.

"Got 'em!"

I pulled a dazed Kenneth back up and dragged him toward the car. Unlocking it, I chucked him in the passenger side. He slumped over and passed out.

Thank God for small favors.

Back home, I pulled into a parking spot beside my garage. What should I do about Kenneth? I didn't want to leave the keys because he was too drunk to drive but decided to set them on the right back tire. If he found them, he would be sober enough.

I went inside.

What a night!

As I changed into sweats, I continued my attempt to identify Rashid. Thoughts came and went, but nothing connected. Something about Rashid was wrong, but I couldn't put my finger on it.

Why did he seem so familiar, but not?

After a futile hour wracking my brain, I drifted off and dreamed about Darth Vader from Star Wars. Instead of James Earl Jones's voice, he sounded like Kenneth Clayton. Darth Clayton spoke to a one-armed Adair Monroe, who hung above an endless drop-off, "I am your father."

Warden appeared, dressed as Princess Leia, complete with her iconic donut hairstyle and white robes. Warden's lightsaber began beeping.

Why did Princess Warden hold a lightsaber?

Coming more awake, I realized the sound wasn't from a noisy lightsaber but my alarm system. I hurtled out of bed. The security monitor indicated a breach on the grid near Kenneth's parked car. One of Badger's hired men might find a passed-out Kenneth and take him hostage.

Grabbing a gun, I shut down the alarm and slipped out a side door. Dashing to the wall, I passed through a well-oiled gate.

Someone edged up the driveway.

Jose. Carrying a machete.

"Jose," I whispered.

He joined me. "Your alarm woke me," he said in Spanish. A duplicate of my monitoring system was in his residence.

A shout for help rang out.

It was Kenneth.

I rushed toward his desperate cries, gun at the ready, but stopped. Kenneth dangled by a leg from a tree, snared in one of my intruder traps. His head hung four feet above the ground, pants unzipped. His shriveled penis was exposed for all to see.

"Get me down!" he demanded.

I put my gun behind my back and a hand to my mouth to stop the laughter.

The sight of Jose's machete made Kenneth change his tune. He begged us not to kill him and offered inconceivable sums of money if I would help him. I let Kenneth swing for a few seconds, then motioned for Jose to cut him down. As he plummeted, I performed an act of charity and caught the end of the rope, although part of me wanted to let go.

Kenneth pulled his feet free from the rope, then tucked himself back where he belonged. Ignoring the wet spot on his pants, he got up.

"Why are there traps on your property?" he demanded.

"Coyotes."

"Coyotes? Why in the hell do you need to trap coyotes?"

"My neighbor's daughter lost her cat to one of them."

"You talk to your neighbors?" He looked at me like I'd lost my mind.

"You need to go home. I bet you have some business deals tomorrow."

"What deals?"

"The kind you told me about tonight." *All* night.

"Oh, well, of course."

Jose went back toward his quarters. Kenneth lurched in the direction of his car, and I didn't bother to help him navigate in the dark.

Retrieving the keys from the wheel well, I handed them to him.

"Thank you for dinner," I said without sincerity.

"You're welcome, um—"

"Davia."

"Yeah, Davia." He hesitated. "Are you holding a gun?"

"Yes." I pulled my arm around and pointed the barrel toward the ground.

"That's an enormous gun," Kenneth said.

"I like to be careful."

He pried his eyes from my weapon.

"We need to get together again sometime," he said, forcing out the words.

"No, we don't."

He stayed rooted to the spot, all pretension gone.

"No, we don't," he echoed.

"Drive carefully."

Kenneth didn't reply. He opened the car door, got in, and left.

17

The next day, I slogged through early morning traffic to qualify for my concealed weapon permit and allow enough time to meet Francis at the Ladies' League. Sleep eluded me until the wee hours due to the alarms triggered by Kenneth and the still-unsolved mystery of Rashid. I was tired and cranky.

At the sheriff's range, located on a military installation, a Marine guard stepped out of his hut and asked the purpose of my visit. The ID from my previous job would've made him salute and duck back inside. Today, I presented as a bimbo in a Maserati who needed directions to the pistol range. If he broke into laughter, I wouldn't blame him.

I parked at the location and popped the trunk. Three uniformed deputies talked to some other early-birds, all men.

"Miss, you need to take this written test," said one of the more senior deputies, his white mustache stained with coffee. He handed me a paper attached to a clipboard.

The test was twenty-five true or false questions. One stated: "If people are in front of you on the range, it is safe to shoot." *False*, but I wanted to write "Depends on who they are" in the margin.

In less than three minutes, I returned the completed test to the deputy.

"Don't you need more time?" he asked.

"No."

"You can only miss two."

"I'm in a hurry today."

The deputy reviewed the test. "You got them all right. Huh."

Four men were ahead of me, so I took a seat on a hard bench and popped in my ear protection. The men's shooting stances were incorrect, and they took ages between shots. After they finished, a lengthy review ensued. I assumed they passed, given their cocky attitudes. In the time it takes a glacier to move, they left.

"You're up," The deputy told me and returned to his coffee.

A man about my age limped toward me. "I'm Deputy Moore. Please bring your weapons."

"Aren't you too young for this job?" I asked, following.

"I got injured in a foot pursuit. This assignment is better than answering phones at a desk."

"Are you sure?"

We stopped near a small wooden table. I put my case down and displayed my weapons to him.

Deputy Moore said, "You'll qualify at ten yards, then at three yards with your left hand. I choose the gun. I want you to load when I say and fire when I ask you to. Any questions?"

"Which gun first?"

"The .22 Magnum revolver."

The smallest and least accurate.

"Load your weapon and put seven rounds in the ten-yard target."

"Any place in particular?"

"The silhouette of the target." He enunciated each word like I was beyond dumb.

"The center mass is torn to shreds from the previous shooters."

"I can tell how well you do. Go ahead."

I fired in quick succession. Finished, I popped the chamber and ejected my spent rounds.

"Did you do that on purpose?" The deputy squinted at the target. It now had two eyes, a nose, and four holes for a smile.

I didn't reply, so he said, "Let's move up to the three-yard line."

"Why?"

He stopped in his tracks. "What?"

"Can't we stay here?"

Dark Terminator sunglasses hid his reaction.

"Okay, Hot Shot. Do you want a blindfold?"

"If you have one."

"I'm joking. Go ahead."

I fired left-handed and ejected the spent rounds.

"Fancy shooting," someone said from behind me.

Detective Montoya.

He wore black jeans, boots, and a tight gray t-shirt with the sheriff's department logo. They accentuated his fit body better than his usual attire.

"Booted out of homicide?" I gestured to his clothes.

"Nope, I was at our other range today and recognized you as I drove past. I think you scared the staff."

"Me?"

Deputy Moore and the others surrounded my target and began an animated discussion.

"Not many people can shoot a gun like yours at seven yards with their left hand and put every bullet through the same hole."

"My lucky day."

His lips twitched. "I won't believe your lines much longer."

"Lines?"

"Any more thoughts on who might be trying to kill you?"

"I thought about it a lot, but nothing surfaced."

"Nothing?"

"I tried. Truly, I have."

Montoya was disbelieving, but he didn't say more.

"Enjoy the rest of your day."

He left, and I joined the deputies.

"Did I pass?" I feigned concern.

"Where'd you learn to do that?" Coffee-stained Moustache choked out.

"An old family friend."

A hillbilly with a musket.

"Wish he'd teach me!" Deputy Moore said, and the men all laughed.

"Why do you think it was a he?" I said.

They grew quiet again.

Afterward, I was treated with respect and deference while I qualified with the other guns. Finished, with forty-five minutes to spare until I needed to meet Francis, I found a drive-thru Starbucks and ordered a hot tea.

Francis was late. In my previous profession, a second late, and you were history. Around here, meeting at a specific time was a suggestion. I positioned myself on a bench with a view of my surroundings. The red X photo and Rashid's unresolved identity remained at the forefront of my thoughts.

"Good morning!" Francis called when she arrived, fumbling in her purse for the keys. She was half an hour past our scheduled time but made no apologies for her tardiness.

I gave a forced smile.

"Here they are!" She held up the keys and unlocked one side of the double doors. Inside, dust particles floated in the light shining through the picture windows on the room's opposite side. "I need to sign in. I'll show you where the register is, and I hope you don't mind signing me out. Pull the door tight when you leave."

At the office, she took a register out of the center desk drawer. She wrote the date, time, and her name in the margin and left the book open on the desk.

"Well, do you need me anymore? I'm late for my next appointment."

As if it matters.

"No, I'm fine."

"Thanks again! Talk soon."

Small, dirty windows lit the disorganized storage room. The cluttered space was the perfect setting for some horror flick. Perhaps the ghost of a spurned socialite would pop out of a dark corner.

It would be a long day.

Was this my new purpose in life? Would my future be consumed by meaningless tasks performed for charitable purposes?

Shaking the thoughts away, I dug through decades of junk.

I should've majored in archaeology.

A cloud of dust exploded each time I touched something. My black shirt grew filthy, and much of my time became devoted to sneezing, coughing, and swearing. After several long hours, my digging produced nothing salable at an auction other than antique office supplies.

Deciding I needed a break to wash up and find Kleenex, I stepped into the hall.

Footsteps rang through the quiet corridor, and a couple from the club meeting appeared before me. I recognized the man and recalled him talking about Willie Weston's death at the meeting. His female companion was around his age with curly dark hair worn in a fashionable cut.

"Hi, I'm Davia Glenn. I'm on the auction committee and spent the morning searching for the gala donations in the storage room. Mr. Weston didn't tell anyone where he put them."

"How frustrating!" The woman appeared sympathetic.

"I'm Tom Stenton, and this is my wife, Alice," Tom said.

"We were discussing the auction on our drive over, right, Tom?" Alice twirled a five-carat diamond ring around and around her finger.

"Yes. Too bad about Willie," Tom said. "He was a friend of ours, and he spent the months leading up to the gala working hard so it would go off without a hitch. Now, the gala's in a few days. How will everything be ready?"

"I don't know much about galas, so I'm not sure," I said. "Do you think someone murdered Mr. Weston?"

Tom didn't seem upset by the question. "At first I wondered that too, but now most of us think it was a heart attack. The Rancho rumor mill would find it juicier if someone murdered him, of course."

"Well, *I* think Amelia Meadows killed him,"Alice declared. "Rumor has it she might inherit his property,"

"Oh, now, she's worth more than he ever was," Tom cut in.

"Some people never can get enough," Alice said. "And then there's the rumor that he was seeing Christa Matthews."

"Speculation doesn't help things," Tom said, and I concluded this was an ongoing disagreement.

"Any idea where Mr. Weston stored the auction items?"

"No. Did you find anything?" Tom asked.

"Not in two hours, but I'm not clear on what I'm trying to locate. Do you have any idea?"

"We don't," Alice said.

"Do you know anyone who might?"

"I can't think of anyone," Tom said. "Sorry."

Could they take over for me?

"Are you helping with the gala?" I asked.

"No, but we attend each year, a lovely affair," Alice said.

"Are you on the Board?" *Why were they here?*

"No, but Alice coordinates the Mah Jong meetings."

I had no idea what that was, but I wasn't going to ask. "Oh, is there one today?"

"We play every other week, so we meet next week. In truth, we get together and gossip." Alice went on to enumerate all the Ladies' League activities: watercolor instruction, flower arranging, bridge, ballroom dancing lessons, lectures, and more.

Was she telling me this to give me nightmares?

I stuck to my primary concern.

"Does anyone come to mind when thinking about the auction items?"

"Try Amelia Meadows," Alice said.

"Yes, " Tom chimed in.

They discussed Amelia as a potential murderer, and now they recommend I talk to her? Did anything make sense around here?

"We must be going," Tom said. "We need to find Beatrice Gibbs."

"Try the ledger."

"I will," he said.

"Nice meeting you," Alice said.

My original intent recalled, I found the women's restroom and spent some time trying to clean the dust from my hair, face, arms, and clothing. I blew my nose on tissue from a gilt-edged box then went to the office. No one was there.

The phone rang. Instinctively, I answered.

"Is this the Ladies' League?"

"Yes."

"This is Monique from Haverfield Galleries. We learned Mr. Weston died and wished to express our condolences. We hope the painting we donated for the gala brings in money used in his memory."

Painting?

"I'm new here. What does the painting look like?"

"An abstract of varied blue tones. Some think the shapes suggest nude women," Monique said.

Gee, what a surprise.

"The artist is an upcoming and talented painter." She mentioned a name I didn't recognize.

"Yes, well, what size?"

"About two by three feet. We donated a complimentary framing for the winning bidder." She spelled the gallery's and artist's names and gave me her full name and phone number, which I wrote down.

Beatrice Gibbs's shoplifting made me wonder if someone stole the painting. Was Willie Weston murdered because he discovered the identity of the thief?

You are not starring in True Detective.

Concluding the conversation, I closed the roster as Amelia Meadows entered.

"Leave that out," she commanded.

A perverse side of me wanted to shove the ledger in a drawer. Instead, I said, "I need your help."

She pursed her lips at me, posture rigid.

"I'm helping organize the silent auction items for Francis Downs and can't find them."

"How preposterous! Willie cataloged everything."

"Would you mind pointing out where things are?"

"What a waste of my time." She turned on her heel and marched out, me pursuing.

Amelia entered the storage room and made straight for the back. The space grew darker, Amelia's mood sucking the light out of the atmosphere. She laid aside some moldy wreaths concealing a steamer trunk and flipped open the lid.

"Here they are. Why couldn't you find them?"

"I don't have x-ray vision."

"*Hmph*! I can't help what people stacked on top."

Before I could thank her, she brushed past me and left.

A typed page cataloged the trunk's contents, but a speed read showed nothing about the painting. Paper in hand, I went to find Amelia. She was in the office logging out.

"One more question."

"Lovely," Amelia muttered, not raising her head.

"Is this everything?" I waved the page at her.

Amelia straightened, pushing a stray hair from her rouged cheek.

"Of course not. I swear you're a complete moron! There are displays to be assembled."

"That's not my problem, but I do need to account for everything, so would you *please* check this list?"

"Has anyone ever told you that you're annoying?"

"Yes, and a moron."

Amelia let out another put-upon huff. Reaching into her purse, she pulled out a pair of snazzy red-jeweled reading glasses, snatched the paper from my hand, and ran a blood-red fingernail down the document. Removing the glasses, she shoved the list back at me.

"Nothing's missing."

"Did Mr. Weston mention a painting, by chance?"

"A what?"

"An abstract painting donated by a gallery?"

"No, but we weren't—" Amelia quit talking.

Always on speaking terms, I silently finished.

Amelia left without another word. I could put up with her disagreeable personality since it netted me what I came to find, and I was finally done.

As I stepped out of the office, Mrs. McGregor appeared. She wore an apron and dried her hands on the dishtowel she carried.

"I spent hours in the kitchen this morning cleaning the china and forgot to log in. What are you doing here?"

"Attempting to locate the silent auction donations."

"Did you find them?"

"I spent ages and couldn't, but Amelia Meadows showed me where they were. The storage room is a mess."

"I've told Beatrice to clean it on numerous occasions, but she never listens. I'm tired of doing everything. I'm getting old."

I made sympathetic noises, but this appeared to be a long-standing issue for the diligent Lydia McGregor, and I didn't care. "Did Mr. Weston ever mention anything to you about a painting he secured for the auction?"

"No. Why?"

"I can't find it."

"Oh, dear! The club should keep better records, but no one's interested. They use this ledger, but people are lackadaisical about logging in and out. We've never recorded donations for the gala despite my urgings."

"Have previous donations gone missing?"

"Yes. People complained they donated artwork, collectibles, jewelry, or other valuables to the club, and they disappeared. We've never tried to find out what happened to them."

"Really? How long has that been happening?"

"Several years or more. I'm not certain."

"Is someone stealing them?"

"I don't think so. Bad record-keeping and disorganization are likely the cause. No one wants to work anymore. In the beginnings of this club, everyone pitched in, but no one wants to maintain our grand traditions."

"It happens." I tried to be sympathetic, but my nose itched.

"For instance, this year, Willie planned to change our gala's formality."

I rubbed my finger back and forth under my nose. "Oh?"

"He wanted to bring in some models to hold the auction items and remove the limit on some of the alcoholic beverages."

I sneezed.

"Oh, bless you! You need a tissue." Mrs. McGregor pulled a packet out of a pocket, ripped off the closure, and gave me one. I blew my nose but went into another fit of sneezing.

"The storage room dust got to me."

"I think you should go home."

"I agree." I wiped at my nose again, attempting to hold back a deluge of snot.

"It was uncharitable of me to speak about Willie in such disparaging terms. The board wouldn't have let him proceed," she said, chastened. "It's just his death has left so much more work for everyone, and I'm overwhelmed."

I bet this was another ongoing feud at the Ladies' League. Threats to my life made their in-fighting feel like pre-school.

"Enough of this chit-chat! I need to go back to the kitchens," Mrs. McGregor said. "You go home and take a shower."

I forged Francis's signature in the ledger, coming to the realization the record was worthless.

Once outside the building, I let the sun warm my face. Note to self: *Never volunteer to inventory a storage room.* Amended note to self: *Never volunteer.* There were reasons these jobs didn't get done, even if Mrs. McGregor would disagree.

A few minutes later, I sped home, anxious to get cleaned up.

As I punched the accelerator, a delivery truck headed down the drive right at me.

Stomping on the brakes, I backed up and pulled into a side road leading to the barn and Jose's quarters. Jose ran up to my window, explaining he let in the truck and my interior designer.

Sherilyn's car blocked the garage entry, so I went in through the house's front door, grumpiness level at Def Con One. An object in the foyer halted me. A seven-foot pine tree pierced through by bird feathers and dead branches blocked the entry. A ball of feathers crowned the horrific item.

My vivacious designer appeared from the kitchen.

"What do you think?" she asked.

I turned hard eyes on her.

"What in the hell is that?"

18

"**A** conversation piece!" Sherilyn said. "This will give people something to talk about. There will be no awkward pauses—"

"My friends communicate just fine."

K would haul the abomination into the courtyard and detonate it.

"Yes, but what about new acquaintances?" Sherilyn gave me a strained smile.

I moved closer to her. "Please remove this from my house."

She froze, a mouse to my cobra.

"Um, of course," she squeaked, terrified.

Regaining my composure, I stepped back. "Why don't you show me what else you've done?"

Sherilyn rebooted in an instant. "Yes! I think you'll *love* what I did in the master bedroom, and I outfitted three of the other bedrooms. I found the most *divine* faux fur comforter for your guests to enjoy."

The furnished rooms were a pleasant surprise. The guest bedrooms now included beds *with* mattresses, pillows, sheets, blankets, and comforters. One bedroom held an inviting faux fur, brown mink comforter.

I pictured Warden lying across it in a provocative position.

Sherilyn pulled me out of the room to continue the tour. She pointed out scented decanters of bath oils, candles, towels, and rugs in the guest bathrooms. The master bath was outfitted with opulent, burgundy rugs and matching bath sheets. She also added plants and decorative containers, everything classy. Off my bedroom, a stone lounge chair covered by thick, removable cushions, two matching chairs, and a small table faced an outdoor fireplace.

"I think we need some potted trees here, a honeysuckle or jasmine vine to bring in some fragrance, plus a rug. Wait! I'm undecided about the rug. They can mildew and become infested with bugs and, like, black, spreading mold and—we won't do the rug."

"Can we hurry along? I need to take a shower," I interrupted, stifling a sneeze.

"Come this way!" Sherilyn dragged me toward the kitchen. She revealed dishes, glasses, dishtowels, and pots filling the drawers and cupboards. On the counter sat a mixer, a blender, and a state-of-the-art espresso machine.

"Sherilyn, I appreciate your hard work, but I don't drink coffee."

Her face fell.

"Again, what about your guests? You need the best equipment!"

What guests?

Davia, wait. She accomplished in a day what I wouldn't achieve in months, if ever.

"Fine."

Sherilyn jumped up and down, clapping her hands. "I'm so glad! First, I contacted this guy who owns a restaurant, and I sort of was in a relationship with him once, but it didn't go anywhere because he, like, never talked about *anything!* Can you imagine? I asked him, *So, can you find a first-class espresso machine for me?* He didn't respond. I mean, I had to drive over to his place and ask him in person!"

She paused and my cell phone rang, thank the merciful gods.

"Excuse me." I stepped outside.

"Davia? This is Beatrice Gibbs. I understand you were at the club today."

What did she want?

"Yes?"

"Is everything in order? The gala's almost upon us."

"I found the auction items."

"Excellent! I need you and Francis at my house today to discuss them. I'll expect you at three p.m. 5150 Sonora Lane."

I stared at the phone in disbelief.

Who did she think she was, the queen?

I stopped myself from throwing my phone. "Are we done? I need to take a shower."

"We should talk about the rest of the house. What your priorities are and—"

"Yes, but not today. I need to get in the shower."

"What's your schedule like for the rest of the week?"

"Why don't you decide what to finish? I trust you."

"You do?"

"I do." *Sort of, but I could make her change anything I didn't like.*

"Thank you! I'm so excited to be able to—"

"Sherilyn, I truly appreciate you, but I need to go."

Three big sneezes followed this statement, so Sherilyn shut her mouth and walked to the front door. "I'll see you again soon."

"Hey!" I called.

"Yes?"

I pointed to the tree. "Please take that with you."

"It won't fit in my car."

"Put it outside, at least."

She hefted the offending object toward the front door, listing to one side due to its weight. "I'll try to put it in my trunk." The branches muffled her voice.

"Leave it outside and arrange for someone to come pick it up."

"Okay." She wrestled the immense tree out, and I stood by with no inclination to help.

As the front door closed, I sprinted for the bathroom and stripped. A bar of organic mint soap sat on the shower's shelf, provided by my decorator. I lathered up and let the steaming water pour over my body until I was lobster red. Drying off with a thick towel the size of a throw rug, I paused to appreciate the perks of my new life.

Living in gratitude puts everything in perspective—my mother's oft-repeated statement, especially when something got me down.

Wrapped in the towel, I went outside to recline on the new patio divan and enjoy the sun, needing to recharge before obeying my summons to the Evil Queen's lair.

I PARKED in front of Beatrice Gibbs's home at half-past three, taking care to arrive extra late. Another car was in the driveway.

Was I later than Francis?

Flower beds framed Beatrice's white ranch-style house. I rang the doorbell, and the ticking of numerous toenails resounded. What form of beasts lurked inside—besides Beatrice? The door opened, and a herd of eight Toy Pomeranians swarmed around me. They wore a rainbow of multi-colored bows around their necks.

"*Darlings!* Do come back here!" Beatrice called over the din of barking and the snapping of sharp teeth.

"Beatrice." I gave her a cool nod, ignoring the chaos at my ankles.

"Darlings!" Beatrice's wheedling didn't affect her rampaging horde.

We went inside. The dogs spun around and pursued me like mayhem always did. They renewed their cacophony of barks and snarls but finally quieted down and went to shred shoes, pee on plants, or plot the demise of civilization.

"Come this way," Beatrice directed me, back in form. She led me to a formal living room. Francis perched on a loveseat, ready to take flight.

"Hey, Francis." I sat next to her.

Beatrice indicated a pitcher and glasses. "I made some lemonade."

Not poisoned red apples?

I poured a glass, took a dainty napkin, and sat back.

"Today, I want to discuss the gala and what we need to pull it all together by Saturday. We're short on time, and the programs need to be printed," Beatrice said.

Francis put her glass down and gave Beatrice a small smile. "Jane Pierce said if we give her the info by tomorrow, it won't be a problem."

"I'm glad to hear you did something right," Beatrice said, and her mean remark made me fight the urge to hurl my drink at her. "Davia, what's left to be done with the donations?"

"Mr. Weston left a list of everything, and the donations are in a trunk in the storage room."

Both women smiled at the news.

"I forgot. We're missing one item, a painting." I braced for a lecture.

"It will turn up. This kind of thing was bound to happen, considering Willie's death." Beatrice said, tone airy. She began to quiz Francis about their assembly for the display.

What just happened?

"Where's your bathroom?" I asked.

"Down the hall on the right," Beatrice directed.

Finding it, I turned on the water in the sink and closed the door from the outside.

Where would I hide a painting if I were Beatrice Gibbs?

I gave each bedroom a cursory inspection but found nothing of note except ugly, patterned wallpaper. Returning to the bathroom, I shut off the water and flushed the toilet.

Beatrice and Francis paused their conversation on my return.

"Do you need me for anything else? I have a tennis lesson in a few minutes," I improvised.

Francis said. "Let's meet an hour before the beginning of the gala."

"Sounds good to me."

"We'll nominate you for Vice President and vote at our next meeting," Beatrice said. "Amelia Meadows is bowing out."

"I'm so excited for you to be on the board!" Francis said. "We need new, enthusiastic members."

She got the *new* right.

My Ladies' League duties finished; I went to the Suprema Market for chicken, spinach, and a gallon of water. After paying, I exited, balancing the grocery bag on one arm and the water on the other. The sun blinded me—and I rammed right into someone.

The plastic jug of water whirled from my grasp and exploded on the someone's foot.

The person being Adair Monroe.

"*Ow!*" He grasped my shoulder, keeping most of his weight on me.

"Sorry! Are you all right?"

"I think you broke something." Adair held the injured foot and sodden leg of his jeans aloft. "Will you help me to my car?"

"Of course."

Unflattering terms like wimp and sissy leaped to mind, but I told myself to give him a break. He pointed out a two-door, black Aston Martin parked a couple of spots over, the same car preferred by James Bond.

Don't make a snarky remark.

I snaked a supporting arm around Adair's waist, sending a shiver through me as we started forward.

He stopped.

"Not going to carry me?"

"If you want me to." I was unable to suppress a smile.

"If the paparazzi captured that photo, it would be quite the cover story."

My eyes grew wide in horror. "No!"

"I'm teasing."

At his car, he sat and ran a hand over his foot.

"Not broken, is it?" I noted.

"Aren't you an angel of mercy?"

"I'm truly sorry."

Adair rubbed his foot. "The feeling's starting to come back."

He stood, and I put my hand on his elbow to support him if he was too optimistic. Up close, the light stubble on his face only enhanced his appeal.

This guy was a Pied Piper for women.

A flat package in the backseat of his car drew my attention from exploring that dangerous avenue. "What's that?"

"A new painting. I just picked it up from the gallery. Would you like to see it?"

"Sure." People in my circle got their art at Home Goods.

He reached past his interior's custom-inlaid, piano-black wood for a manila envelope on the front passenger seat.

"I don't want to unwrap it here, but I have a photo." He eased out a thick, colored card. "The artist is being hailed as the next Picasso."

The painting was of blue abstract nudes done by the artist the woman from the gallery mentioned.

"Does he always paint blue nudes?"

"No, this is his only one, a unique acquisition for my collection."

"Who did you buy it from?"

"An art dealer friend. She sometimes comes into rare pieces."

"Is her name Beatrice Gibbs?"

"Beatrice, the Ladies' League President? What are you on about? No."

"Adair, Haverfield Gallery donated this painting to the Ladies' League for the upcoming gala."

"What are you saying?"

"Someone stole the painting,"

"No way!"

Before I could respond further, something shiny near the top of a wall at the parking lot's end drew my attention. Catching Adair by the shoulders, I pulled him to the ground.

A bullet shattered the side window of his car.

19

I landed on Adair, and dropped the remainder of my groceries. At least he wore casual clothes this time, so I didn't mess up another suit.

"What did you do that for?" he demanded.

"Stay here." I jumped up, pulling the gun from my ankle holster.

A car moved through the lot, and I ran alongside it until the driver turned to park. Sprinting to the wall, I stuck my head over it and observed a man running toward a distant building. Doing a one-armed vault, I crashed down face-first into a garden.

WTF?

Who was the target—me or Adair?

How much to repair the flowers I crushed?

My pursuit brought me to the Suprema Resort and Spa's grounds, a luxury property dotted with cottages and charming gardens. Racing for a tree to hide behind, I prayed my leg would hold up.

A round zipped past my nose.

Plastered against the tree, I sneaked a quick look. When no one shot, I ran as fast as possible and plastered myself against the front wall of a cottage. Edging to the corner, I bolted around it and ran right into a maid carrying a stack of folded towels.

"*¡Dios mio!*" She dropped everything.

"*Lo siento!*"

Beyond, gardens surrounded a free-standing fountain and more guest cottages. When I stepped out from cover, the gunman fired. I made an Olympic-level dive and landed behind the skinny fountain. Its water spit drops on my head as bullets sprayed gravel into my face.

When there was a lull, I dared fate and made a break for the cottage.

A dashing couple in tennis clothes exited.

"Go back inside!" I ordered.

They froze for a second, but the sight of my gun made them obey. I darted down the side of the building and turned a corner.

A laundry cart hit me, knocking me to the ground as a muzzle flared.

The slug missed.

Taking hold of the cart, I slammed it left, connecting with the shooter. When I got around it, he was halfway to another cottage.

At least he limped.

My gun up and sighted, I gave chase. My quarry was blonde with light eyes and fair skin. He spun, aiming his automatic handgun at me. Deadly rounds were about to be emptied in my direction, but I couldn't fire back because of possible innocent bystanders.

Time slowed like in *The Matrix*, and I braced myself.

His finger began to squeeze the trigger when a man ran in from the street, sailed through the air, and tackled the shooter. Both men fell to the ground.

It was Adair.

He punched the gunman in the face.

I didn't move, shocked.

My foe lifted his arm and clocked Adair in the temple with his gun. Blood sprayed from a gash, and Adair's head lolled to the side. The man rose and kicked him hard in the chest, sending Adair sprawling.

When I sped forward, a crowd began to gather outside their cottages. The gunman ran toward the street.

Adair lay on his back, moaning. His wound bled profusely, dripping down his face and onto his dirt-and-grass stained polo shirt.

"You're an idiot!" I told him, kneeling. "What exactly were you thinking?"

"You're welcome." He struggled to sit up, and I helped him, doing a quick assessment of his injuries.

"Where's your car?"

"Huh?"

"Your car. Where is it?" I guessed he didn't run here on his injured foot.

"Over there." He pointed toward the street.

"Give me your keys!"

"What?"

"Give me your keys!"

"Why?"

"I need to go after the bastard you just tackled."

"Are you taking the piss? You can't go after that—that madman! Best to let the police pursue him."

"Ah!" I exclaimed in frustration. "Adair, I'm not like most women."

"No, most don't have a death wish."

"Don't argue. Your window is busted. What more can happen?"

He rubbed at a rivulet of blood dripping into his right eye.

"I think I'm bleeding."

A comment of sheer irrelevance. Well, irrelevant to me.

He'd live.

I reached to search his pockets, but he snagged my wrist and hauled me down to eye level.

"You're the most exasperating woman I've ever met."

He pressed his keys into my hand.

"Thank you." I ran for the street, arms pumping like a stunt double. My leg tingled, but I ignored the possible complication.

Adair's Aston sat in the center of the street, the driver's door still open. I slid in, turned on the engine, and peeled away. The gunman roared past in a black Mercedes sedan.

Was he the same guy who tried to run me over near Bryce's

Boutique? Attack me at the pistol range? If so, I would put some hurt on him.

The hitman headed for downtown Rancho Suprema, blazing along at dangerous speeds. He blew right through a four-way stop, almost hitting an SUV driven by a startled woman on her cell phone.

I eased past.

Ahead, the Mercedes didn't stop for another four-way intersection.

Beyond was an open road.

A man talking on his cell phone and holding a drink crossed in front of me at mid-block. I wrenched the steering wheel to the left, veered into the center divider, and obliterated the landscaping. The frightened pedestrian jumped back in shock, dumped his drink all over himself, and dropped his phone.

The Mercedes vanished around a curve.

The route was Switchback City. The winding roads were designed in the 1920s and allowed people to meander and enjoy the scenery. Now they made the perfect slalom course for high-performance cars. The Aston hummed a throaty roar, leaping to eighty miles per hour. I held ideal trajectories on every curve, tires squealing, gaining on the Mercedes.

The moment I was in range, gunfire began.

My front windshield cracked, and I swerved.

Ahead, a delivery truck driver at an intersection pulled out. The Mercedes did a hard drift, missing it. I pulled the emergency brake and side-skidded, the Aston sliding forward at an alarming speed. I braced for impact, but the car shuddered to a halt less than an inch away, straddling both lanes.

The truck ambled on.

Reversing, I maneuvered into the correct lane and gassed it.

An empty road lay ahead.

Had I lost him?

A blur of black accelerated from a side road, slamming into my right back bumper with a nauseating crunch. The contact sent the Aston into a spin, tires squealing in a three-hundred-sixty-degree turn. I clutched the steering wheel, praying the car wouldn't flip or hit a phone pole. At last, the car stuttered to a stop, facing oncoming traffic.

A driver in a spiffy red sports car kept his hand on the horn, impatient. I reversed, raced backward, and flipped around.

The Mercedes accelerated away.

If I were the assailant? I would have jumped out, waited for the car to cease spinning, and popped a round off through the windshield. This gunman failed on his follow-through, lucky for me.

The freeway loomed ahead, a chance for him to disappear.

Taking a shortcut, I stopped and backed into position. When the Mercedes appeared, I put the pedal to the floor. The Aston sped forward, the resulting collision and inertia shoving the Mercedes down a nearby street. My foe's car slammed against a guardrail and bounced to a stop, facing me. I lifted my gun to fire through the windshield, but the driver accelerated backward.

Was he a stunt driver doubling as an assassin?

Stepping on the gas, I caught up and rammed him. The man rotated the car around and sped off.

We returned to light speed, scenery a blur. It was time to test the upper limits of Adair's Aston. I maneuvered to the right of the Mercedes, nosed my car into his back-right quarter panel, and hit him.

The Mercedes spiraled, then straightened.

The man aimed at me through his window, but we crashed through a wooden fence and were on the back nine of the famed Rancho Suprema golf course. We raced past a threesome of golfers. Any missed swing would be an excuse for the history books.

Another round struck my windshield, the additional crack killing visibility. I stuck my head and gun out the driver's side window.

My opponent prepared to fire when the Mercedes zoomed through a dip. The car flew into the air, tilted, and cartwheeled on its side at high speed. Parts flew off, and the roof collapsed. Something black fluttered at the driver's window.

The Mercedes impacted another hill, rotated, and landed roof first in a water hazard.

A flock of swimming ducks scattered.

I skidded to a halt, bailed out, and ran to the submerged vehicle, not giving the driver a chance to regroup and start firing.

The black object trapped outside the car in all those flips was the assassin. He lay partly out the driver's side window, dead.

My team would say, *You saved some ammo,* but I'm not that cold-blooded.

The golfers stared in shock at the wreckage. One spoke frantically into his cell phone. Local law enforcement meant trouble for me, so I punched a number programmed into my speed dial. A gruff man's voice answered.

"Agent Wills."

Wills was my California handler to call for clean-up and emergencies only. If this didn't fit that requirement, I didn't know what would.

"Davia Glenn. I terminated a hostile at the bottom nine of the Rancho Suprema Golf Course. I'm requesting assistance."

The line went dead.

I turned my attention to Adair's car. The back and side windows were gone, the front windshield shattered, the right side crumpled, the left front quarter panel demolished, and the front bumper dragged the ground.

Well, the roof was still pristine.

Sirens screamed. Two fire trucks, an ambulance, and a whole station's worth of police cars headed my way.

I began to consider what to do, unable to cry or act distraught. I decided to get in the driver's seat, put my head back, and close my eyes. Pretending to be unresponsive might buy me some time.

A battalion of deputy sheriffs ran forward, guns drawn. Most went toward the Mercedes, and they quickly deduced the driver was dead.

"Don't move," a deputy instructed, keeping his firearm fixed on me.

Five minutes later, they let the paramedics enter the scene. I put my head back and stayed limp. This trick would only work for a few minutes because my eyes would be responsive if anyone shone a flashlight at my pupils.

An earnest paramedic and his partner began assessing me under the vigilant eye of the deputy. I spent a few minutes acting dazed before "reviving" and complaining about fictional pains in my leg, ankle, right arm, and head. The younger paramedic touched my leg near the gun holster, and I jerked back.

"I need to splint your leg to be safe." He turned to gather the necessary supplies.

"No, I'm fine," I told him.

His partner said. "Miss, splinting the injury is a necessary precaution."

I opened my mouth to argue when a certain detective stepped from behind the paramedics.

"Ms. Glenn, we meet again," Montoya said. He spread his arms to indicate the scene. "Don't tell me. A stranger attacked you, and for some weird reason, you pursued him."

"How'd you guess?"

"Did you shoot him, or did he lose control of his car?"

"No idea."

Montoya clenched his jaw.

"I think you and I will get to spend a lot of time together," he said ominously.

Personally, I considered him too cute to do ominous.

Montoya was about to say more when five men in black suits holding badges came towards us.

"National Security," one said. "This is our investigation now. Thank you for your assistance, but this crime scene is closed."

Montoya stared at them. "Excuse me?"

"National Security, sir," said a tall, older man who resembled Harrison Ford. "I'm Agent Wills, in charge of this investigation. The deceased in the Mercedes is a terrorist, and we're taking over."

"Uh, you're what?" breathed Montoya, confused.

"Taking. Over," the man repeated.

Montoya didn't move, dumbfounded.

My eyes fell on the still-intact package in the backseat of the Aston. *The painting!*

"Detective, in the back of this car is a painting stolen from the Ladies' League." I removed the artwork from the back.

"So? I don't think I'll be able to arrest you for possession of stolen property, which would be the least of the charges you racked up today."

"*I* didn't steal it, but I have someone who might be able to tell you who did."

Montoya exhaled with resignation. "I have a contact in property crimes."

"The Ladies' League would probably be grateful if you found the thief and give you tickets to their gala."

"Is this a peace offering?"

I nodded. "Here you go."

Montoya balanced the package.

"Sometime over coffee, will you tell me what happened?"

"I don't drink coffee."

He left, not looking back.

The paramedics hovered. Two suits spoke to them, and they packed up.

I turned to the agent nearest me. "Would you find out the whereabouts and condition of Adair Monroe? He let me borrow this car, and I need to return it to him."

The agent did a survey of the destroyed Aston.

"I don't think he'll want it."

Getting on his radio to check, he told me paramedics took Adair to the ER at a nearby hospital.

"How is he?"

"He's not critical, but they didn't provide specifics."

I thanked him for the information, and Agent Wills approached. "We were put on alert by Streeter's office after your move but given no specifics," he said.

"What more do you need?"

Silence stretched.

"You ops agents are an informative bunch," he finally commented.

"Aren't we? Who can give me a ride to my car?"

Wills shouted to the youngest agent, the one still stuck doing errands, "Diehl! I need you to take Ms. Glenn to her car."

"Yes, Sir." He left his study of the deceased man and the wreckage.

"Thank you," I said to Wills and went with Diehl to his car.

A parade of TV crews raced toward the wreck, and a TV helicopter swooped in overhead, missing my exit.

We arrived at my Maserati, still parked in front of the Suprema Market. I thanked Diehl for the ride and headed for the hospital. Once inside, a person at information directed me to a private room. On the correct floor, I searched for too many nurses hovering near a door.

"Excuse me."

The crowd dispersed.

Adair lay in bed wearing a hospital gown, an IV drip attached to his arm, and his head wound bandaged. The monitors signaled his heart was strong.

Thank heaven—the news about his car might give him a stroke.

"Hey." I moved to his bedside.

"Hey, yourself." He gazed at me through a haze of painkillers.

He lay still, not smiling or inhabiting the space with his typical high energy. It struck me like a punch to the gut. He was in this condition because he tried to save my life.

Collateral damage.

"Here's your key back," I said, not knowing what else to say.

"What happened?"

Rather than explain, I used the remote to turn on the television. We stared at a small screen mounted on a high stand in the corner.

"Details are scant about a high-speed car chase this afternoon, ending in a fatality on the Rancho Suprema golf course," a female news anchor reported. Aerial videos of the upside-down Mercedes in the pond and a stretcher holding a body bag played in the background. The view widened to include Adair's mangled Aston.

Adair's eyes bulged. "How are you standing here?"

"I got lucky. Sorry about the car."

"I don't care about the car."

"No?"

"No!" he assured me. "We're both alive, and that's all that matters."

His sympathy and understanding struck me at a level I didn't want to examine. He didn't expect me to handle anything and everything, which was both baffling and appealing.

"Why was that man shooting at us? Who was he?" He put a hand to his forehead, trying to remember.

"A terrorist of some kind."

"A *terrorist*?" he echoed. "Why would he want to kill us?"

"You should hire a bodyguard."

"I've never needed one. Most people are polite around me, asking for selfies. Nothing like this."

"You might want to increase security for a while." Until someone neutralized the Badger threat, anyone I came in contact with could wind up right where he was, or worse.

"I'll consider it."

"Adair, how do you know the men you met at Chateau Rouge?"

"An ex-pat friend of mine living in Dubai connected us about a business opportunity. Since the region has proliferated quickly, I thought I would at least listen."

"What kind of business, if you don't mind me asking?"

"Some major development, luxury homes. Are they behind this terrorist?"

I ignored his question. "Do you recall Rashid's last name?"

He thought about it. "Sorry, I can't remember. I'm having problems concentrating."

"No worries. It's not important."

He lay back, eyes half-closed. "Why did you chase that man, Davia?" His words began to slur.

"You should rest." Turning to go, I remembered something else. "Oh, by the way, I gave your painting to a sheriff's detective."

Adair sat straight up, revived. "You what?"

"I told you somebody stole it from the Ladies' League, but we never finished the conversation due to being interrupted, remember?" I made my hand into a gun and pointed at him.

"I can't forget. Ever. But the painting! The transaction was through a reputable dealer."

"Maybe, but today I spoke to a person from Haverfield Galleries, and the painting was a donation. I'm on the Ladies' League auction committee."

"*You're* on a gala committee?"

"Hard to believe, right?"

"Yes, very." He shook his head and immediately put a hand against his temple. "Ouch."

I placed an arm behind his back and eased him down. Adair took hold of my shoulders, pulled me to him, and kissed me gently on the lips.

"I'm glad you're okay," he said.

Being this close to him made me want to lay my head against his chest and remain.

What was wrong with me?

Ignoring how his kiss made me feel, I straightened. "As I said, you need to rest."

Retreat can be a good option.

"Davia?"

"Yes?"

"Thank you for saving my life."

"Same to you."

We held eye contact for too long, so I broke off.

"Goodnight," I said and left.

Fatigue caught me while I waited for the elevator. Today contained a CCW test, a dusty storage room, ditzy decorators, maddened Pomeranians, a high-speed pursuit, and a kiss from Adair.

The elevator dinged.

As my mother would say, tomorrow would be better.

If not, I would take out Badger by myself.

20

The insistent vibration of my cell phone woke me at two a.m.

"Glenn?"

"Colonel Streeter." I rubbed my eyes. The world should leave the West Coast alone at this hour.

"There was an incident?"

I sat up and yawned. "Yes, Sir."

"Agent Wills could give me no details, except the ID of the deceased, an associate of Badger."

"Yes, Sir."

"Excellent work."

"Is the case closed?"

A brief pause.

"Negative. Whoever put out the info deleted their tracks."

"Hm." In the old days, I woke aware and alert. Now I barely made intelligible noises.

"We're not secure." Streeter reminded me of old protocols.

"No, Sir. Did you get my message?" Did bonehead Luke remember to give Streeter the info?

"Yes, but I can't discuss."

Can't you give me a hint?

The colonel continued, "Email's not secure, so I'll send someone to you. Please complete your report by 0900 hours."

Nine?

"Yes, Sir."

"Excellent work, Glenn."

The line went dead.

Streeter was the master of terminating needless discussion.

Lying back, I wondered about my team and their families. If someone were injured or dead, Streeter would tell me, wouldn't he? Was I on the outside for information? One neutralized hitman didn't mean the end unless Badger ran out of money or assassins, which was unlikely. Spinning everything around in my head, running through all the possibilities, I fell asleep.

At six, I decided on a quick workout before pounding out the report. Phoning the hospital and asking to speak to Adair was considered and discarded. He might change his mind about forgiving me for the damage to his car. At least, that's what I told myself.

Why had his kiss affected me? I hardly knew him.

Contrasting Adair to Warden, I realized Adair brought forward a part of me I rarely allowed out, the sensitive person underneath my steely exterior.

Deciding not to dwell on the subject, I strolled to the kitchen, pulling up the news on my phone. The headline of the local coverage trumpeted, "*Terror on Rancho Suprema Golf Course!*" I read the accompanying article and viewed the video footage again. The piece held mostly speculation, reports of an unidentified woman driving Adair Monroe's car, and a crisp "No comment" from Monroe's people. It was the stock reply given by important personages, for which I was thankful.

After putting water in the kettle, I selected a tea packet and protein bar from the near-empty pantry. Following breakfast, I took advantage of my in-home gym, now fully equipped by Sherilyn. I sprinted on the treadmill, lifted weights, and did two hundred incline sit-ups to increase my conditioning.

The gate buzzed as I transferred my report to a thumb drive. The monitor displayed a clean-cut man driving a plain wrap government vehicle.

"I'm Agent Morris."

I went out carrying a sealed manila envelope containing the drive. Agent Morris drove up and extended an ID, which I examined. I gave him the envelope, and he put it on the front seat.

"Thank you," he said, and I could tell he burned my image into his brain like any well-trained agent.

"Welcome."

He drove out the gate.

I took the gun from the back of my waistband and relaxed.

Free time! Maybe Ace would enjoy a trail ride.

What if Badger sent a replacement assassin?

After some debate, I settled on a ride around the arena.

Ace nickered when I entered the barn. I fed him a carrot and put on his halter. Tying him in the alley, I retrieved the bucket containing brushes and combs from the tack room and brushed his glossy coat. There were a few tangles in his mane and tail to unsnarl. Once saddled, I walked him around in case he held his breath, and rechecked the cinch. Leading Ace to a mounting block, I walked up the stairs and put my foot in the stirrup. Tennis shoes substituted for a proper pair of boots.

The arena was well-groomed thanks to a small tractor used weekly by Jose. Ace stayed still when I unhooked the gate, leaning down from the saddle. He also did a perfect side-pass to allow me to close and re-latch it once we were inside. I worried he might be rambunctious, but he was gentle because Jose turned him out to play in the arena each day to burn off some of his energy and hay-belly. Soon, we moved from a sedate walk to a jog and a lope. His gait was smooth, like sitting in a giant rocking chair.

Nostalgic memories of my childhood and the hours spent on horseback made the stress and worries over recent events dissipate. After an hour, I dismounted and undid Ace's cinch. Taking him back to the barn, I unsaddled then led him to the wash rack for a bath.

"Ready for a snack?" I tied him in the alley, retrieved some grain from the feed room, and dumped the treat in his feeder. Hopefully, he would hold off from rolling until he was dry.

I was satisfied at being dirty, wet, and smelling of horse. Lunchtime neared. Happy, I walked back up the drive toward the house, I crested the hill and saw something on the ground.

A crumpled body.

Jose.

I RUSHED to him and knelt, scanning the surroundings but seeing no one.

"Jose! Jose?" I shook him, but he didn't respond. A shovel lay nearby, discarded.

A quick check of his body revealed no apparent injuries and his breathing was steady.

Was it heatstroke?

I kept shaking him, wondering if I should call an ambulance. "Can you hear me?"

Jose's eyelids fluttered and he came awake, confused. He sat up, his body jerking spasmodically. I held his shoulders to steady him.

"What happened?" I asked in Spanish.

Panic crossed his face, and he attempted to stand.

"Don't." I grabbed his arm, but he pulled back.

"*Peligro.*"

Danger.

Still crouched, I rechecked our surroundings, but nothing stood out.

Shoving an arm under Jose, I directed us toward the courtyard and potential cover. When he saw where we were headed, he pulled back and stopped.

"He might be there," he told me, pointing a shaky hand at the courtyard doorway.

"Who?"

Jose's face was ashen. "He got me in—" He mimed an arm around his neck. "I lost consciousness."

My blood ran cold. Someone gained access to the property, caught Jose unawares, and choked him out?

I reversed course, making for the barn. Adding Jose's weight to my own caused pinprick pain to run down my bad leg. The incline made the trek even more difficult.

"Was he alone?" I whispered as we went.

"I—I think so."

"What did he look like?"

"It happened *rapido*. Dark clothes, my size."

"A man?"

"*Si.*"

Jose pulled his keys out, and I unlocked his quarters. Once inside, I relocked the door and helped him to his neatly-made bed, where he lay down. A shelf housed a monitor containing security camera footage. Hurrying over, I checked the views of both driveways, the front and back of the house, and the barn area.

Nothing.

Was he inside my home?

Had I locked all the doors?

I considered my options.

"How do you feel?"

"Head is *no bueno*." He closed his eyes.

Jose required medical care, so I made the call. After opening the entry gates, I said, "I'll lock your door, but don't open it unless you're sure it's either me, paramedics, or police."

I left, pulling the locked door closed.

I need to find the intruder before the police arrive, and I don't have a weapon.

Scolding myself for not taking a gun when I went to ride, I performed a quick search of the tack room. A double-edged farrier's knife, used to trim long horse hooves, lay in a bin. It was rusty from disuse and covered in a layer of dust. Picking it up, I blew off the dirt.

The wood handle was about five inches, and the blade around two, ending in a curved hook. It would have to work.

My path to the house was up the hillside through dense vegetation, with brush and trees for cover. I thought of Kyle teaching me how to move undetected while sensing someone else's presence. "You don't want to be the first person to die in a horror movie," he had said.

Carry nothing that makes noise.

Watch where you step.

Move with caution.

It took time to be stealthy, and I didn't have that luxury. Which entry point should I try? Deciding on a spare bedroom window, I pried at the screen. It popped off. Setting it aside, I moved the blade up between the panes. The latch groaned against the intrusion. I waited, listening, but the closed door to the room didn't open.

Keeping low, taking quick checks around me, I resumed my task.

Scrape. Screech. Creak.

The latch came loose.

After another survey behind me, I eased the window forward and I pulled myself up and over. The plush carpeting muffled any noise from my entry. Concerned my cell phone might give me away, I shut the sound off and placed it in a dresser drawer.

Before turning the room's wrought iron doorknob, I pressed an eye to the keyhole. No one was in the visible portion of the hall, and nothing betrayed the presence of an intruder. Perhaps we missed each other, me coming in while he went out.

Blade gripped; I stepped into the hall.

Someone crashed into me.

My back thudded against the tiled floor, my improvised weapon skittering away. A lean man straddled me, a horrific scar extending from a pale eyebrow down his cheek. Bringing up a knee, I kicked out, launching him off me.

I bolted forward to slam my hand into his throat. He blocked my arm with ease and attempted to punch me in the face. I deflected the blow, but he followed up with a fierce kick to my hip. The impact made me stumble backward, and I sucked in a hard breath. The man ran forward to kick me again, but I spun and deflected his blow with a roundhouse kick.

Our legs connected, and we crashed to the ground.

My hands gripped one of my attacker's legs. He lashed out with his other foot to strike me in the face, but I dodged the blow. In a split second, another vicious kick connected with the side of my head. The impact dazed me, and my hold loosened.

The man threw himself atop me. He landed a series of ferocious punches to my kidneys before directing his fists toward my face. I raised my hands to block the incoming blows. With surprising speed, he pinned my arms in one strong hand. Withdrawing a syringe from his jacket, he popped the cap off a long needle with his teeth.

The end dripped with whatever was about to be injected into my body.

Fear supercharged me. I drove my knee up close enough to my assailant's groin to cause an *oomph* exhalation. His hand relaxed a fraction, but a sharp pain stung my neck, deep and unforgiving. His thumb poised on the plunger of the syringe.

Rolling over, gripping his legs with mine, I fought to break his hold, desperate to free myself. He clung to me, hyper-focused on his mission.

The liquid descended, some spilling on my neck due to my evasive efforts. I pushed the needle out, but the fluid entered my bloodstream, its contents speeding through me.

A headbutt to my foe's face caused the syringe to fly into the air and land near my blade. The cylinder still contained half its liquid. Throwing the man off me, I staggered forward. My breathing grew shallow, and I began to lose control. I reached out a hand, and it multiplied in my vision like the arms of an octopus.

My assailant tackled me from behind, and we fell to the floor. My fingers closed around the syringe. Spinning, I plunged the contents directly into the man's chest. He let forth a roar of rage, pulled back, and reached for my farrier's knife.

Distant sirens wailed.

My eyelids grew weighted, vision blurring.
A blink.
He drew near with an arm above his head, knife high.
Another heavy-lidded blink. I raised my arms for the block.
Blackness.

21

———————

Bang! Bang! Bang!

My brain registered the noise.

Bang! Bang! Bang!

With effort, I opened my eyes. I lay on my back in the hall.

What happened? Why was I on the floor?

A man with a jagged scar down his face lay on his stomach close beside me, a farrier's knife in his hand.

Who was he? What was he doing in my house?

I couldn't remember anything.

"Sheriff's Department! Open the door!"

Could I stand? Could I even *move*? I pressed both palms into the floor, levering up to my elbows. The effort made me nauseous, and the room rotated. I felt trapped inside a glass box, like a taxidermied animal. Falling on my side, I stretched out to place two fingers on the man's neck.

No pulse.

I searched his waxy face, trying to remember. He must have attacked me. Why else would I be in this position?

Crawling across the floor, I inched up the wall. Still dizzy, I rested against it for support. Taking a tentative step, I stumbled forward on rubbery legs.

Nearing the door, I called, "I'm coming, just a second!"

The banging and yelling stopped.

Piercing pain burst across my head and I put my hand to its side. The action caused my knees to buckle, and I almost fell.

Come on, come on, come on.

Straightening my clothes and smoothing my hair, I pulled the heavy front door towards me and stepped outside.

Two uniformed deputy sheriffs, a man and a woman, backed up, watchful.

Closing the door, I put my hands up, trying not to collapse.

"Hello, I'm Davia Glenn." I hoped my voice remained steady.

Keep it friendly.

"Yes, Ms. Glenn. We received your call about the assault on Mr. Macias. We wanted to check on your safety," said the older of the pair. Lines around his eyes framed a steady gaze.

"Is-is he okay?"

"Yes. The paramedics are assisting him now, and he's declining transport to a hospital,"

"Do you know what happened?" the other asked, an athletic Latina woman.

Memories rushed back. "I was riding, and afterward, I walked back from the barn and found Jose collapsed in the drive. He told me a man on the property attacked him. I helped him to his quarters and called you."

Think fast.

Why did I come back to the house?

Why did I leave the safety of the barn?

"Did you see anyone?" the older man asked.

"No. The house alarm was on and not triggered. I have a CCW, but I left my guns because I was riding. I thought I should retrieve a weapon."

The woman tensed. "Are you armed?"

"No. I heard your sirens, so I left the weapons in their safe."

"We didn't find anyone. Do you know why this occurred?" the man said.

"No. I'm shaken by everything that happened."

Please write me off as a nervy Rancho girl, the kind who falls apart when she breaks a nail.

"Does Mr. Macias have any enemies?" he continued.

"I just bought this place, and he stayed on as caregiver for the property. So, no idea."

They took my details and handed me business cards.

"Let us know if you think of anything else," the male deputy said.

"I will."

"One last question," he said.

"Yes?"

"What is that?" He pointed to the tree Sherilyn still needed to remove. It looked even worse by daylight, limbs drooping.

"A conversation piece."

"I wouldn't want to have a conversation about that," the man replied.

"Me either," said the woman.

Jose came through the courtyard gate holding the shovel he had dropped in the drive.

Our eyes met.

"How are you?" I asked.

"*Bueno.*"

I somehow walked forward, and the deputies followed.

"*Gracias,*" Jose told them.

"Thank you for your statement, Mr. Macias. If you think of anything else, give us a call," the woman said.

The deputies went to their patrol car.

"I need to make a call." I slumped, dropping the business cards. "A man's inside. Dead."

"What happened?"

"I don't remember, but I don't feel right."

We entered the house and went down the hall, Jose supporting me.

All that remained was an empty syringe and a discarded farrier's knife.

The man was gone.

HAD I BEEN SO GROGGY, I mistook a low pulse for *no* pulse?

"*No esta aqui*?" Jose frowned. He's not here?

"He was right there." I pointed to the spot. "I think he injected me with something."

"Will you be all right alone?" Jose's hands clenched the shovel handle. He inclined his head toward the door.

"Yes. Go."

He set off to search the grounds.

I picked up the knife. It was absurd to clear each room carrying the inadequate weapon, so I hurried to my bedroom. The fast movement almost made me fall, but I caught myself and scanned the room.

Nothing.

A check of the outside surveillance cameras yielded the same result. Only Jose moved along, searching. In the closet, I pulled open the drawer containing my gun lockbox to retrieve my .45.

"Before I teach you to fire a gun, I want you to decide something," Kyle said to young me. "If someone comes at you with deadly intent, what will you do? Can you pull the trigger? I'm not talking about scaring them with a shot in the air. I mean aiming for center mass and firing."

I hesitated. "You mean, could I kill them?"

"Yes. You need to decide now. When or if the time comes, you won't have the luxury of thinking about anything."

Holding the heavy weapon, I wanted to sink to the carpeted closet floor and lean back against the island cabinet. The after-effects of whatever was in that empty syringe caused my vision to go in and out of focus. My stomach heaved again, and bile entered my throat.

Move, or you never will.

More long breaths. More pep talks from my brain.

One-two-three

Out of the closet, back into the master bedroom and bathroom.

Clear.

The other closet and bathroom.

Clear.

Down the hall, I checked each room. Bedrooms, bathrooms, gym, movie theater, living room, office, and kitchen.

Clear.

In the pantry, I picked up a bottle of water and gulped the contents. It made me retch. After several minutes spent bent over hacking, my stomach quieted. I choked another bottle of water down, hoping to flush the drug's contents out of my system. My head ached, and I felt a considerable lump near its top right side.

How did I get injured?

As I moved back into the kitchen, my vision blurred and transposed the setting.

A remote village appeared.

"Bombshell, you're with me," Warden said. He ran forward toward a warehouse. Behind me, Savant and K followed. I charged after Warden—and crashed into a barrier at full speed, knocking myself to the ground. I lay gasping with the wind knocked out of me.

The kitchen swam back into view.

I charged into a wall!

Hallucinations.

Were my memories even real? They had to be. I wouldn't feel like this otherwise. But how did my attacker get out? A thought struck me as I rose. Was there more than one assassin?

Oh god.

Telling myself to focus, I went through the mudroom and into the garage.

No one was there.

Back inside, I crossed the living room and exited through the French doors into the backyard. A tile-lined path led to a gate separating the guest house, pool, and pool house. Calla lilies bloomed in deep reds and oranges, red and white geraniums spilled over the edges of pots, and mature trees cast shade on the lawn.

Nearing the gate, I ducked down, legs shaking with the effort of squatting. Pushing the gate forward, I checked the path. Ahead, the water of the pool reflected the clear sky. Its infinity edge faced the valley, giving the illusion of water spilling off a cliff.

I inched down the path. When the house ended, I turned the corner.

Someone tackled me to the ground.

I lost hold of my gun—and stared up at the scar-faced man.

22

A fist came at my head, but I twisted, broke free, and stood.

"Why do they want me to bring you in alive?" he sneered with a German accent as he got to his feet.

"Who?"

"Someone who paid me a lot of money, but I'm not interested in keeping you alive anymore since you attacked me." He motioned like he stabbed his chest.

I got him, too. No wonder we both moved like punch-drunk fighters.

I dove for my gun, but impaired coordination made me miss.

The German sprang forward and kicked the weapon. It flew in an arc, landed in the pool, and sank to the bottom.

We moved away from the water's edge, keeping our distance, sizing each other up.

He came at me with a balled fist.

"You killed my little brother."

"Your *brother*?" I moved out of his path without much effort, and he lurched past.

"*Der Hammer,*" he said in German.

The Hammer.

"When was this?" Was he speaking of collateral damage from some mission, like Badger's son?

"Yesterday, in this snooty town, thanks to you."

The driver of the Mercedes.

"Yeah, well, I don't know why you call him *Der Hammer*. He was *Der Tor*." The fool. "He couldn't rig explosives, shoot, drive, *or* finish a job."

Enraged, my opponent launched himself at me. I planned to avoid him, run to the pool house, and grab up any improvised weapon I could find. Instead, my altered reaction time made me unable to execute, and his body clipped me in the shoulder as he sailed past. I lost my footing, almost falling into the pool. Balance regained, I threw myself forward toward my original goal. Behind me, the man corrected as well, close on my heels.

As I neared the pool house, Sherilyn Silvers strode through the side gate, wearing a silk blouse and slacks, her glossy blonde hair swept into a high ponytail.

"Hi, Davia! What are you doing?"

My foe stopped chasing me and threw an arm around Sherilyn's neck, elbow tight against her throat. Sherilyn's eyes grew big, her mouth forming an O.

Horror filled me. Would he hold her hostage in an attempt to get me to comply or simply snap her neck?

"Let her go!" I demanded.

"If she's important to you, even better." He tightened his grip.

The German's hideous scar became more pronounced as he increased his arm's pressure. All color left Sherilyn's face as her air supply was cut off.

"*No!*" I shouted as my designer's face grew slack.

Another person in my orbit, a victim of collateral damage.

Sherilyn went still, her body dropping as my enemy looked exultant.

Then her face transformed.

She jabbed an elbow into her attacker's ribs.

The assassin doubled over with a harsh grunt.

Sherilyn grasped his forearm and flipped him to the ground. Taking his wrist, she twisted his arm and kicked him in the head over and over.

"Take that, you bastard!" she shouted.

The man collapsed, unconscious.

Was this another hallucination? I shut my eyes and reopened them.

The scene remained unchanged.

"What in the hell, Davia?" Sherilyn still held the assailant's arm. "I mean, I come in here to take some measurements in the guest house for curtains, and the next thing I know, some maniac has me by the throat! Getting assaulted was *not* what I expected! At least those self-defense classes worked. It made my parents happy when I took them because I'm the only girl in the family, but geez. Who knew?"

I grabbed Sherilyn, giving her a quick hug, and she released the prostrate assassin's arm.

Jose appeared, still holding the shovel.

"I saw Ms. Designer drive in through the gates and wanted to—" he paused, noticing the prone man on the ground.

"Oh, hi, Jose. This guy," Sherilyn gave the still-unmoving man a solid kick to the ribs, "*attacked* me, and I put him down. Why would he do something like that, Davia? Who is he?"

"Uh—." With my brain scrambled, a cover story was out of reach.

"I'll call the police." Sherilyn took her cell phone out of her fallen tote bag.

"No." I put my hand on her phone.

"What do you mean, *no*? Is he a friend of yours or something? If so, this was like, what, a prank?"

"It's complicated. Think of him as a stalker. A connection of mine is aware of the situation and will come to collect him. Can you tie him up, Jose?"

"A connection?" Sherilyn asked as Jose left to retrieve some rope. "Are you, like, dating a cop, and he's aware of things? Or are you some important person who's given VIP treatment from law enforcement?"

"Difficult to explain," I said and waited until Jose returned, then excused myself to go back into the house and retrieve my phone to call Agent Wills.

"This is Davia Glenn," I said, detailing events. "He's alive. Please update Colonel Streeter." I hoped an interrogation specialist would extract intel on the breach and any further plans by Badger.

Back outside, the attacker sat trussed up against the wall of the pool house. Jose stood over him, his shovel poised to strike. My designer was gone.

"Where's Sherilyn?" I asked Jose.

He motioned to the guest house.

"Measurements."

We were both surprised. I never would've guessed this side of Sherilyn existed. She dealt with the assault and went right back to work, unfazed.

The German began to fight against the bindings.

"You're about as ineffectual as your brother," I said to him, kneeling. "What's *your* nickname, *Der Idiot*?"

"*Du Schlampe!*"

"Karma's a bitch, too, so I'm in excellent company."

Agents arrived, picked him up, and took him to their car. I gave them the syringe, which they put in an evidence bag. I hoped they might tell me what it contained or the bad guy would say since he also got to experience the contents.

I sagged, energy depleted. Jose leaned against the shovel, still pale. I picked up a pool cleaning net and went to scoop out my gun. As I swept downward, the water morphed into a churning, dark whirlpool. Phantasms swirled in its depths, racing toward the surface. Startled, I let go of the net.

"Are you all right?" Jose came toward me.

The pool returned to peaceful blue.

"We both need to get some rest."

Jose helped me retrieve my weapon, and I dried the gun with a towel from the pool house and stuck it in my waistband. We parted company. I would thank Sherilyn, then lie down.

When I entered the guest house, Sherilyn said, "I hope they do the lockup, key-thrown-away thing with that guy. People like him shouldn't be allowed to be free in the world, and he came to Rancho Suprema no less."

"Yes, he's gone now."

My phone rang. The screen read unknown caller.

"Hello?"

"Davia! You're tough to track down."

It was Adair.

"How'd you get my number?" My tone was curious, not hostile.

"You told me you joined the Ladies' League, so I called Beatrice Gibbs. Unpleasant woman."

"I agree. What's up?"

"I'm having a little gathering and would love for you to come."

I tried not to groan at the thought. "When?"

"Tonight. My invite is late, but you're so exclusive with your digits."

"Yeah, well—"

"The party starts around eight. You know my address, and you can bring a friend."

"How many people are coming?"

"Oh, just a few. See you soon!"

Why was this happening? And why tonight? I questioned whether I could walk back into the house unaided, let alone attend a party.

"What was that about?" Sherilyn fixed me with an inquisitive stare.

"Want to go to a party tonight? You could network."

"Where?"

"If you come here, we could ride over together. I don't recall the exact address, but know how to get there."

"Who's the host?"

"Adair Monroe."

"Shut *up!* Are you for real? *Adair Monroe?* How do you know him? Besides being smokin' hot, he does so much for people and never takes the credit. He lets abused women shop on his dime to help them. And those eyes, I think—"

"Do you want to go or not?" I listened longer than usual because of her heroics but was about to topple to the floor face first.

"Are you kidding? Who would turn down an invitation to Adair Monroe's?"

Me. I wanted to hibernate, only coming out when Badger Season was over.

"The party starts at eight."

"I'll be here around eight-thirty. We don't want to be the first to show up, although I'm tempted to knock on his door right as the clock strikes the hour. I can't believe it! I'm attending a party at *Adair Monroe's!*"

"I'm glad you're going, but I need to lie down. Thanks again for your help."

As I went out, I heard Sherilyn talking about what she would wear and who might be attending, joyous squeals punctuating her words.

Too exhausted to shower, I toppled over on my bed without removing my barn-dirty tennis shoes. In seconds, I was asleep.

The vibration of my cell phone woke me. The sound stopped before I registered the source. I rolled over, noted the gun still in my waistband pressing into my back, and removed it.

What time was it? Groping around on the bed for my phone, I picked it up.

Eight p.m.

The phone buzzed again.

"Hello?" My voice was groggy and unclear.

"Agent Wills here. You got dosed with a custom blend of tranquilizers, including an additive, so it worked faster than normal. We think someone cooked it up in a lab overseas, but we're not sure. We shouldn't talk specifics on the phone."

"Side effects?"

"Loss of body control, nausea, hallucinations, blurred vision, vomiting, drowsiness—"

"Thanks for the info," I didn't want to hear a rehash of what I had already been through. "Did you learn anything else?"

"Negative."

"Thanks."

The scar-faced man's brother tried to kill me, but this guy had orders to bring me in alive. What changed?

The phone vibrated again.

"Hello?"

"Davia! It's Sherilyn. I'm on my way over. Are you ready? I still can't believe we're going to Adair Monroe's for a party! I bet this is how Cinderella felt going to the ball. But that girl was clueless. How you fall in love with someone you only danced with a few times is beyond me. Anyway—" Sherilyn continued talking while I tried to sit up. Hunched on the side of the bed, I wondered if I could stand.

"I'm not ready. I still need to take a shower and have no idea what to wear."

"Oh, that's okay! We'll be even more fashionably late. I'll hang out while you get ready, and if you need me to help you pick something out, that will be so much fun. *Girlfriends forever!*"

Managing a shower was a miracle. A million jackhammers pummeled the inside of my head, and the lump under my hairline was so painful I could scarcely touch it. I pondered whether I should take aspirin, wondering how it would mix with what was already in my system.

Could I cancel on Adair? Why was I doing this? I imagined Sherilyn's miserable expression if I declined to go. She stopped the killer today, so this was the least I could do to repay her.

By the time Sherilyn arrived, my hair was dry, and I did my makeup to the best of my inadequate abilities. I answered the door, still wrapped in a towel. She wore a simple black dress, high heels, and more makeup than usual.

"Let's go check out your closet!" She took my hand and hauled me back to the bedroom. "I saw some bags from Bryce's Boutique, and he always has the trendiest clothes. I bet everything is super fabulous. Did he help you pick things out? I'm sure he did. Every time I shop at his store, I wind up with *way* more than I planned. He keeps handing me things until I give in!"

Her happy chatter made my head pound even more.

"I don't think I can manage heels tonight," I confessed.

"We don't have to be twins. In fact, it doesn't matter what you wear. I mean, Adair phoned you personally!" She went through my clothing-filled hangers.

"So?"

"So? What do you mean, *so*? Billionaires like him pay someone to do that sort of thing, usually by email, evite, text, or something. They don't call you up! He must like you. Are you dating?"

"Uh, it's complicated."

"You say that a lot! You said it was complicated with the stalker guy today, and now it's complicated with Adair Monroe. I mean, your life is a mess!"

"It is."

She handed me dark jeans, a sleeveless black silk turtleneck, a navy-blue blazer, and a pair of Gucci flats.

"Wear these. You'll be chic and won't suffer from aching feet all night, like me. I mean, who created heels? I bet a man. No woman would make anyone wear these wretched things. I swear they crunch my toes like a vise!"

I pulled on the outfit, trying my best not to fall over. I turned so Sherilyn wouldn't spot the bandage on my thigh and the dark bruises forming on my sides.

"How about earrings?" she asked.

"What kind do you think I should wear?"

"Oh, some dangling gold ones. Or diamond studs? You're wearing your hair down, so no one will see them."

I fetched a pair of gold hoops. To me, being dressed and upright was a real victory.

"How about taking this cross-body bag? You can put your house keys and phone in there. Wait! You need some more blush. I don't want to hang around a zombie look-alike." She took me to the bathroom, retrieved a brush, and coated some color on my cheeks. "There! That's much better. Ready?"

"Yes?"

"Tell you what. Why don't you let me drive? You look like you haven't slept in a month."

"I have a headache."

Sherilyn opened my medicine cabinet, found some aspirin, and poured three into my hand. Picking up a glass from the counter, she filled it with water and gave it to me. Relenting, I took them.

Here's hoping these don't do me in.

When I finished, she tucked my arm into hers.

"Let's go knock 'em dead!" she said.

As I hurried to keep up, I hoped her words wouldn't become literal.

ADAIR'S MANSION was ablaze with lights. Cars moved in a steady line up his drive to the entrance, where valets ran between them, opening doors. A grand fountain sprayed water to varying heights. We got out, and a photographer urged us along a red carpet to stand in front of a white screen displaying Adair's company logo. Sherilyn put her cheek against mine, and I did my best to smile.

Click- Click-Click

"I also want a selfie!" Sherilyn took out her phone, and I pulled back.

"Go ahead."

She snapped a few of herself, phone held high.

We ascended the steps. Staff handed us flutes of champagne at the door, and we entered an ivory-yellow room, an intricate black medallion pattern in the marble at our feet. The ceiling was at least twenty-five feet high, and gilt-framed oil paintings depicting scenes of the English countryside graced the walls. Ahead was a living room with couches and chairs placed around a stone fireplace. People filled the space, laughing and talking while an electronic beat played in the background. French doors led outside.

Sherilyn clutched my arm, pointing at one of the paintings.

"That's a real Gainsborough." She put a hand to her mouth in awe.

I gave her an uncomprehending look.

"Don't tell me you've never heard of the artist who painted *The Blue Boy*?"

"No, sorry."

Sherilyn was about to launch into a lecture on art history when the crowd separated for Adair. He wore ripped black jeans and a navy blue pullover hoodie paired with high-top Chucks. His hair had a fresh cut; shaved close on the sides. It made his cheekbones more pronounced, and he was paler than usual. Still, his smile lit up the room.

"He's even more delicious in person!" Sherilyn whispered, nails digging into my arm. "His eyelashes are so thick and long. If it were us, they would be extensions or fake! And his hoodie must be cozy cashmere. He's underdressed for a host, but who cares? He can do whatever he wants."

Adair saw me and immediately disengaged from the people surrounding him. Sherilyn vibrated with excitement beside me.

"Davia, I'm so glad you came. " He kissed my cheeks, and then his aquamarine eyes held mine, glittering like rare stones. The noise and crowd faded as sensual moaning and a rhythmic beat played from hidden speakers.

The room became a kaleidoscope of colors and sound, Adair at the center. He removed his hoodie, revealing a sleek torso with six-pack abs and a tattoo on his left pec right above his heart. He tossed the top to the floor and put his hands in my hair. His tongue entered my mouth, and I pulled him close, kissing him.

What was happening? What about Warden?

"Davia? Davia?" Adair's voice came from a distance, and I concentrated on the sound. He stood before me, fully clothed. His hands clasped my upper arms, keeping me steady.

"She's had a rough day," Sherilyn told him, removing the champagne glass from my hand before I dropped it. "She has a bad headache."

"Yeah, I, uh—" I stammered. My brain was a jumbled mess. "Adair, um, this is Sherilyn Silvers."

The pair exchanged a worried glance.

"Let's go somewhere quiet." Adair put an arm around my waist, and I forced myself not to recoil when his hand brushed my bruised side.

He and Sherilyn spoke, but their words were incomprehensible to my disordered mind. He led me down a long hall with frescoed alcoves. Some contained flower arrangements lit from above, while others displayed graceful statues. I passed in a dreamlike state, removed from reality. People were indistinct, hazy.

A man with dark hair and eyes came into focus. He wore a pink polo shirt and dark trousers. He and a group of people were in a small study, talking. A familiar younger man beside him raised a glass toward Adair.

Who were they? I knew them. From where?

Even in my confused state, a sense of unease gripped me.

Adair unlocked and opened one of a set of heavy double doors. Once inside, he closed and relocked it. The noise from the music and crowd shut off.

"Just a little farther." Adair directed me toward a well-furnished sitting area. It held a couch and two armchairs. An open book and some newspapers lay on a low wooden table beside a vase of fresh flowers. Beyond was a sumptuous four-poster bed.

"Couch or bed?"

Being away from the crush of people and pounding music eased my thoughts.

"Couch is fine."

He helped me to it, and I sat.

"Water?"

"Yes, thanks."

Adair retrieved a bottle from a small, glass-front fridge, twisted off the top, and poured some into a glass from a serving set located nearby.

"Here." He sat beside me.

I took a long drink of the cold water, grateful my mind could process again.

"Where's Sherilyn?"

"She said she'd come to find you later. Of course, I'm boiling this down to the essence because she said a lot more."

"She does tend to ramble."

"How are you? You seemed ready to drop in there."

"I'm better now. I should've stayed home, but Sherilyn was so excited to come, plus she's an interior designer and might get some new business."

"I'll keep her in mind," Adair promised. "What's wrong?"

Everything. Some thug knocked me senseless and drugged me, plus I'm having inappropriate fantasies about you.

"I think I just overexerted myself lately. How are you?" I pointed at the Band-aid peeking out of his hairline.

"This?" He lifted his hair then let it fall. "I recovered fairly quickly. My mum assures me I'm hard-headed."

"I'm glad you're better."

"Yes, well, yesterday you kept it together, even after that gunfight. I felt like a bloody idiot compared to you. You were brilliant, if fool-hardy. Wait, a *lot* foolhardy. I must confess; I'm glad to see you're finally feeling the effects."

"Shock and denial can delay responses."

"I don't want to sound like a misogynist, but I never thought a woman would take on a gunman like you did. You went right after him. No hesitation."

"Your mom says you're hard-headed, and mine says I'm impulsive."

"And you own a gun."

"Yes."

"Why?"

"My parents worried about me out here. I grew up shooting, a common activity in the Midwest."

He took my hand. "Davia, I hope you'll be more careful from now on. You could've ended up in a body bag, not the other guy. I mean, you're brave and all, but your life isn't something you should risk."

I couldn't meet his eyes and concentrated on our clasped hands.

His thumb caressed my palm, and he brought his other hand to my cheek, lifting my face.

"Please promise me you won't do something like that ever again."

Unable to speak, I nodded. Adair cuddled me into his chest. If only we could stay this way. I could pretend this was another night in with my guy, and that my promise to never do anything to put me in harm's way could be the truth. I closed my eyes, listening to his heartbeat, knowing every moment wasn't real.

After much longer than necessary, I straightened. "You should go back to your guests."

"Are you any better now?" He kept an arm about my shoulders.

"Yes. You're the host, and I'm keeping you to myself."

Adair removed his arm, and I pushed regret to the side.

"I doubt they'll even realize I'm gone. My people got carried away. I'll have to redefine 'intimate gathering' for them." He gave a rueful laugh.

"How many people are here? A hundred?"

"More. I think closer to three or four hundred. The outdoor space is immense, and people scatter."

"Really?"

"Unfortunately, but you can stay here and rest. I'll come back and check on you." He got up.

I rose. "I'll be all right."

Would I? I had to be.

"Let me introduce you to a few people from Rancho Suprema. They aren't all like Beatrice Gibbs."

I followed him back into the hall, and he secured the door. This time the noise didn't strike me down. Getting through the crowds was easy because people parted when they saw Adair coming. He smiled greetings at everyone but maintained his forward motion.

We stepped outside onto a covered patio with a view of the grounds. White canvas tents held tables containing food in covered chafing dishes served by staff in white coats. Other servers circulated with hors d'oeuvres on silver trays.

"Are you hungry?" Adair asked.

"A little." My stomach remained unsettled.

A man nearing forty, clad in a suit, walked towards us. He wore his dark brown hair short. Gray eyes keen with intellect shone from his pleasant face, and he bore himself like former military, capable, and confident.

"Mr. Monroe." He had a British accent. "Is there anything you require?"

"No, Jason, except some food. This is Davia Glenn. Davia, this is Jason McCall."

I wondered if Jason was Adair's Alfred Pennyworth and if there was an underground bat cave somewhere on the property.

"Charmed to meet you." He then addressed Adair. "Would you like me to send some plates to your private patio? The food is excellent; local, organic, and sustainably sourced."

Adair looked askance at me.

"I don't think I can eat much," I said.

"Thank you, Jason. We'll get something small and mingle."

"Excellent, sir. Ms. Glenn." He tilted his head and left.

"I see what you're thinking, and I'm not Batman," Adair said.

"I did consider the possibility."

"Jason is my closest friend. He's been with me since the beginning."

A server stopped to let us select from his tray. I chose what appeared to be crab mixed with spices on a piece of endive. The bite tasted terrific; the wasabi, mayonnaise, and cilantro adding to the flavor.

"Mm, that tasted wonderful." I hoped the food would stay down.

"It was." Adair wiped off his fingers. "Why don't we go through the buffet and take a walk around?"

We tossed the napkins in a nearby bin but only got a few feet when three men stopped us. They teased Adair about his casual clothes, one taking a handful of his hoodie. They wore button-down shirts and dress pants.

"I need to find Sherilyn," I told Adair and slipped away. Small talk was impossible right now. I heard footsteps behind me.

"Davia!" It was Adair. "I don't have to—"

"I'm fine. Visit with your friends. I'll find you before I leave."

"You sure?"

"Yes. Go."

He returned, and the men clapped him on the back to raucous laughter.

I went past the tents containing the food and toward another covered pavilion. Inside was a dance floor and DJ. Music blasted, bodies writhed in time to the beat, and strobe lights flashed. My head began to pound again.

In the distance, twinkling lights decorated trees that edged formal gardens. I went toward them, needing silence, solitude, and a place to sit. An inviting bench set back from the path suited my needs, and I nestled into the shadows.

Conversations drifted from people walking past:

Two men discussed golf: *I shot an eighty on that course.*

You're so funny. You've never broken ninety.

A woman to her husband: *Will we go to Yachts Miami this year?*

The husband, indignant: *Our yacht is only two years old. I won't buy a new one every year, no matter what you say.*

Two women: *Did you hear the Remingtons purchased a 4500 square foot house?*

How gauche. Anything under 12,000 square feet is a joke.

These snippets emphasized how much Aunt Lilah's will changed my life. I hadn't lived in Rancho Suprema a month yet, and the only familiar notes were the hitmen pursuing me.

On cue, a man appeared with a gun in his hand.

24

———

I rocketed to my feet and placed my hand atop the weapon. In one practiced move, I wrenched it from his grip. Flipping the muzzle back around, I pointed it at the man.

It was Jason McCall, Adair's most trusted associate.

"What do you want?" I demanded. "Does Adair know about this?"

Jason put up his hands.

"Yes, Ms. Glenn. He does."

Adair was in on this, too? Was the shooting outside the market staged for my benefit? To what purpose?

"Which is why he sent me to check on you and bring you a bottle of water," Jason continued, his voice level.

A regular bottle of water was in my hand.

Not again. Would this drug ever wear off? What could I say?

"I'm sorry," I said. "I thought—"

"I held a gun on you." It was a statement, not a question.

I didn't answer.

"Mr. Monroe told me about someone shooting at him and how you took his car to chase the man down. It didn't make sense unless you're—"

"Overly enthusiastic? Adventure-seeking? Incredibly foolish?"

Jason snorted. "A highly-trained operative."

"I like my explanations better."

Jason considered this.

"I guess that's how we'll keep things," he said at last. "I'm concerned because Mr. Monroe has grown quite fond of you, and he can't handle these types of scenarios."

He was right, of course. He echoed my previous thoughts about why any attachment to Adair would never work.

"I did mention he should hire bodyguards," I said.

"He's nixed the subject on a number of occasions. I do what I can, but I'm not always around him."

"Try again. Maybe he'll listen this time since I discussed a need for bodyguards with him yesterday."

"And what are your feelings for Mr. Monroe?"

How did I feel? I was attracted to him, but my heart remained with the ever-absent Warden.

"I don't know."

"Well, I'll keep everything you said in mind," Jason told me. He would also store any other observations. Highly-trained people recognized others, and Jason McCall was at that level.

"Thanks for the water."

"You're welcome." Jason gave me a last calculating appraisal and left.

The drug clawed at me, refusing to loosen its grip. Should I find Sherilyn and leave or catch an Uber if she wanted to stay? I might bash some innocent person in the throes of my delusions.

Exhaling, I went back down the path.

Where would I find Sherilyn in this mass of hundreds on a property this size?

Not wanting to fight the crowds, I took a deserted walkway that meandered past the back of the mansion. I wondered if the closed French doors led to Adair's master suite, wishing to go in and be alone for a while. There was patio furniture outside, but I resisted the urge to continue my isolation. Marshaling my reserves, I trudged toward the back entrance, deciding to go inside and begin my search.

A man smoking a cigarette was near the steps.

He blew out a mouthful of smoke. "Miss Glenn?"

My face must've conveyed I didn't recognize him.

"I'm Nabil Nasser. I met you at Chateau Rouge a few weeks ago."

"Oh, right."

Nabil took another drag off his cigarette. "Smoking's an unpleasant habit, I know. Not at all popular here in Southern California, where most people stay healthy and fit, like you."

Long lashes framed his dark brown eyes. His high cheekbones and chiseled jawline made him attractive, but his thin lips gave the impression he could be as cruel as he was charming.

"Where are you from?" I wondered how he would answer and whether I would believe him.

"Dubai. I came here on business to convince Mr. Monroe he should invest in our project, but I also have time for some fun."

He emphasized the word fun like an invitation.

"I'm glad," I said. "If you'll excuse me, I need to find a friend."

Nabil responded by taking a long, slow drag off his cigarette, desire plain on his face. Unsettled, I hurried toward the steps. There were more people inside than when I first arrived. The din of conversation was deafening, punctuated by shrill laughter. Dazzling women with long, bare legs and an assortment of men mingled in the room. Servers holding trays threaded through the cramped space, trying their best not to drop anything.

Getting through the vast living room became an ordeal.

Excuse me.

Pardon me.

Would you let me pass?

A man holding a glass of red wine lost his balance, spilling liquid all over my pants.

"Watch it!" I exclaimed.

The red stain soaked in like a bloody wound.

Heading down a long hall in the opposite direction from Adair's master quarters, I searched for a bathroom.

A door swung open, almost hitting me. A man exited, still zipping up his trousers.

Success.

Entering, I found a hand towel and pressed it against my drenched clothes.

It took me a second to realize someone had come in behind me and shut the door.

"HELLO AGAIN," said a familiar voice.

Rashid. Was he real or another figment?

"I can't recall your name," I lied, glancing at the towel now stained from the wine.

Great weapon.

"I'm Rashid Khadem. We met at Chateau Rouge. Don't you remember?"

"Oh, yes." I put a hand on the counter to steady myself as a wave of wooziness hit.

"Too much to drink?" he guessed.

I pulled my shoulders straight. "I think I'm coming down with something. What do you want?"

He raised his hands in a placating gesture. "I saw you being helped by our host earlier and wanted to make sure you're okay."

His features shifted, my vision adjusting itself, like focusing a pair of binoculars. For a split-second, he became another person, someone who gave me the heebie-jeebies. *Who?* I strained to recall but couldn't put a name to whomever it was.

"Well, Rashid, thank you for checking on me." The jolt from my unease provided a much-needed boost.

He stayed between me and the exit, unmoving.

"If you have to fight in a bathroom, it's tricky," said Dean, one of Kyle's Delta Force friends. "There are hard edges you can utilize as weapons. Slam your opponent's head on the sink, counter, or bathtub. Look around for improvised weapons. You can wet a hand towel, add a bar of soap and fold

it around your hand to hit with more force. If there's a shower wand and hose, wrap it around their neck or hit them with the end. If you use the toilet lid, remember the space is often small, and you might not be able to swing it with much force."

A knock at the door. "Would you hurry up? I need to pee," a woman pleaded.

"You good?" Rashid's hand was on the doorknob.

"Yes. Thank you." I placed the used towel on the counter.

When Rashid opened the door, the woman raced in, shooting us an inquiring glance as we exited.

"Nice to see you, Ms. Glenn."

The crowd swallowed him up.

That was strange.

Feeling claustrophobic, I went back outside. Inhaling the night air, appreciating its crispness, I wondered anew where to find Sherilyn.

"Davia!" Adair ran up the steps. "There you are! I got free from those guys at last and wanted to find you."

"Have you seen Sherilyn?"

"No, sorry. Is there anything you need?"

"I'm still not up to par and was considering going home. Sherilyn drove us, and I wanted to see if she was ready to go or if I should schedule a ride."

"We can make a loop, and if we don't find her, I'll take you home."

"Adair, you don't have to. This is your party, and—"

"Stop. As I said, the guests will swing along fine without me."

We began our journey. People enjoyed the food, dancing, or were engrossed in conversation, so no one disturbed us. As we walked, I began to feel better. My head cleared, and my thoughts became more centered.

Adair said, "Did Jason find you? You still didn't seem like you felt good, and I wanted him to check."

"He did, thank you. Was he in the military?"

"Sort of," Adair said.

Sort of? MI6? A real-life James Bond?

Jason materialized beside us.

"Jason, we were just talking about you," Adair said.

A more thorough assessment of Jason confirmed he had the commonplace, almost forgettable appearance necessary to be a spy. James Bond would never cut the job in reality since his looks were too memorable. Was I on the right track?

"I was about to ask Adair again about hiring some bodyguards," I inserted to change the topic.

"That's a wonderful idea," Jason echoed.

"Now you two are ganging up on me," Adair protested. "You're overreacting!"

He took in our serious countenances.

"I'm warning you I might develop a self-important attitude having an entourage following me around," Adair said.

"I'll make some calls," Jason said, visibly relieved at Adair's decision.

"I'm trying to find a friend," I said to Jason and described Sherilyn. "Have you seen her?"

If Jason was MI6, he knew what everyone looked like and what they were doing.

"Yes. She dragged some man out on the dance floor and appeared to be having a good time."

"How long ago?"

"In the last hour. Shall I go fetch her?"

"No. If you wouldn't mind telling her I'm leaving, I'd appreciate it." I was better, but the thought of conversing with Sherilyn in a loud music setting didn't appeal.

"No problem," Jason said.

"Wonderful!" Adair said. "Jason, I'm going to drive Davia home."

"Allow me, sir. You're the host of this party, and you should stay."

"Yes," I agreed. Having him remain behind was better for his safety. Who knew what awaited me back at the property.

"Really?" Adair held a kicked-dog look.

"Yes. I'll see you at the gala," I assured him.

"Okay, I guess. Thanks for coming tonight." He pulled me into a protective embrace and planted a kiss on top of my head. "Promise me you'll rest."

"Promise."

"I worry about you." He stepped back.

"I'll be fine. When you tell Sherilyn I left, would you ask her to dance? You'll make her night."

"I will. Be safe." Adair headed in the direction of the dance pavilion.

"Thank you for doing this," I told Jason.

He led me to an Audi sedan parked at the side of the house in an unobtrusive space. We got in and headed down the drive. People filtered in and out of an open garage displaying some of Adair's supercars. We went past valets running to collect vehicles from the hundreds parked in a pasture. Jason drove in silence, intent on his task. We got to the road, and he began to turn.

"Don't you want my address? Or at least let me direct you?" I asked.

"I already know where your home is."

I stifled a sharp breath, not wanting to reveal my surprise at his announcement. "How?"

"Ms. Glenn, do you think Mr. Monroe's life isn't a priority to me?"

"Um, no?"

Would he try to eliminate me because I was a possible threat to Adair? Why didn't he attack me earlier? Because of where we were and too many witnesses?

"After you defeated that assassin, who was clearly after you, I found out what I could about you."

"So, you learned I was a personal assistant to a CEO who traveled a lot?"

"Creative cover story."

I did a quick inventory of the dimly lit car's interior for a possible weapon. I didn't want to seize the steering wheel and take us off-road because I'd already destroyed one of Adair's cars this week.

Two would be rude.

He whipped the car around a corner, driving fast. Rancho Suprema's roads were challenging to navigate at night due to the lack of street lamps, but Jason handled them like he'd memorized every bend of every route.

Tires squealed.

The centrifugal force threw me against the door.

"What about you?" I asked, my hand gripping the seat to avoid tipping as I considered my options.

"What about me?"

He answered a question with a question—the tried and true dodge.

"MI6?"

His face remained impassive as an answer, and we pulled into my lower entryway.

"Code?" he asked.

I told him. He punched the numbers in, the gate swung open, and he zipped up the drive.

Would he try to kill me on my property?

We crested the top of the hill.

Two men stood before us, guns in their hands.

25

A nondescript car blocked my garage door.

It was Savant and Ned.

Were they real? I needed to believe they were.

"They're friends of mine," I said as Jason reached for what was sure to be a firearm concealed in his clothes.

He braked, and I was out before the car stopped moving, hope and happiness flooding through me.

"What are you guys doing here?"

"Who's that?" Savant kept his eyes on the car.

"He's fine," I told him, and he slid the gun into a pocket. Ned kept his out, still concentrating on the driver.

Jason turned the car around, put up a hand, and blasted back down the drive.

Ned tucked his gun away. "Out on a date, Bombshell?" His tone was playful. "If so, he dumped you to fend off two armed men."

"He's former MI6, and he figured out my background."

Ned gave a disbelieving shake of his head. "Didn't expect to find someone like him in this town. And what's with your hair? Trying to make it easier for someone to kill you?"

"No, I—hey! You've worn your man bun forever. Don't start. And you didn't answer. Why are you here?"

"Streeter sent us out to quiz that German asshole. We jumped a military transport, five hours to here, then three more questioning that bozo. We're not making much progress on finding the mole, and we didn't get anywhere with him," Ned said. "Thought we should stop by for a quick 411. Your handler gave us your address."

"Where's everyone else?" I tried for a casual tone.

"Warden, K, and H are pursuing separate lines of inquiry. We've been relentless since the whole leak got exposed," Savant said. "Anyway, your hired man let us in. We needed to be pretty persuasive to convince him to open the gate."

"He got caught in the Badger crossfire, too. Come inside, and I'll fill you in."

The men helped themselves to what they could scrounge from my fridge and pantry while I told them about the inheritance and the assassination attempts. We settled at the kitchen table.

"If you have a bunch of money, you could spare some for food." Ned twisted off the cap to a bottle of warm beer and lifted his chin at the assortment of protein bars and one bag of popcorn.

"No time to shop." I didn't want to divert the topic to my eventful problems at the Suprema Market.

Two shrugs.

Wrappers were ripped open.

Kyle's voice was in my head: Eat when you can, sleep when you can, and never stop figuring out how to stay alive.

They munched while I caught them up.

"Still experiencing the effects of the drug cocktail?" Savant asked.

"I'm better now." My answer defaulted to the *everything's coming up roses* front of being an operative. In truth, I wanted to barf, sleep for six weeks, and hope I might be back to normal after that.

"How long has the drug been in your system?" Savant checked his watch. "Twelve hours so far?"

I nodded. "Not a fun ride, plus I took a solid kick to the head and some blows to my kidneys, or at least that's what the bruises tells me."

"You've taken down Warden, but some hired gun almost got you?" Savant's tone was censorious.

"I—" I stopped. *It didn't matter if I wasn't one-hundred percent. No excuses.*

"I think you did well for being out here injured and naked," Ned said, using slang for no backup. "Taking out two hitters in short order by yourself is impressive."

"Do I get a gold star?" I didn't want to relay the story of being saved by Adair and Sherilyn. I would never hear the end of it.

Ned tossed me a protein bar. "There's your reward. Anything else we should know about?"

"I met a man named Rashid Khadem through a businessman here, Adair Monroe. Rashid pitched Adair on a luxury development in Dubai. Something is—well—*off* about him. His buddy's named Nabil Nasser. He has a businessman/playboy vibe, but nothing else."

"We'll check their bona fides, do a deep dive," Savant said.

Something niggled around in the back of my brain. I couldn't bring it to the surface, so I let it go.

"Anything you can share about developments?" I asked. Would they give me information?

"We would if there were any. Some second-rate mercenaries came at us in our off-time, but we swatted them like the pests they were, as you have." Ned tipped his chair back and stretched.

"We should roll." Savant stifled a yawn.

"If you need to sleep, there are plenty of guest rooms."

"Can't. Need to go collect up little Hitler there and have a further get-acquainted session on our flight back," Ned said, setting his empty beer bottle down.

I handed Ned a paper towel to blot some of the droplets out of his beard. When he finished, I followed them out.

A bright full moon lighted the courtyard.

"It was great to see you guys." I missed the easy banter and companionship, the team's courage and character making our bond unbreakable.

They paused.

"We didn't know you were leaving the team, so we never got to say goodbye," Ned told me. "At first, I thought you quit because of your injury, but that didn't make sense. You're meaner than a wildcat in a bag."

"Hanging out with Hodge too much lately?" I teased.

"Anyhow, I guess you're not coming back? Hell, I wouldn't if I owned a spread like this." Ned gestured to the surroundings.

"The inheritance isn't all that made me leave, and—"

"We know about you and Warden," Savant interrupted.

"You do?"

"Girl, you haven't been stuck around that mopey bastard like we have. Even Savant here figured it out in the first, what, hour?" Ned said, and Savant gave a quick nod of agreement. "He's been intolerable. Even K had words with him about his attitude."

Savant said, "We've all talked to the colonel, separately and as a group. We told him we don't care if you two stay on the team together, but he's still mulling the situation over. He told us he has a year to decide."

They stood with Warden and me? "Really?"

"Of course," Ned said, and Savant nodded.

Relief flooded through me.

"In the meantime, this Badger debacle needs sorting," Savant said, rubbing at his tired eyes.

"Warden reached out to me once, said he thought Badger sent people out here, but the connection was garbled," I told them. "Any ideas what intelligence he had?"

"As I said, we've come up mostly goose eggs, except fifteenth-hand information, which Warden must have passed on to you. Even Kilburn hasn't scored much," Ned said.

"I guess we'll just keep knocking 'em down as they pop up." It seemed like a never-ending game of whack-an-assassin.

Ned threw an arm around me and drew me in, ruffling my hair.

"Glad to see you," he said.

"You too." Tears threatened, and I fought to hold them back.

Savant raised a hand. "Later, Davia."

Emotion engulfed me as they drove off. I was grateful for the time with my teammates but lonely and distressed without them. Back in the house, I checked all the windows and doors and set the security. My body ached like a grizzly bear's chew toy. Another wave of queasiness threatened. I rushed to the closest toilet and threw up, heaving until my insides were empty. Releasing my hold on the porcelain, I crumpled to the floor, the tile against my cheek.

IN THE EARLY HOURS, I dragged myself to my room, stripped, and crawled into bed. My dreams were tumultuous. I was at the Suprema Market, and Rashid appeared at the end of an aisle. He morphed into a giant, pink bullfrog and hopped toward me, uttering a menacing *ribbit- ribbit.*

I woke with a start.

Were the drug's after-effects giving me nightmares?

Morning arrived like an unwelcome guest. Semi-awake, I began to consider what to do. The visit from Savant and Ned shone a spotlight on the emptiness inside me. What was my role in this community? The most important decision people made here was whether to choose Botox or Dysport.

My cell phone rang.

"Davia, I need your help." It was Lydia McGregor. "Francis called to say some people she counted on took an unexpected vacation. I volunteered to do half of the gift baskets, but the task will take too long alone."

"I've never done anything like that." I hoped Lydia would call someone else.

"I'll show you. Can you be at my house around 1 p.m.?"

"What's your address?" I put the info in my contacts, resentful of the call despite my admiration for Lydia.

Now, I'm stuck with more gala nonsense.

My doorbell rang.

Outside, Sherilyn greeted me. "Hi! I'm here to meet the movers coming to cart off the tree." She pointed to where the eyesore still blighted my porch.

Despite staying out partying, Sherilyn brimmed with energy, pink lipstick setting off her complexion. She wore jeans, a t-shirt, and tennies, making her resemble a high-schooler.

"Did you have fun last night?" I propped myself against the doorframe.

"That event was unreal! And when Adair came to tell me you were getting a lift home, he asked me to dance! *Me!* Every other woman there, and even some of the men, were jealous-mealous. He let me snap a photo of us, see?"

She shoved her phone at me, displaying a photo of herself posed with a pout next to a bemused Adair.

"This photo will bring me a lot of business. Everyone will want to work with me because of him. I mean, he's not interested in me because, like, all he did was talk about you, at least when I could hear him over the music. And he is such a first-rate dancer. I couldn't stop staring at him! He made this move where he crossed his arms over his chest like he held someone tight and brought his hips forward and back. I wanted to *faint* because he looked so seductive! Men who dance well are usually *incredible* in bed!"

I don't let my thoughts go down the road of what Adair might be like between the sheets. "I'm glad you had fun."

"How about you? Did you come home and sleep? I mean, you look dreadful, Davia. Are you prone to migraines or something?"

"No. I think this whole week wore me out."

Sherilyn studied me. "Have you had breakfast?"

"No. My pantry's nearly bare."

She took my elbow and led me to the kitchen, sitting me in a bar chair at the island.

Sherilyn opened my refrigerator.

"You weren't kidding! How do you even exist? I swear the expensive Swiss Diamond cookware I got you is gathering dust!" She shut the fridge, did a cursory look at the pantry, then began to dig around in her tote bag, muttering to herself. "I always keep something with me in case of emergencies. I hope I still have them in here."

"Sherilyn, it's fine."

She turned doe eyes to me. "It's not, Davia. We're friends, and friends watch out for each other."

While she continued to search through her bag, I looked on in wonderment. Were we friends? When we first met, I could never have foreseen she held so many facets. Preconceived notions had colored my expectations of the people who lived and worked in Rancho Suprema.

"Here we go!" She held up two packets of instant oatmeal, put water in a copper tea kettle, and ignited a burner.

"Why do you keep those in your purse?"

"You never know where you'll end up, and you might need food. I was a Girl Scout, and their motto is *Be Prepared*." She opened a cabinet and brought out a bowl.

Did being prepared require oatmeal, not weapons? The contrast in our upbringing brought me up short. What had I missed out on by choosing to be trained in the skills I developed rather than the more traditional route of girls' clubs, music, and ballet dancing? What if I had never delivered that cake to Kyle?

I was eleven. Mom tasked me to welcome Kyle Kavanagh to the neighborhood with a homemade cake. I trekked through the summer heat to his small, white farmhouse.

There was no answer at his front door.

Continuing the search, I carried the gift around the side of the house. My pink tennis shoe clad feet scuffed through dried patches of grass, and flies circled me. I couldn't swat them and carry the cake.

The whole errand was a pain.

Rounding a corner into the backyard, I found him. Mr. Kavanagh sat in a wheelchair with a shotgun pointed at his chin.

I froze.

My feet twitched, my hands prepared to drop the homemade cake on the lawn, and I almost bolted back home, screaming my lungs out, when the voice of my mother stopped me.

Remember your manners!

Despite the situation, I didn't want to explain not completing the delivery to Mom. Searching inside myself for the slightest ounce of courage, I stretched my arms out half an inch.

"Mr. Kavanagh, would you like some c-cake?" I squeaked.

His piercing blue scary eyes, split between seeing me and a final destination, didn't flicker. Neither I nor my cake could change whether he stayed or went.

My last bit of courage left me, running for its life. I almost gave in and followed when Mr. Kavanagh's finger moved in the best direction—away from the trigger.

An eternity passed before he settled the shotgun across his knees.

We regarded each other, me a blonde girl in dusty coverall shorts ready to puke from fright, he a red-headed Irishman stepping back from the edge of an afterlife.

He finally said, "What kind of cake is it?"

"L-lemon."

He didn't say anything more.

Searching for something else to talk about, I hit on the obvious. "So, what kind of gun is that?"

This question, and our subsequent friendship, changed my life forever.

Now, Sherilyn ripped open the oatmeal packets, dumped their contents into a dish, and brought me out of my memories.

"You should at least have your meals delivered," she lectured, adding boiling water to the oatmeal. "A place in town offers grass-fed lamb and beef, free-range chicken, and wild salmon. No hormones, antibiotics, canola oil, or gluten! I mean, what is gluten? And why is gluten such a problem?"

"Got me."

Sherilyn set the oatmeal before me with a mug of steaming hot tea.

"Thanks." I dug in. The warm food made me sigh with contentment. "You were right. I need to eat more regularly."

"See? I told you." Sherilyn poured herself a cup of tea and joined me. "So, tell me about you and Adair. How did you meet? Are you a couple? You need to spill!" She took a sip of her drink, peering at me over the rim.

I swallowed the bit of oatmeal in my mouth, not sure how to answer. "We've run into each other a few times and went to lunch once. We don't know each other that well."

"You don't?" She put her cup down, disbelieving.

"No."

"Is there someone else?"

What should I say? After considering my options, I went with the truth.

"Yes."

"There is? Who? He must be something if—"

"He is," I said before she could continue.

"What's his name? What does he look like? Where did you meet him?" Sherilyn rapid-fired her questions.

"His name is James Warden. He's six-three, has dark brown hair and green eyes. We met at, um, work three years ago. We became involved right before I moved here."

"Do you have a photo?"

I scrolled up a surreptitious picture I took of Warden weight-lifting shirtless.

Sherilyn gaped. "Oh my god! He's quite the hunk of beefcake. Where does he live?"

"Virginia."

A small crease appeared between Sherilyn's eyebrows

"That far away? All I'd want between a man who looks like that and me is some oil I rubbed all over his body! Warden could be a movie star, but a long-distance romance is difficult. I mean, considering what you have right here—"

"As I said, Adair and I have met a few times, which is different than the bond I have with Warden."

"By bond, I hope you mean mind-blowing sex. The whole of the kama sutra and tantric positions or anything else you can—"

"I haven't slept with him."

"*What*? Are you acting unavailable because it makes you more enticing? Warden isn't a man I would want to hold out on too long. And by too long, I mean more than a few seconds."

"Uh, it's—"

"Don't you dare say complicated! I swear, Davia. Whatever's happening with this Warden guy, I think Adair's really interested in you, and he *lives here.* He kept going on about how brave you are."

"He did?" I couldn't stop myself.

"Yes! And you're different from most women here or who might run in his circles. First, you're not on social media. I mean, at all. Like, I looked you up to friend you and couldn't find you anywhere. Snapchat, Twitter, Instagram, Tiktok, Clubhouse. I even tried Facebook. Nothing! People constantly post about everything, photos of themselves in all kinds of poses, and even photos of what they're eating or where they are. You're a ghost!"

"Yes, well—"

"And when you wear designer clothes, it's like you're headed to the dentist to get a cavity filled. Are you a tomboy? Of course, that's fine. You rock this understated look, but with those laser-blue eyes of yours, you look ready to take on the world! You're a lady boss, mega-power in one package. No wonder Adair can't stop talking about you."

"I—"

Sherilyn kept going. "Since we're friends, I'll tell you a secret. Your house was my first job as an interior designer."

"It was?"

"Yes! Which is why I picked out that stupid tree. I got too enthusiastic about finding unique objects and didn't consider the overall perspective. I appreciate how much you let me do, and with little supervision."

"Living here has been a new experience for me as well. I might not have conveyed my gratitude enough, but I appreciate everything you've done."

"You do? I'm so glad! Since we're sharing, and I told you my secret, you need to share something more about you and Warden and why you haven't been all over him yet." She gave me an expectant look.

Fortunately, the gate buzzer rang. The company hired to haul off the wretched tree had arrived.

"Thanks for breakfast." I indicated my empty bowl.

"You're welcome. We'll talk more later!" Sherilyn picked up her bag and hustled out to order the poor movers around.

Standing, I took my mug and bowl to the sink and rinsed them out. Was this what it was like to have a close girlfriend? Still uncomfortable with sharing anything about my life, I didn't know how to feel. And Warden covered in oil? Damn.

I checked the time. It was only ten a.m.

My phone dinged with a text.

Hey, Beautiful! I hope you got some rest.

I typed: *Who's this?*

Adair. Guess I forgot to unblock my # before. (Embarrassed emoji.)

I'm fine, I responded.

Tomorrow's the gala. Save me a dance? (Heart emoji.)

Heart emoji? I could ask Sherilyn about its significance but knew her shriek would break the sound barrier and decided against it.

A dance? One dance.

Yes.

Yes! See you soon—three blowing-a-kiss emojis.

Most women would kill for the number I added to my contacts. I turned off the phone, not wishing to dwell on the subject.

Worn out, I went back to my room and fell asleep.

THE DRIVE to Mrs. McGregor's hilltop house was narrow, with overgrown bushes running leafy fingers along the side of my car. Towering trees surrounded the residence, dropping dead leaves on the roof. Three vegetable garden beds blossomed with summer corn, lettuce, tomatoes, squash, and zucchini.

Lydia met me at the front door. "I heard your car. I'm so glad you're here!" She shoved some ribbon into a front apron pocket. "Do come in."

The house carried a musty odor, with knick-knacks displayed on every available surface. Old photos of a youthful Lydia and a good-looking man, likely Mr. McGregor, were framed on the walls.

"Where are we working?" I tried not to knock anything over.

"Let's go into the kitchen. I laid everything out on the counters and dining table."

We crossed the room, went down a dark corridor, and emerged into a brightly lit, cheery kitchen. Fresh vegetables lay on the white-tiled counter, near a small bowl containing homemade tea bags.

"What are these? Beatrice and Willie had some in their homes."

"I made my Ladies' League friends a batch of special-blend tea in appreciation for all their work."

"Beatrice put them in a bowl in her entry."

Mrs. McGregor sniffed. "She doesn't possess a lot of sense."

Her spacious table held ribbons, clear and colored cellophane rolls, paper grass, and a couple of baskets.

"I don't have any experience with projects like this."

"Here, I'll teach you." Lydia selected a pale-blue basket, filling the bottom with dark blue paper grass. She placed an engraved card describing dinner at a Caribbean restaurant in the center, and surrounded it with ceramic tropical fish, and a Caribbean Rum bottle. Wrapping light blue cellophane around the outside, she tied the top with a cascading ribbon.

The whole enterprise took her about two minutes.

"I told you this is easy!" she declared.

For you.

Lydia began work on another. I selected a trip for two to Paris. Choosing a dark green basket, I added light green confetti paper to the bottom and tried to center the card, but it kept falling over. I propped it against a miniature Eiffel Tower, but it slid down again. Giving up, I put a bottle of Dom Perignon and two glasses at the back. The bottle fell over with a loud clang.

Lydia looked up. "Do you need some help?"

"I'm failing at this, sorry."

She came over and showed me how to tuck things into the confetti paper so they stayed secure, and I thanked her for the help.

Selecting light green cellophane, I cut off the correct amount and wrapped it around the basket. I now held a bunch of wadded paper at the top with nothing to secure it. I should've entered the battle with better preparation.

"This isn't a skill set you have, is it?" Lydia noted.

"No." This admission was embarrassing for reasons I couldn't fathom. Was this one of the life-expanding experiences Aunt Lilah wanted for me?

I pictured a business card:

Davia Glenn, Gunfights and Gift Baskets.

"What did you do before you moved here?" Lydia asked.

"Oh, my job required a lot of travel." I let go of the cellophane and prepared tape and ribbon.

"Where did you go?"

Places I don't want to talk about with you.

"You mentioned you've been to South America?" I asked.

"Yes, I toured some rain forests in Colombia."

"Why did you vacation there?" Colombia was safer than during Pablo Escobar's era running the Medellin cartel, but tourists might get caught in a narco-terrorist crisis. My last mission there involved an intense operation. I doubted Mrs. McGregor slipped across the border like me, illegally.

"I needed a break from the politics at the Ladies' League."

"So, you went to a potentially dangerous place instead?"

Which in this insane Rancho world actually made sense.

"I joined a group of scientists doing some studies of an amphibian located in the rain forest. I have a degree in biology."

"Oh." Of course, her life extended beyond the Ladies' League.

We lapsed into silence, concentrating on the task at hand. Halfway through, we took a break.

"I made some miniature poppy-seed muffins and iced tea. We can sit at the picnic table in my backyard," Lydia said.

"Sounds wonderful." I needed to stretch and stop thinking about coordinating colors, making everything balance, and other artistic skills I didn't possess.

An old pepper tree grew next to a picnic table where we placed plates and glasses.

"Have you lived here for a long time?" I asked, taking a sip of the refreshing tea. Some yellow butterflies flitted around the flower bed.

"Frank and I moved here after we got married, so about fifty-five years. I was twenty, and Frank was much older. He finished a career in the Navy and founded a successful engineering firm."

"Do you have kids?"

"No. Do you have anyone special?"

It was an officially mystifying question. My bond to Warden stayed firm, without a committed relationship, with the recent attentions of Adair Monroe thrown in.

"No. Tell me about your garden."

Lydia gave me a discerning look. "You'll meet someone soon."

An immediate subject change was necessary.

"May I ask you something?"

"Yes?"

"I learned someone here in town bought a painting donated for our auction from a private dealer. Who do you think is stealing items donated for the gala?"

"This again? As we discussed, I have no idea."

"How about Willie Weston?"

She pondered. "Willie had some odd ideas, but I don't think he stole anything."

"How about Beatrice Gibbs?"

"She spends lots of time running the organization and also tends to several greenhouses on her property. I don't like to say she's a thief."

"Maybe Amelia Meadows?"

Lydia laughed. "The only thing Amelia's guilty of is her bad taste in men. She's not an easy person to like, but I feel sorry for her."

"Why?"

"She truly loved Willie, and took the breakup pretty hard. When he started seeing that young realtor, well!"

The afternoon sun waned, and the air grew chilly.

"We need to finish our project." Lydia collected her plate and the now-empty pitcher while I took up the rest of the dishes and carried them back to the kitchen.

Several hours later, we finished. I put the final basket in the storage room with relief. Lydia stood beside me, and we admired our handiwork, an assortment of temptations for those with expendable income.

"Thanks for the help." Lydia showed me out and promised to meet up at the gala the next day.

UNABLE TO FACE GOING HOME to my empty pantry, I picked up my mail and made for the closest Mexican restaurant. I sorted through the post and ate a steaming plate of pollo asada with refried beans, rice, and flour tortillas.

A front-page *Suprema Gazette* newspaper article touted the Ladies' League Gala. The story expanded to page three, where a photo of Beatrice Gibbs was featured. She posed in front of a greenhouse holding a potted plant of some kind.

I scanned the article: *Beatrice Gibbs, President of the Ladies' League, is an active horticulturist. When she's not occupied with the League's many demands, Mrs. Gibbs attends to her rare and exotic plants.*

"I developed a love for gardening as a child," Mrs. Gibbs reminisced— (blah, blah, skipping forward) *Some of the plants in her private greenhouses include Yellow Kaner, Foxglove—"*

I stopped reading. Although the few plants I owned through the years died from inattention, pre-mission briefings included discussions of poisonous and non-poisonous plants, important information if we needed to forage off the land. I reread the list. Some of her plants were poisonous.

What if Beatrice poisoned Willie?

After considering the evidence for a while, I almost dialed Detective Montoya but put my phone down. I didn't want back on his radar.

Another section of the paper featured photographs taken at various events. The women had perfect teeth, hair, and cleavage. A man had deer-in-headlights eyes from too much indulgence in plastic surgery.

A photo on the next page kept me from taking another bite: Beatrice Gibbs, Alice and Tom Stenton, Willie Weston, and Amelia Meadows posed at a previous gala. Despite the formal attire, Willie reminded me of Hugh Hefner in a smoking jacket but sleazier. His hand rested a fraction below Amelia's left breast, pulling her tight against him. I was surprised to see a soft, adoring look on Amelia's face as she gazed up at Willie. Perhaps she did love him.

Finishing my meal, my phone rang as I started the car.

"Ms. Glenn? Detective Montoya. I'm following up on the painting."

"Isn't Adair Monroe cooperating?"

"His people keep saying he'll get back to me, but he doesn't. They did provide me with the art dealer's information, but I got nowhere with her."

"You didn't hand this off to the property crimes people?"

"Well, I assumed this theft was important."

Translation: The case involved you, and I need to find out more.

If I laid out my suspicions about Beatrice, perhaps Detective Super Glue would come unstuck from trying to figure out my past.

"Was Weston's body tested for poison?"

"Is there something you want to tell me?"

"I suspect a ring of thieves are working at the Ladies' League, and one might have poisoned Weston if he discovered them."

"Who?"

"I don't want to say. Tell me if poison was in his system, and I might tell you who I suspect."

"The samples from his blood and tissues are still at the lab. We're understaffed, so we don't have results yet. I'll roust a toxicologist who owes me if you tell me more about your suspicions."

"Off the record?"

"I'm not a reporter."

"Oh, you know what I mean," I snapped. "Everything is circumstantial."

"Lay the facts out for me."

"This might be complete conjecture on my part."

"Let me decide."

I gave him my conclusions and the potential suspect's name, telling Montoya to test for a plant-based poison.

"Plant poison can cause nausea and other unpleasant symptoms. I don't remember any evidence at the scene."

"A certain plant can mimic a heart attack. Since Weston had a bad heart, maybe that's what the murderer planned."

If somebody murdered him, which was a stretch.

"C4, superior firearms skills, high-speed chases, terrorists and, now, poison expert," Montoya summarized. "You're an unusual addition to the social scene in Rancho Suprema."

"Think of me as a Renaissance girl."

"I stopped believing the *it's all a coincidence* line from you a long time ago."

"Mm."

"I'll tell you if they find anything in the tox results."

"So, you'll ask for those tests?"

"What else do I have to do?"

Loosen up? Have some fun? He was too young to be married to the job like this.

"Are you attending the gala tomorrow night?"

"I got a ticket as thanks for recovering the painting, but I'm undecided about going."

"Might be the only time you can wear a tux and arrest someone for murder."

"Tempting. More tempting if you'll save a dance for me."

"I will. See you there."

26

Salon Divine was a madhouse. Women hustled between hair, makeup, and nails while more packed the lounge. Tense customers demanded Bambi freshen their drinks or bring them more snacks.

I hoped I was the only one packing a gun.

Two assistants washed and dried hair in an assembly-line process. Ramon bustled past, carrying something long and glossy. He pinned a faux ponytail to the back of a client's head. Waiting, I caught up with celebrities' latest indiscretions featured in a magazine. Finally, it was my turn.

One of Ramon's assistants washed my hair. I cringed when her scrubbing hands hit the bruised part of my scalp but said nothing.

"Are your extensions holding up?" she asked.

"What do you mean?"

"When you brush your hair, do any pieces pull free?"

"No."

"Great!"

If my hair shed like a dog in summer, Ramon would have been stuck spending valuable time putting in replacements.

A different assistant took me to another room, where a beautician began the drying process. She styled my hair with a round brush, moving it in sync with the screaming hand dryer. I studied her technique, hoping to recreate the style but knowing I would fail. With my hair dried, she started on another client.

Bambi paused in her unending quest for drinks and food. She held two Perrier bottles and balanced bowls of snacks for the customers.

"How are you doing since the explosion?" she asked.

"What explos—oh." With recent events, the car bomb was gone from my mind. "I'm fine. You?"

"I still have nightmares!" She began to pale.

A patron saved me.

"You, girl! Where's my drink?" Entitlement Botox hardened the woman's face.

"Be right there!" Bambi said. "We can talk later." She rushed back away, and an assistant manicurist buffed and polished my nails.

When she finished, the blow-dryer pro reappeared.

"Time for Ramon."

"Hello, Davia." Ramon's shoulders sagged from exhaustion.

"Are you holding up?"

"I think so because we're nearing the end of the day. Earlier, two clients got in a physical altercation."

"About what?"

"I think the argument was about whose plastic surgeon was the best."

"Sounds important."

"So, what would you like me to do for you?"

"Why are you asking me?"

"Everyone else has had decided opinions."

"My sole goal is to fit in at the gala."

"Don't worry."

In less than twenty minutes, he twisted and curled my hair into an elaborate up-do. He used so much hair spray a hurricane wouldn't move anything. Admiring the results, he snapped his fingers. "Oh, I almost forgot! I'll be back in a minute."

He retreated into a side room, returning with a black velvet box.

"Adair Monroe sent this for you."

"What is it?"

He placed the box in my hand.

"Something for your hair. Bryce told me Adair called him to find out what you were wearing, and a delivery person came this by this morning. It almost slipped my mind in all the madness."

I didn't want to open it. The contents might prove explosive in a not-quite-so-literal way, our kiss igniting the fuse. Lifting the lid, I beheld an ornate silver comb with an intricate flower pattern. The flower centers were sapphires sparkling in the light. *Jumbo* sapphires.

Ramon was floored like me. "I think Adair Monroe likes you very much."

"What should I do with this?" Return the gift with a note saying, *Don't I still owe you for the Aston?*

"Wear it, of course!"

Ramon took the comb and placed it on the left side of my elaborate coiffure. He turned my chair, and the mirror reflected the brilliant gems.

"Spectacular!" he said.

"Isn't this a bit much?"

"This is an understated, tasteful piece. Trust me."

What should I do?

Another assistant led me to a private workspace inhabited by a trendy makeup artist from Beverly Hills. She knocked at the door, and a harassed voice told us to enter. A thin young man with a shaved head stood next to a chair facing a lighted mirror. Open cases surrounded him holding various types of cosmetics.

"Sit!" He wore eye shadow, glamour radiating from him. He studied me in silence. I forced myself to stop obsessing about the comb.

"I'm Davia," I finally said.

"Hmm?" He came out of his reverie.

"I'm Davia."

"I'm Christian. Sorry, I was just mulling the possibilities. Not every girl receives a sapphire comb from Adair Monroe."

"Is nothing secret around here?" I asked, indignant.

"Don't worry." Christian selected a small paint gun. "The package arrived early this morning, so Bambi and I peeked."

"For a man with a near-endless supply of money, this is a trinket, I'm sure."

"Girl, you don't realize what he gave you, do you?"

"A silver comb with sapphires?"

"A *vintage* silver comb with sapphires valued at, I'd guess, $200,000 minimum."

"Two hundred *what*?" My hand flew to touch the comb.

"He doesn't do jewelry unless he's serious."

"Why do you say that?"

"Darling, too-hot-for-words women are in limited supply in this world. I do thirty percent of their makeup, and my friends do the rest. We hear it all, believe me."

So, the comb was far more than a small token of regard? I wanted to yank it from my hair as Adair might believe he was entitled to more of me than I wanted to give.

What could I do?

"What other jewelry are you wearing?" Christian interrupted my thoughts, daubing something along my cheekbones.

"I don't know."

He straightened in disbelief. "You don't know?"

I strained to remember what was in Aunt Lilah's jewelry box. "I might have some drop sapphire earrings and a couple of necklaces."

Christian resumed dabbing at my face.

"Describe them."

"One necklace is elaborate, with lots of sapphires. The other is a fine silver chain with a sapphire pendant."

"Wear the simple one," he advised. "You don't need to gild the lily."

Christian continued his work in silence, and I returned to my quandary. The best thing would be to talk to Adair at the gala, thank him for the comb, and give it back. How to accomplish that was another matter.

The next time I looked in the mirror, a stranger sat in my chair. Christian had laid on dark and smoldering eye shadow, accented my high cheekbones, and made my lips appear large and pouty.

"I can't believe this is me."

"I didn't need to do much. Here." He handed me a small case.

"What's this?"

"A kit for touch-ups. Refresh and gloss your lips often. I added some eyelashes at the edges of your lash line and put in a tube of glue in case they start to lift."

"Fixing false eyelashes is beyond my capabilities."

"Please keep it."

Perhaps eyelash glue meant to him what my guns meant to me. I relented, thanking him.

"You're welcome. You'll be the star."

At reception, dozens of judging eyes bored into me. Did Christian leave a smudge on my nose or something?

Bambi exclaimed, "No wonder Adair Monroe is captivated with you!"

"He's not."

Bambi gave me a knowing wink. "Oh, I understand if you're trying to keep your relationship quiet," she whispered. "Who wants paparazzi dogging their every move?"

Paparazzi? Yes, situations can always get worse.

ONCE HOME, I removed my gown from its garment bag, the vibrant blue hues sparkling in the light. Retrieving the jewelry case from the safe, I looped the simple sapphire necklace on the coat hanger and got out the deep blue strapless bra and matching panties Bryce made me purchase. Slipping into high-heeled pumps, I did a few stretches to check my leg and was pleased nothing cramped.

Half an hour later, I was ready to leave and felt confident.

Beauty was a weapon.

I tucked the kit Christian gave me into a small beaded clutch along with my cell phone. I hesitated. *Should I take a gun?* The revolver might fit in the elegant bag, but I also needed room for my keys. Nothing else I owned would work, and I was not wearing an ankle holster. My luck, it would tangle in my gown, and I'd trip and fall in front of everyone.

Beauty might be a weapon, but fashion was a pain.

Was a new assassin waiting for me already? Quite possibly, but it was unlikely he'd choose a well-attended event for an attack. In the end, I decided to take a folding knife.

An hour before the gala began, I parked my car and stowed everything in my bag, ensuring the weapon sat on top. The transformation of the building's interior was remarkable. Half the room held tables covered by crisp white tablecloths and laid with china, cutlery, and crystal glasses. In the center of each table sat a wreath of perennials in vivid colors. The wreath centers held bowls with lit candles, creating a cozy, romantic atmosphere. The room buzzed with activity. Members of the Ladies' League added finishing touches while the hired wait staff arrived and started their jobs.

"Davia!" Francis called. Her green shift flowed straight to the floor, and she wore her hair pulled up to display emerald and diamond drop earrings. Her tiny heart beat like a frightened sparrow.

"What's wrong?"

"I can't take this!" she cried. "Everyone comes to me for answers, and I don't know what to say half the time. Oh, if only Willie were still alive."

Part of me considered taking hold of Francis, maneuvering her to a chair, and telling her about a few atrocious world events to put this in perspective. The rest of me completely understood her anxiety. Gala mania could make the most formidable person run off the rails.

"You have this under control," I said, attempting to soothe her frenetic energy.

"Oh, thank you, Davia." She calmed a bit.

"What did you need me to do?"

She nodded to a doorway. "If you would take charge of monitoring the silent auction in the Davenport room, I need to meet with our emcee."

"You go take care of whatever you need to do. I'll handle it."

Thanking me, Francis moved on to her next task.

The recent assaults made me pay more attention to my surroundings and any potential hidey-hole a sniper might use. I scanned the entrances and exits, the tables, dance floor, and stage, but nothing stood out.

"Davia!" Lydia McGregor joined me from across the room. She closed the distance between us with purposeful strides. "An attendant won't tell you your seating assignment because they're setting up now. We're at table four over by the front. Numbers are clipped to the centerpiece of each table."

"I'll find you. You look lovely."

She wore a pale blue floor-length dress with a matching jacket. Tiny rhinestones set into diamond shapes at the collar and cuffs sparkled. Her hair shone, and she wore mascara, revealing pretty eyes. Despite her elegant attire, she persisted in wearing sensible shoes with rubber soles and her black-framed glasses.

"Thank you, Davia. And you!" Something across the room drew Lydia's attention. "Oh! I told them not to start bringing out the wine so soon! Excuse me."

Making my way to the Davenport Room, I grew envious of Lydia's shoes. My torture device heels and restrictive get-up were a misery. The gift baskets sat on long tables, a few on risers to vary their height and add dimension to the display. I went down each aisle, pausing to peruse the most expensive items. A spectacular diamond bracelet was on a table by itself. After assessing security, I laughed at myself. The Ladies' League thieves specialized in pre-emptive strikes, not blatant snatch and runs.

Couples began to enter the room. The men wore tuxedos with corsages at their lapels, while the willowy women wore couture gowns and glittered with jewels. One had gems woven into her hair.

She gave me one of those once-overs I received since moving here. This time, the woman's face registered approval.

Had I achieved a socialite's appearance?

Music began playing over hidden speakers, the festivities now underway. The room soon grew crowded, and servers passed among the attendees carrying champagne glasses and trays of hors d'oeuvres.

As the guests imbibed alcohol, the conversation grew louder, and laughter rang out more often. I patrolled the aisles, maneuvered around people, and waited for questions. Everyone appeared more interested in visiting with each other than talking to me.

Then the crowd paused almost as one. Adair entered with a silver-haired lady on his arm. She wore a black and white gown with white orchids pinned at the left breast. Adair's tuxedo molded to his athletic frame, and sapphire cufflinks sparkled at his wrists. His slicked-back hairstyle evoked glamorous movie stars from the early days of Hollywood. If there were bodyguards, I didn't see them. Not ready for an awkward discussion about his gift and its implications, I prayed the crowds would stay between us until he finished bidding and left.

Adair walked forward, and I went the opposite direction, keeping people between us. He and his mother were popular, pausing to converse often. They examined the displays and occasionally placed a bid. My tormented feet ached, but there was nowhere to sit.

After what seemed an eternity, Adair neared the exit. I began to sigh with relief when two women started a loud argument in the center of the room.

"I let you win the trip last year!" The declarant wore a tight, hot pink gown, hair teased to scary heights.

"You are so selfish!" the other shouted. "I can outbid you if I want!"

Profanities followed. One of the women reached out to slap at the other, jostling a server. A drink tray hit the floor, splattering the tables.

"Excuse me." I came up behind the younger of the combatants.

She turned, hostility plain on her face. "What do you want?"

"Yeah, who are you?" The other questioned, face more suited to a dive bar than a gala.

"I'm a member of the auction committee."

"Well, tell Andrea I can have the vacation!" the younger woman said.

I recited the rules. "The trip goes to the highest bidder."

"Samantha thinks she should win because she's younger and spoiled!" Andrea said. "Isn't that right, *Sis?*"

The last word simmered in the stew of a long-standing family feud.

Samantha struck her older sister in the face, causing Andrea to yelp. Andrea launched forward and tackled Samantha, the women crashing to the ground. They pulled hair and scratched each other. I seized Samantha's hand as she moved to yank off one of Andrea's earrings. Wrenching her arm behind her back, I pulled her upright and tight against me.

"Knock it off," I ordered. Samantha continued her flail about, so I increased pressure until she focused more on the pain than fighting.

Andrea took advantage of the situation and kicked Samantha's ankle.

"*Ouch!*" Samantha squealed.

Removal was the best option, so I stiff-leg walked Samantha toward the door.

A shrill wail issued from behind me, and Andrea barreled toward us. Before I could react, Adair reached out and swung her into his arms. She squirmed and protested until she realized who held her.

"Oh, Adair." She morphed from hellion to simpering socialite in an instant.

I gave him a grateful smile, and he grinned.

Darn. Well, I guess I couldn't hide forever.

People gave me room to maneuver the young firebrand out. Two men met us near the door.

"Samantha, what were you doing?" the younger of the two asked.

"I bet you fought with Andrea again," the older man guessed, disgusted, and went past us into the room.

"You can let her go," the younger man told me.

"If I do, you need to leave and not attack me," I warned Samantha.

"I'll make sure she calms down," the man promised.

I released Samantha, and he took hold of her.

She rubbed at her arm. "That hurt!"

"You need to behave yourself," I said.

"You-you-*bitch!*" Samantha wrestled to get free, but the man kept a firm hold and dragged her toward the front doors.

Once they left the building and she didn't run back in and throw herself at me, I straightened my gown and ran a hand up to my hair. Everything was in place from Ramon's super-hold hairspray. I started back, but Adair came into the hall and towards me.

"Davia! Are you all right?"

"Yes, I appreciate your help. Again."

"This is becoming a distressing habit."

Adair's mother came out of the Davenport room.

"What an uproar!" Her words carried with refined, British elocution. She reached us and paused. "You handled yourself well in there. Are you new to Rancho Suprema?"

"Yes, I'm Davia Glenn."

"Kate Monroe."

"Pleasure to meet you," I said.

"Those Simmons sisters are so unruly. They're always bickering and fighting about something. If I were their mother, I would lock them in a room and throw away the key!"

"Mum," Adair said in an admonishing but amused tone.

"People should remember their manners," she continued.

"You sound like my mom," I said.

"I bet I would like her." Kate's shrewd gaze moved between her son and me. "I'll be at our table, Adair."

"I'll be there soon."

"Take your time; don't rush. Lovely to meet you, Miss Glenn."

"Likewise."

She walked toward the dining area, posture graceful as a ballet dancer.

"I'm glad you're wearing what I sent. The perfect gift for the perfect woman." Adair's lips parted in a satisfied smile.

"I am *not* perfect."

Adair's arm went around my waist, and he pulled me close. My traitorous body melted into him. I searched for a way to bring up the gift, but his proximity made it difficult to think. He kissed me on the forehead, each cheek, and moved towards my lips.

"Where are your bodyguards?" I asked, putting my hand against his chest and stepping back.

He let out an exaggerated sigh.

"What is it with you and Jason?" He sounded like a put-upon teenager. "I had a row with him tonight. What's going to happen at a gala?"

Please, Universe. Don't take his words as a challenge.

Before I could respond, Beatrice Gibbs appeared. Her deep purple gown and a small tiara of amethysts matched her pompous attitude. "Davia!" She proclaimed my name like a royal command. "Go into the Davenport Room, and announce dinner is served."

Was I relieved or resentful of the interruption?

"Monroe, escort me to my seat," Beatrice demanded.

"My pleasure." Adair somehow sounded sincere.

Beatrice attached herself to his arm like a leech. They started for the dining room when Adair turned his head. "Davia! Remember the dance you promised."

"Of course." *A dance where I would discuss the comb.*

In the Davenport Room, I tapped a pen against a glass several times, and everyone quieted down.

Huh, that trick worked precisely like in the movies.

"Attention, please! Dinner's being served. Make your final bids, and please enjoy your meals," I announced.

People headed out, their conversations resuming. I recalled my original task of checking on the silent auction items. Their cellophane wrapping repelled most of the liquid from the spilled tray of drinks, and I wiped any stubborn drops with a discarded napkin. The broken glasses were already swept up and removed. Disposing of the napkin in a trash can, I decided to wash my hands in the kitchen, which was a shorter distance than the ladies' room; welcome news to my feet. I rushed down the hall, not wanting to be late for dinner.

Movement ahead.

A man in black stepped out from a shadowed corner.

He held a razor-sharp butcher's knife.

27

I ndiana Jones's line about not bringing a knife to a gunfight sprang to mind, but I didn't have a gun. I pulled my knife from my clutch and flipped it open, sure my attacker would laugh.

The blade was three inches long.

A white jacket lay discarded on the floor. My latest opponent had disguised himself as hired help and likely stole his weapon from the kitchen. The man's complexion was swarthy, and he broadcast lethal confidence. He held his weapon in a fist in his right hand and ran toward me.

I dove left, hindered by my attire.

He stopped, reversed, and slashed at my side. The sharp tip passed within a hair's breadth. To back him up, I waved my knife, cutting the air in broad swathes.

"I'm not worth the money," I told him.

He replied in Arabic. He didn't care about money; he wanted to kill me.

My own psycho.

Launching himself at me again, the man drove the ten-inch blade toward my abdomen. I jumped back, pulled my stomach in, and struck his arm with my knife. He yelped with surprise. A line of red soaked through his sleeve as anger clouded his face.

I backed up when he advanced, but one of my heels caught in the carpet, and I almost fell. My hand slammed down on a decorative table for balance. The surface held a vase.

A *brass* vase.

Transferring my blade to my left hand, I grabbed the pot and whacked my assailant in the head with it. He fell to the floor as water and flowers scattered everywhere. I slammed the vase into his right arm, hoping he would drop his knife, but he held on.

He got up and pivoted toward me.

I slashed his chest.

"Ready to quit?" I asked in Arabic, those language classes paying off at last. "A woman is kicking your ass."

He let out a cry of outrage and rushed toward me, knife high over his head, planning to plunge its length into my wicked little heart. Dropping the vase and my knife, I captured his arm, swung it behind his body, and flung him to the floor.

Dropping down, I shoved a knee into his back. Reaching out, I grabbed the fallen vase.

Bash! Bash! Bash!

On the third strike, he went down, unconscious.

What should I do?

Retrieving my decorative clutch from the hall floor, I pulled out my cell phone and dialed.

"Agent Wills."

"This is Glenn. I neutralized a hostile at the Ladies' League building in Rancho Suprema. I'll stash him in—" I glanced around, "—a closet off the kitchen."

I dragged my unconscious attacker the short distance. As I did, a curl slipped down the side of my face. The small closet held vacuums and brooms but also enough room for my defeated enemy, so I chucked him inside and closed the door. Hustling to the office, I retrieved some duct tape from one of the drawers. Despite being ready for a frontal assault when I opened the door, he was still unconscious. I taped his wrists, ankles, and mouth. His eyes opened, and he began to struggle.

"Someone will be here shortly." I patted him on the cheek and closed the door.

Phone and knife back in the clutch, I returned the vase to the table. After gathering the scattered flowers, I used them to conceal the man's discarded knife in a bit of unbalanced floral arranging. Catching sight of myself in a mirror above the table, I recalled Christian's admonitions and reapplied my lipstick and lip gloss. The fake lashes held, and the errant curl didn't detract. I was almost good to go except for my hands, sticky from bubbly and blood.

A noise came from behind me.

I spun, thinking my attacker was loose.

Amelia Meadows moved back fast enough to avoid the underside of my hand.

"What is wrong with you?" She paired her unhappy countenance with a crimson red gown and ruby jewelry.

"Sorry. You startled me."

"Why is there blood all over your hands?"

"I cut myself on a glass. I'm going to the kitchen to wash them."

She wrinkled her nose. "The kitchen?"

"I need a sink."

"I don't even want to know why you make the decisions you do." She turned around to leave.

"Wait! Look, we don't know each other well, but I meant to tell you I can't imagine how you feel losing Mr. Weston. I'm truly sorry."

Amelia looked down, and when her eyes met mine again, her callous exterior disappeared. Now, she seemed like a regular, grieving woman.

"Thank you," she said.

We parted company without further conversation. As I went toward my original destination, I realized I wasn't the only person who put on a brave front, and let go of another judgmental view.

As I entered the kitchen, a waiter hurried past with a tray.

"Excuse me, Miss!" he apologized after nearly colliding with me.

I washed my hands, dried them on a dishtowel, and proceeded to the dining room. Smiling apologetically, I slipped into my seat at table four next to Lydia McGregor.

"I was starting to worry about you, Davia," Lydia said. "You missed the salad course."

"Some of the baskets got splashed when a server dropped a tray of glasses, and I wiped them off."

"You're such a worker, dear. I hope the Ladies' League realizes how lucky they are to have you."

Lydia introduced me to the others at our table. An ancient couple sat on her right, a Mr. and Mrs. Edward Spencer. Mrs. Spencer repeated everything by shouting into her husband's right ear.

Two empty chairs sat to my left.

"Who's supposed to be sitting here?" I asked Lydia. A server placed a dinner plate in front of me.

"I can't say. Sometimes people pay but don't attend. They're so inconsiderate."

Continuing this theme, Lydia began a conversation with the Spencers about the difficulty of finding people to help with the gala. Thankful I didn't need to make polite conversation, I ate.

My waistline became uncomfortable, but at least my feet got a break. Bussers cleared dinner plates while other wait staff stood in the distance with dessert trays. I scanned their faces, but no one was out of place.

"Ladies and gentlemen. May I have your attention, please?" Our emcee, local TV anchorman Rick Coleridge, held a microphone onstage. He spoke with the practiced voice of an announcer.

People paused, and any conversation dimmed to a murmur.

"In a few minutes, we'll begin our live auction. All the money raised is used for the Ladies' League philanthropic work. But first, here's your president Beatrice Gibbs with a few words."

Beatrice, seated on stage, rose to a smattering of applause. She took the microphone, put on reading glasses, and checked her prepared notes.

"Welcome to the Fiftieth Annual Ladies' League Gala! First, let's all pause for a minute of silence and remember our much-missed chairman, Willie Weston."

My dessert arrived, a piece of cake with lavender icing and real violets.

Yum.

Was it wrong to think about dessert instead of the deceased Willie?

After the remembrance, Beatrice talked about club traditions and thanked the people who helped with the gala. I applauded at the mention of Francis Downs and Lydia McGregor. She didn't mention me, so I tuned her out and ate some of the cake. It was delicious.

A loud round of applause signified the end. Beatrice returned the mike to the emcee.

"And now, what we've all been waiting for—the auction!" Coleridge said. "I'm sure everyone's consulted their programs, and you're ready to open your wallets for a good cause."

"Are you bidding on anything tonight?" Lydia asked.

"I don't have a program."

"Here, take mine."

Ten items were up for auction. Among them were a private yacht excursion, a week-long stay in a castle in Ireland, and a two-week trip to New York City with tickets to a sold-out Broadway musical. The final item was the purloined painting.

"Find anything you like?" Lydia asked when I returned her program.

"I don't need anything."

"Too bad."

"How about you?"

"Oh, no. I don't need anything either."

The bidding was a frenzy, and the excitement tempted me to join. Each item's total was much higher than the actual value, and Lydia wore a pleased expression.

"Our final item is a painting by a promising young artist. Your dearly departed Willie Weston secured its donation from Haverfield Galleries."

At Coleridge's words, Beatrice pulled off a black sheet covering the painting. The bidding became fast and furious. Adair, who sat at a table across the dance floor from me, waited for the furor to decrease before raising his hand and keeping it extended. After a time, the people bidding against him gave up.

"Sold to Adair Monroe," Coleridge declared, and the audience burst into applause. Adair gave me a quick thumbs up. "And now, if you'll give us a few minutes, we'll be back to announce who won the silent auctions. The Flaming Hot Flamingos are setting up so we can start dancing!"

Patrons turned back to their dinner companions, resuming conversations.

"Did you enjoy the auction?" Lydia asked.

"Yes, that was fun." I poured some wine into my glass and relaxed, thinking galas weren't so bad. Once the attempts on my life were over, that is.

Was this the world Aunt Lilah wanted me to embrace? Would I come to think raising money for charity—while spending even more money on wardrobe, hair, and makeup—was a fulfilling endeavor?

The announcer returned to the stage.

"Excuse me." Coleridge appeared strained, and the crowd quieted. "Detective Montoya of the Sheriff's Department would like your attention."

Montoya, replete in a black tuxedo, took the microphone. Uniformed deputies guarded the building's exits.

"I'm sorry to interrupt the festivities, but I'll be brief. Are Tom and Alice Stenton in attendance?"

The Stentons stood, nervous and pale. Two deputies bent their heads and gave them instructions. Alice picked up her handbag and clutched Tom for support. Whispered conversations began throughout the room.

"Thank you, and enjoy the rest of your evening." Detective Montoya left the stage.

Speculation exploded.

"What happened? Eh?" Edward Spencer thundered. His wife yelled into his ear, attempting to explain.

"Is this about the painting theft?" Lydia asked me.

"I think so." Actually, I knew so.

"I shouldn't be surprised. The Stentons acted so, well, entitled. Besides, I think they're only renters."

Coleridge retook the stage and began to announce the silent auction winners. Soon everyone forgot about the Stentons. The room erupted with laughter when the trip the Simmons sisters fought over went to the elder sister's husband. Samantha got up to protest, but my admonishing look made her sit back down.

After all the winners claimed their prizes, the Flaming Hot Flamingos launched into "Jailhouse Rock," an appropriate choice. The oldie band's lead singer wore a white tuxedo with a red shirt, the drummer and guitar player wore red tuxedos, and the female keyboard player wore a red sequined gown. They twisted and danced with enthusiasm while they played, making up for occasional off-key notes.

"Would you like to dance?" It was Detective Montoya.

We made our way to the crowded dance floor.

"Surprised by the arrest?"

"Nope."

"Of course not."

The Stentons might crack under questioning and give up others in the Ladies' League. Who knew? I wanted to have a good time. Montoya turned out to be an experienced dancer, swiveling his hips in time to the music. Bob Brooks and his wife shimmied close by and smiled at me. The song ended, and the band went right into "Great Balls of Fire."

Montoya inclined his head at the band, asking to continue. I nodded.

Keep dancing. You deserve to enjoy a night out after everything Badger's thrown at you.

When the song concluded, a hand tapped my shoulder, and I

turned to see Sherilyn wearing a pale pink gown. Bryce stood beside her in a dark navy tuxedo with black lapels, elegant as always.

"I thought I would surprise you!" she said. "Bryce needed a companion because Ramon is *exhausted*, so we came together."

"Perfection," Bryce said when he took in my overall look. He leaned forward to kiss my cheek.

I introduced them to Detective Montoya, who kept his dark eyes on my designer's face as he indicated his pleasure to meet them both. As Sherilyn flushed with interest, Montoya got a call. The band had begun another number, so he excused himself to answer his cell phone; a hand cupped over his ear to dull the noise.

"That was the toxicologist with the report on the Weston case," he said to me. "I need to call him back."

"Excuse us," I said, giving Bryce's arm a squeeze and a hug to Sherilyn. The pair resumed dancing, but Sherilyn continued to watch the detective.

I crooked my head to Montoya to indicate we should go outside.

We exited into the relative quiet of the front courtyard, and Montoya dialed. I went further into the gardens to give him space.

"Glenn!" a voice called.

Agent Wills and several others loaded my duct-taped foe into a black SUV. I gave them a wave as they left.

Montoya rejoined me. "Who was that?"

"Some old friends."

"They're the guys who took over the golf course crime scene when the terrorist crashed his car."

"You think so?"

"Yes, I do. Is there something else going on?"

"Maybe."

Annoyance played across his face while mine revealed nothing.

"Well, I got some results," he said when I didn't speak.

"Plant poison?"

"No. The toxicologist had trouble running down the substance he found in Weston's blood."

"What was it?"

"Turns out to be a poison secreted by some amphibian."

"What type?"

"A Golden Dart Frog. It resides in—"

"Colombia?" I finished for him.

"How'd you know?"

The one person in the Ladies' League I admired, Lydia McGregor, was the culprit. She sailed beneath my radar because of her kindness to me.

"I know who killed Weston."

"Who? Beatrice Gibbs?" Montoya recalled the person I initially suspected.

"No, I was dead wrong. The murderer is Lydia McGregor."

"Who?"

"One of the most dedicated members of the Ladies' League, someone not happy with Weston because of all the changes he planned to make to her beloved club."

"Interesting motive," Montoya remarked. "Change can be a difficult thing, but murdering someone is extreme."

"She went to Colombia to study a rare type of amphibian. I think she put the poison inside homemade tea bags she gave out to some members of this organization."

"Do you think she put poison in all the bags?"

"No idea, but the others are still alive."

"Is she here?"

"Yes," I disclosed, reluctant.

"I need to take her in for questioning and prepare a search warrant for her residence. Guess I won't be dancing anymore, even though I hoped to ask Ms. Silvers."

"She'll be disappointed."

"And, I didn't have a chance to say you look stunning," he continued, "For an operative."

"I'm not an—" I paused. "I'm one of the good guys."

Montoya got swept away in my aftermath too many times to keep up my protests.

"Which is why I never arrested you."

"Gee, thanks?"

"You're welcome. Perhaps someday you'll tell me the full story over coffee."

"I don't drink coffee."

"You say that, but I'll figure out some way to learn the full truth."

I bet he would try.

We went back inside.

28

"She was at table four," I told Montoya.

Please, Lydia. Be supervising something in the kitchen, chewing out a valet for dinging a car, anything.

But there she sat, watching the dancing.

"Mrs. McGregor?" Montoya said.

"Yes?"

"I'm Detective Montoya of the Sheriff's Department."

"Yes, dreadful about the Stentons stealing from our organization."

"Yes, well, I'm arresting you for the murder of William Weston."

Her eyes closed and reopened. Did she realize this was coming? Was the arrest a relief?

"I'm sorry, Lydia," I said.

"Would you escort me out, Detective?"

Lydia rose and took Montoya's arm. As they started for the exit, she paused beside me. "Take care of the Ladies' League for me, will you, Davia?"

"I'll do the best I can."

Sinking into my chair, I tossed back the remaining red wine in my glass. At least Montoya let Mrs. McGregor leave with dignity, and I was grateful. The night was a roller coaster of nerves, irritation, and, now, sadness.

Adair appeared beside me. "I wondered where you were. You owe me a dance."

"Yes." I returned to the present. "If you don't mind, I need to rest for a few minutes first."

He lowered himself into the chair vacated by Lydia. "I saw you dancing with that detective. Was he too much for you?"

"Ah, no. We met when my car blew up." I didn't want to give him the whole story. "He's the one who figured out who stole the painting you bought tonight. Are you happy to get it back?"

"Yes, although it cost me a lot more than the price I paid the dealer. It survived a wild ride without being damaged, and I survived a crack to the head. We're made for each other!"

I started to launch into the much-delayed discussion of his gift, but the hard-rocking band chose to slow down and began a rendition of "I Will Always Love You."

"Please dance with me." Adair put out his hand, which I accepted. Once on the dance floor, he put an arm about my waist, we clasped hands and began to sway to the music.

"Mr. Monroe, would you mind if I took your picture?" A short, plump young man asked. He carried a camera and wore a friendly smile.

"Sure, Dennis."

We held a pose, and Dennis took several photos. He took a notepad from a rumpled jacket pocket. "Name?" he inquired of me.

"Davia Glenn."

"I'm Dennis from the *Suprema Gazette*. Thank you for letting me interrupt."

He resumed photographing couples, and we returned to dancing. The photo would appear on the society pages fulfilling another will requirement.

You have eleven more months to decide whether that matters.

"You're the most beautiful woman here," Adair said.

"Thank you." I fought the undeniable chemistry, infatuation, or whatever this was.

What would it be like to kiss him until we were both breathless? To wake and feel his naked body beside mine? To set aside my harsh reality and commit myself to his world?

I stepped back, taking a firm grip on my wandering thoughts. "I was about to thank you for the comb."

He twirled me under an arm and back into a close embrace.

"I'm glad you like it." His voice was warm as he kissed close to where it graced my hair.

I put distance between us once more. Meeting his eyes, I said, "I can't keep it."

Adair frowned. "Why not?"

"I can't accept such an extravagant gift."

"It's not extravagant."

"Not to you, but—"

"Davia—"

"This gift is too much for the time we've known each other."

"I disagree. We've been through a lot, and events have brought us close."

"True, but being in life-threatening situations isn't a basis for a relationship."

Yes, I was a hypocrite, but Warden and I spent *years* in life-threatening situations, not a few encounters in scarcely a month.

"Let's take time to know each other better. We would make a great couple," Adair said.

He was right; we probably would. *If I was just a girl living the life of Riley, and he was, well, who he was. A sexy billionaire with a big heart.*

The music ended, and Adair kissed me. The room disappeared, and I surrendered to his sweet mouth.

I can't do this! I need to stop.

Flashes burst before my closed eyelids, startling me.

It was Dennis, snapping more photos.

Disentangling myself from Adair took most of my willpower. Confusion crossed his face as I pushed him away.

"Davia." He put out a hand, but I took a step back.

"Thank you for the dance. Excuse me." I snaked past the other dancers.

This is simply a flirtation, nothing else. Most men I dated felt I didn't need them, and he won't be any different in the long run.

A set of double doors beckoned, revealing a long, quiet hallway. Stepping through and reclosing them, the sound of music and the crowd's conversation became muted. I needed to be alone, to regain control over my turbulent emotions.

Getting to the truth of what would be best for my future would require some solemn self-examination. Operatives were a particular type of person. At our core, we accepted the necessity of killing people, even if we lost a piece of our humanity each time we did. In the end, what remained? Regret? A thousand-yard stare? Satisfaction from helping our country? Would living here, and being with a man like Adair, be better in the long run? Or could I resume my old job and keep from going over the edge?

Continuing along the corridor, head down, I rammed straight into someone. I stopped, surprised to find another person in the closed-off space.

"Sorry, I—"

"Davia?"

It was Aubrey Elliot from Colonel Streeter's office, dressed as one of the wait staff.

"Aubrey! What are you doing here?" I perked up at seeing her. "Is everything—"

She held a gun with a suppressor in her hand—pointed at me.

"Don't move," she ordered.

"What?"

"I said, don't move."

For a moment, nothing in the world made sense.

"I learned Badger's latest hitman failed," she said.

"Yes. My handler already took him. The problem's solved."

"It's not!" she spat, disgusted. "Three assassins botched the job, so I have to kill you myself!"

"You have to *what*?"

She must be joking.

"Kill you. Myself," she repeated. I provided Badger intel on the team, practically served you all up on a silver platter, and what happened? He got most of the ACE team, but only you and Ned got shot in Africa, but not fatally."

I stared, speechless.

How had no one discovered the traitor was right among us? Had anyone realized she also leaked info to betray the ACE team?

Aubrey gave a satisfied laugh. "Fooled you, didn't I? And you're supposed to be so smart."

"Why are you doing this?"

"Why do you think? Badger paid me extremely well."

Money? Only money?

"It has to be more than that." I hoped it was a reason I could understand, like a relative held captive or some other dire predicament that compelled Aubrey to comply.

"We all can't inherit a fortune, can we, Davia? I mean, look at you. I scarcely believe what I'm seeing. Makeup, jewels, haute couture. Who knew you had it in you?"

"It isn't that simple."

"Just like my situation and my choices."

"I don't think inheriting money is like choosing to betray your country."

She let out a disdainful breath. "Perhaps not."

"What about honor, loyalty, duty? Don't those concepts mean anything to you?" I persisted.

"No. What have they done for you? You worked yourself into the ground daily to keep up with men who never considered you their equal, even if they never admitted that to you. Our country ordered you to do dirty deeds it didn't acknowledge, ones that might have gotten you killed. For what? Honor, loyalty, and duty?"

Her words stung, echoing my earlier thoughts.

I lifted my chin. "I worked hard to be in my position on the team."

"For *what*? The government barely pays you enough to scrape together a down payment for a two-bedroom house to enjoy during your retirement. Do I want *that*?" She laughed at the thought. "Whatever Badger pays me is more than I'll ever make as a 'Yes, Sir' gopher to Colonel Streeter."

"So, what's the plan?" I would keep her talking while considering my limited options. The gun in Aubrey's hand didn't waver, and she was too far away. She could shoot before I got close enough.

"When this job's finished, I'll enjoy the rest of my life. I won't stay awake at night, beset by conscience and regret." Aubrey meant every word.

Aubrey Elliot, the in-the-background, dutiful assistant to Colonel Streeter. Every day confidential memos and top-secret information littered her desk. Her computer provided unlimited access to intel wanted by our enemies.

I kept stalling. "One hired gun told me Badger wanted me alive. The last guy wanted to kill me. Are you going to take me somewhere, maybe let me talk to your boss?"

"No. Badger flip-flops on what he wants. He's so overcome with grief at losing his only son; he's not exactly stable. I mean, he came up with the red X photo idea thinking you would panic and make a mistake."

We both understood how absurd Badger's red X photo idea was. Another time, Aubrey might have said, "You? Panic?"

We would have laughed.

But not now.

Aubrey continued. "Those other idiots failed, so I told Badger I wanted double the money upfront. When I add it to what he's already paid me, I'll be substantially well-off. Besides, killing you is so much easier than fulfilling his revenge drama."

"And the rest of the team?"

"That's Badger's problem. I'm one and done, ready to disappear and enjoy my future."

She was going to kill me. I recognized the implacable determination on her face, her formerly soft brown eyes grim with purpose. I would die pretending to be a society girl instead of one of the best covert agents in the world.

"Aubrey, I'm so—" I mumbled.

"What did you say?" She took a step toward me.

Leaping forward, I locked my hand on her pistol.

Aubrey wrenched the weapon back, aimed it at my chest, and fired.

Nothing happened.

"What the—" She stared at the gun.

Her fifteen-shot capacity automatic was familiar to me. I set the safety in a split second. Pulling my knife from my clutch, I shoved Aubrey's gun away with one arm and slashed the edge of my trusty blade across her wrist.

She cried out, blood gushing from the deep wound.

Closing the distance, I swept her legs from underneath her. She crashed to the floor. Driving my stiletto heel into the underside of her forearm, I dropped my knife and wrenched the gun from her hand. Flipping it, I used the butt like a baseball bat full-force against her temple.

She folded into a pile on the carpet.

"And you're another failure, just like the rest," I snarled.

Fury raged in my veins.

She cooperated with a terrorist for personal gain, and people died in the process.

I flipped the gun over and disengaged the safety, pointing the muzzle at her head.

My body shook from the storm of anger erupting within me.

My finger moved toward the trigger.

A hand covered mine.

"Don't, Dav."

It was Warden.

29

He wore a dark, expensive-looking suit with a white shirt and bow tie, a fresh scar cutting across an eyebrow. He removed the gun from my hand before pulling me against him. Neither of us said anything as we leaned into each other, a reunion scenario neither of us had envisioned.

Warden reached into a pocket for his cell phone.

"We need one hostile collected and a cleanup crew, back west entry to the Ladies' League."

He ended the call.

"Agent Wills?" I guessed.

He nodded, pulled some zip ties out of his coat pocket, and secured Aubrey. I doubted anyone else attending the gala carried those.

"He's having a busy night," I said.

"What do you mean?"

"I'll tell you later. What are you doing here?"

"I'll fill you in, but I need to let the agents in the back." Warden left, looking purposeful and dangerous despite his formal attire.

Moving in a fog, I retrieved my knife, grateful it had saved me once again. Picking up my bag, I put the weapon inside, thankful my clutch was dark and wouldn't show stains from my bloody hands. A hysterical laugh escaped me at the thought.

Aubrey Elliot. Memories of us spotting each other in the gym, making snarky remarks behind Luke's back, and enjoying meals after work with the team sped past. I believed her to be an ally, a woman also making her way in a man's world. And she sold us out for money.

Be careful who you trust, Davia. The advice came from my parents, Kyle, and life experience, but it still stung to be betrayed by someone I thought was a friend.

Terrible exhaustion threatened my composure. I wanted Warden to return and for this to be over. The truth was, I was in shock. Warden hadn't asked how I was because the event concluded success-fully, and there was no need for discussion. My mind drifted to Adair and his reaction. He might say, "I'm gob-smacked, Davia. I don't know how you're standing!" Would he wrap me in a blanket, settle me in with a strong cup of tea, and cater to my every need? Would I want that?

Which was better? To be accepted as a warrior or pampered like a princess? Some version of both? Neither?

I focused on Aubrey again. Would I have shot her if Warden hadn't stopped me? Blood oozed from the knife wound and the blow to her head, staining the carpet where she lay unmoving. My heel had punctured her flesh, and a deep purple bruise was forming. I examined everything as if I were viewing the scene through a distant window, and shut down my feelings.

Warden returned with four agents. Two of them lifted Aubrey without a word and carried her out. The other two began cleaning to eliminate the bloodstains.

"We don't need to stand here and supervise," Warden said.

"I need to go to the ladies' room."

His green eyes glinted with humor. "Drinking too much?"

I held up my bloody hands. "Wash your hands after defeating your enemies."

He shook his head at my macabre attempt at humor.

"Where should I meet you?"

"Table four."

"See you there." He strolled off, and I headed for my destination.

Francis Downs was drying her hands when I entered. "Davia! I saw you dancing with Adair Monroe. You're a lucky girl."

"Well, I—"

"He's every woman's fantasy, isn't he?"

"I guess so."

She pointed to the blood on my hands. "What happened?"

"I nicked myself on a broken glass."

"Oh, no! Well, don't let me keep you."

She leaned in for a quick hug and left.

Still aghast at the traitor's identity, I let the warm water run over my hands and checked my reflection. Dampening a tissue, I washed specks of blood from my face. After, I reapplied lipstick and gloss.

As I finished, Beatrice Gibbs entered.

"Davia, the caterer has a problem. Have you seen Lydia McGregor?"

"No, I haven't."

I tried to move past her, but she stood in my path.

"I saw you dancing with that detective. Why were the Stentons arrested?"

"Don't you know?"

"I don't."

"Me either."

I went out, leaving her alone with her questions. Perhaps the Stentons would give her up if she were involved. If there was information to be had, Detective Montoya was the man to extract a full confession.

When I drew near the main room, Warden sat in Lydia's chair, and I almost lost control again.

On seeing me, Warden stood. "Would you like to dance?"

Before I could answer, Adair pushed past people, face creased with worry.

"Davia! Where did you go?"

He paused when he noticed Warden.

"Have we met?" Adair asked.

"No." Warden's reply was steely.

The two men appraised each other.

Would the wonders of this night ever cease?

"Adair, this is James Warden, he's my—"

"Boyfriend," Warden finished, the word firm and final.

Co-worker! I was about to say, co-worker!

Adair's posture stiffened.

"You never said you were involved with someone."

"You never said?" Warden glowered at me.

"Life's been rather, uh, complicated." The most over-used word of my life sounded lame, even to my ears.

"I can't wait to hear what you've been doing," Warden spoke with caution, his face a mask.

"I'll let you tell him." Adair backed away, reading the tension, a mixture of disappointment and hope on his face.

I rounded on Warden when Adair was out of earshot. "*Boyfriend*?"

He ignored my question.

"Who was that guy? What are you doing hanging out with a Brit?"

"You're not my boyfriend!"

"Only because of the circumstances," Warden replied.

Adair crossed the room, took his mother's hand, and she rose to dance with her son.

Warden followed my eyes.

"Is he important to you?"

Not having any idea how to answer, I said, "Since I left the team, my life's been both complex and confusing."

"Do you want to be with him?"

"I don't know anything anymore." The words came out in a bitter rush.

Warden took my hand in his. His face turned toward mine, eyes filled with understanding. "Why don't we go somewhere and talk?"

"That's a great idea." Closing the chapter on the gala and all the night's surprises was a welcome thought. "Did you rent a car?"

"No, I flew in and had one of Agent Will's men drive me here. I learned someone might attempt to take you out tonight, intel from Kilburn."

"Is the person he got the info from still alive?"

"What do you think?"

"Well, you were too late. Let's go to my place," I said. "We can catch up there."

We left, with women checking out Warden as we passed.

"What did you mean by too late?" Warden asked as we walked toward my car.

"Aubrey was the *second* attacker."

"You got a twofer? Good job."

Yes, the men in my two worlds were dramatically different.

"Would you like to drive a Maserati?"

Warden's face lit up like a little boy getting a new bicycle. "You own one?"

"Yes."

"Cool."

I pressed the key into his hand. He slipped it in his pocket and retook my hand, his grip firm and reassuring. The night sky was dark, cloud cover masking the moonlight. My car sat backed into a spot at the end of the lot.

A limo blocked our exit.

"We need to ask the chauffeur to move," I said.

We approached the driver's side, and Warden gave a polite tap on the glass.

The tinted window rolled down, revealing a man pointing an automatic rifle at us. He backed us up as he got out.

"Drop the clutch," he told me. He then instructed Warden to remove the gun in his shoulder holster, put it on the ground, and slide it under the car. After Warden complied, the man had him lift his pant legs and did a pat down to ensure he didn't have a secondary weapon.

"Get in." He directed us toward the open rear door.

We shuffled into the back bench seat opposite the car's sole inhabitant.

Inside the lush interior was Rashid Khadem.

30

"Hello," he said in a resonant voice tinged with venom, an automatic handgun trained on us. The driver stood outside the now-closed door, ready to kill us if we escaped.

My instincts had been right. Here was another Badger affiliate, but he moved freely in the same circles as me.

"Who are you?" Warden's voice was commanding despite the circumstances. He sat hunched forward, ready to pounce.

Rashid's eyes crinkled with amusement. "I thought your team was the best, James Warden."

Warden didn't rise to the bait.

How foolish was Rashid to think he had a chance alone against two trained agents?

Kyle: Let's talk about close-quarters combat. What should you do first?

Me: Keep a survival mindset.

Kyle: How?

Me: Stay frosty and figure out how to remain alive.

The limo door opened once more, and Nabil Nasser slid in next to Rashid. He faced me, a languid smile on his face.

"Hello, Miss Glenn. Lovely to see you again." His hand touched a button on the center console, and an automatic pistol appeared. He picked it up with casual ease, pointing the barrel at me. "You remember my uncle, Rashid," he continued like we were in a polite social situation.

His *uncle*? My mind raced, focusing on Rashid's deferential body language.

How had I missed it? The out-of-context settings? The drugs?

I suddenly saw Nabil for who he truly was— Badger. Now aware, I noticed that a deft hand had shaved years off Nabil/Badger's face, but the height, build, and underlying malevolence lingered.

"Plastic surgery, huh?" I said.

Badger's lips pressed flat like I had blurted out what was inside a wrapped present and ruined the surprise.

"In retrospect, I should have figured you were Badger sooner," I commented for Warden's benefit. He gave a slight start upon hearing this, but I only noticed because he was so close to me. He was now aware of who this was and that our chances of surviving were dwindling. His body coiled with tension, ready to explode.

"Badger? So that's my code name, I suppose? I like it. Badgers are hard to kill."

"Unlike your son," Warden said.

Badger's face became cold. "I was told it was either you or Ms. Glenn who made the killing shot."

"We didn't know," I said.

"Don't you think you *should* know who you destroy? These are real people's lives you're affecting, people with families who love them. But, no matter. Ever since, I've worked to make everyone on that mission pay."

"Yes," I replied. "We kept being reminded every time a cut-rate punk showed up and tried to kill us. Whoever's in charge of your hire-a-bad-guy department needs to be fired."

Would my words goad him into a mistake?

Instead, he did the unexpected.

He smiled.

Aubrey's words: He's not exactly stable.

Determined to provoke a response, I said, "Even though you knew where we would be on our last mission, you failed. This has been one long march toward your downfall."

"Has it?" He remained magnanimous. "You two are here, now. The prize members of your supposedly infallible team. You can't call that a victory."

Beside him, Rashid was quiet and unmoving. He wore the stony look of an experienced killer. While I tossed barbs at his nephew, not a flicker of emotion crossed his face.

"So, what's been your deal?" I said. "Schmoozing up to Adair Monroe, hanging out at his parties—"

"Rashid or I could have killed you there, of course," Badger interrupted. "But I enjoyed delaying your death, watching you try to function after the German injected you with the drug I provided."

"Even with the drug in my system, you wouldn't have won."

"You think?" He remained smug. "I knew if I waited long enough, your man Warden here would show up, and tonight I have you both where I want."

"Maybe, but let's circle back to your ironic lecture about how we should know the people whose lives we destroy. Whose lives do *you* destroy? You take small children from poor parents and sell them to be sex slaves. I highly doubt their fate has ever given you pause."

Badger maintained his nonchalant attitude, waving off my words with a *Who cares?* gesture.

I went on. "Okay. Perhaps dealing with *adults* isn't your skillset, which is why you pick on kids."

"Ms. Glenn, I run a global network." His words were tight and controlled. "My clients are well-placed, influential people. I'm afraid you're not aware of the extent of my reach."

"Despite your reach, we were able to kill your son," Warden said. "I guess you didn't tell him how you make money could be perilous for him."

Badger smiled again, but this time, he bared his teeth like a wolf spying its prey. "You don't know anything about my son."

"I do, actually," I replied. "He saw a group of highly-trained operatives on a joint mission with equally deadly operators, and was such a numbskull he got in our way."

When Badger spoke, his voice was almost a whisper. "Stop talking."

"Or what? Will you shoot us at one of the most noteworthy events in Rancho Suprema? Your goons don't have suppressors, so, yeah, that won't attract attention or anything," I said.

The sarcastic remark lingered.

Badger's eyes shifted from me to Rashid. He gave a quick lift of his chin. Rashid's hand went to the limo door, opening it a crack. He bent forward to communicate something to the driver outside.

In an instant, I launched forward and threw out my left arm. A jab grazed Badger's throat at the same time my right hand circled his wrist and pushed the gun up.

Warden's reach was superior. His right hand was on Rashid's weapon while his left landed a blow to his head.

Badger kicked out and connected, throwing me backward. I retained my firm hold on his gun arm, pulling down and twisting as I fell. His body came forward, and I stomped his foot with a heel.

He screamed a wild, primal sound.

The momentum of falling to the floor brought Badger on top of me. His weight pressed me against the lower seat with limited ability to move.

Next to us, there was a blur of activity; elbows, headbutts, strikes, and counter-strikes.

A rush of air.

The front door of the limo opened. The driver got in and pointed his gun through the window divider. He couldn't pull the trigger on the moving, flailing, fighting bodies without possibly shooting his boss.

Warden threw Rashid out the side door, continuing their fight on the blacktop.

It was an advantage to remain beneath Badger now to keep from being a target. He struggled against me, fighting to take a shot. His finger moved for the trigger, and I threw his hand up.

Bang!

The driver fell, lying halfway through the window. The assault rifle fell from his lifeless hands, landing on the seat.

"No!" Badger shouted as blood spilled from the driver's head.

I rolled us over and slammed Badger's gun arm against the door frame. Outside, I glimpsed Warden and his opponent. Warden's belt was off, and he whipped it across Rashid's startled face.

The death of the driver reenergized Badger. He slammed me in the stomach with an elbow, did a quick roll, and was back astride me. He abandoned his gun and wrapped his hands around my throat. My dress and the tight space trapped my arms and legs.

Badger threw his weight and rage into his task, cutting off my oxygen supply. I choked, twisting and writhing to escape, but nothing worked. In a last-ditch effort, I ducked my chin, attempting to squeak a bit of air past his fevered hold.

"You. Killed. My. Son." Badger accompanied every word with a savage squeeze to my windpipe.

Tiny lights sparkled across the limo's ceiling, and the interior started to revolve. My chest grew tight, and I became dizzier and dizzier. Soft whimpers emanated from my throat as my surroundings darkened.

Time was about to run out.

Kyle's voice surfaced, repeating a favorite saying.

Kill first, die last.

I scrabbled to find some purchase and strained to lift my hips as Badger's features faded like a closing shot at the end of a movie.

The slight position change allowed for an infinitesimal amount of space between me and the seat. Yanking my right arm free, I drove my thumb into his left eye.

Badger's bellow of pain was so deafening, the men fighting outside paused. His hands flew to his mangled face.

I sucked in air, coughing from the effort. Badger's body contorted, and he continued to shriek in agony.

Extricating myself, I seized Badger by the front of his shirt and shoved him out of the limo. He fell to the ground but got to his feet, one hand clutching his injured eye. I picked up the abandoned rifle and followed.

Warden had Rashid backed against the limo, an arm locked around his neck. He slammed the man's head into the side of the car repeatedly. Rashid had dropped his gun at some point, and I recovered it from the pavement where it lay. Holding a weapon in each hand like Annie Oakley, I tossed Rashid's gun to Warden, and he caught it like a star football player. Warden put the gun barrel tight against his foe's head, and Rashid's hands went up.

"You good?" Warden asked me, breathing hard.

"Yes, but if my dress got ripped, I'll be so upset."

Warden grinned.

I moved to Badger.

"On the ground." I pushed his shoulders.

He went to his knees.

"You are going to pay for this!" he swore, glaring as best he could.

"I don't think so," I said. "But hey, you'll get to rock a villain eye patch from now on."

Warden zip-tied Rashid, whose face was a bruised and bloodied mess, and pushed him down to sit against the limo. He then secured Badger.

Time for another call to Agent Wills.

WE GOT INTO MY CAR, Warden in the driver's seat, knees pinned against his chest. His hand went down to the controls. "You're a shrimp."

"A shrimp who's still ahead of you," I retorted, and we both took a breath. We were disheveled, cut, and bruised but feeling the euphoria of survival.

The parking lot was closed. Men in suits secured the weapons, piled Badger and Rashid into a dark SUV, and were in the process of moving the limo containing the dead driver to another location. Warden's gun had been recovered and returned to him.

Warden started the Maserati, and I gave him directions. After an agent let us pass, he roared out of the lot.

"Do you think Badger has anyone left to send after us?" I wanted this to be over.

"I don't think there's a trusted number two to take over except maybe his uncle, who we also neutralized. I got the impression Badger was a one-boss show," Warden said as he tested the car's limits.

"Let's hope so. Badger says he's connected, but the only course is to continue our daily situational awareness and wait, I guess."

"All we can do."

"How'd you find me?"

"Your handler kept tabs on your dailies, so I came straight here. I entered through the back of the building, and chance brought me to where you were."

"I think you crossed air paths with Savant and Ned, returning to base with another Badger bozo. The past few days have been like old home week."

"And Aubrey. Did she tell you why she did it?"

"Money."

Warden did a double-take. "What? That's all?"

"America's most notorious double agent spied for Russia for money and diamonds. For twenty-two years, I think."

"Yeah, that was Robert Hanssen, and there was some other guy whose name I'm not coming up with."

"And Aubrey was just a disgruntled government employee who hit the lotto by selling us out. Turn here."

Warden spun the wheel and pulled into my drive. I touched the gate remote, pondering what motivated people to make certain decisions.

Would money cause me to leave my team and stop protecting my country?

Was Aunt Lilah cruel or caring when she left me the inheritance?

Did I want to return to a life of unquestioned orders, surrounded by the types of people who carried them out?

Aunt Lilah filled my life with both money and unanswered questions.

"I can't believe you were at a gala," Warden said, interrupting my thoughts.

"I can't believe it either."

"Well, you were the most beautiful woman there tonight."

Adair said those exact words earlier.

Parking in the garage, Warden stopped me from exiting the car. "Let me open the door for you."

"Are you messing with me?"

"I can be a gentleman." He helped me out and wrapped me in his arms. I nestled into him, allowing myself to relax.

When we stepped apart, Warden kept hold of my shoulders.

"Your neck doesn't look so good." He turned my head gently side to side to survey the damage.

I put a hand up to touch the area and grimaced. "Yeah, well, Badger got the worst of it. You have a cut on your jaw, by the way."

Warden brushed a hand along his face, then surveyed his bloody fingers.

"We're quite the pair to draw to," he said with a sly smile.

"Hodge," I said, noting how the Texan's phrases had insinuated themselves into our lives.

After turning off the alarm system, I unlocked the side door, and we went in. Warden looked around.

"How big is this place?"

"Beyond comprehension-sized. Would you like some coffee?"

Warden's eyebrows raised when he spotted the espresso machine. "Since when do you drink coffee?"

"My interior designer thinks I should be prepared for guests."

"Your designer?"

"Like I said, long story. I'll be right back." Hurrying to my bathroom, I washed up and tended my injuries. My neck was beginning to bruise, so I downed a few aspirin.

Next, I removed Adair's comb from where it somehow remained in my hair and placed it on the counter. Although I still needed to return it to him, the multi-dimensional Adair had also made me reconsider my black-and-white prejudgments of the people of Rancho Suprema. Perhaps Aunt Lilah tried to help my life in her way, and I would choose to let go of some of my anger towards her.

Picking up a washcloth and a first aid kit, I returned to the kitchen. Wetting the cloth under the kitchen sink tap, I dabbed at Warden's cut.

"Will I live?" he asked.

I applied some antibiotic ointment.

"It's a long way from your heart. I think you'll be fine."

His suit was a mess; his jacket ripped at an elbow, dirt down the side of a pant leg. The destruction didn't matter. Being this close to his much-missed face filled me with contentment.

"What about the guy at the gala? What's the deal?" Warden folded his arms across his chest.

How could I explain Adair?

"He's been supportive and kind to me since we met."

Warden mulled this over, gaze unfocused. He often wore the same expression when tackling a complex issue.

"This is my fault," he said. "After you left, I didn't know what to do. I wanted to give you space and time to decide if getting out might suit you better, although not calling you was difficult."

"Is that why you didn't contact me, except the one time?"

"Yes." His face was troubled. "I missed you every minute of every day. After I got here and saw you fitting right in at the ball in your gown, with a guy obviously in love with you—"

"He's not in love with me," I corrected. "I'm just a change of pace."

"I'm not sure I agree with that, but it doesn't matter. How do you feel about him?"

"Adair's a lot of fun, has a good heart, and is likely to become cannon fodder if my life continues its current course. He treats me like I'm normal."

"Like a woman who doesn't have uncommon skills?"

"Yes."

Warden considered this. "Is living here better for you?"

"Aren't there times in your life you wish you didn't make all the decisions? Didn't have to pretend you were always fine?"

"Of course, but our jobs don't allow us that luxury, as you're aware. If you stay here, you might be able to step back, relax, and live a peaceful existence. Is this new path what you want?"

"I missed you and the team and what we do."

"I hope you missed me a bit more than the rest of the guys." He brought me close to him.

"I did miss you. So much," I said.

Warden's eyes became a deeper green, and he placed a soft kiss on my forehead.

"Honestly, I don't see things working with the other guy, Bombshell." He used my nickname in playful tones. "He doubtless wants to put you in bubble wrap and place you with the breakables. After the novelty wears off, you'll be pulling your hair out—and his!"

I smiled up at him. "You're probably right."

"Let's talk about things more in the morning." He pulled me even closer. "I like your dress, but I'd like it better if it were on the floor."

My thoughts went back to our first kiss forever ago. Now, when our lips met, we channeled an even higher level of desire than our last embrace before I left the team.

"Let's go somewhere more comfortable." I took Warden's hand, starting toward the room with the faux fur blanket. My cell phone vibrated from inside the clutch I abandoned on the kitchen island, stopping me.

I went back.

"Hello?" My voice was terse despite knowing who it would be.

"Glenn?"

"Yes, Sir."

Colonel Streeter. I put him on speaker.

Warden, his back against the door frame, listened.

"There was another incident?" Streeter asked.

"Yes, Sir."

"One of our own?"

"Yes, Sir."

"Neutralized?"

"Yes, Sir."

A pause.

"And Badger?"

"On his way to you, Sir, along with his uncle and another hired gun."

I imagined Colonel Streeter pumping his fist in the air and doing a victory dance in his office. Colonel Streeter wouldn't, but I was sure Mean Streets would.

"Is Warden there?"

"Yes, Sir."

And he's kissing me along my bodice.

"I'll expect your report at 1200 hours tomorrow."

"Wouldn't 1700 work?"

A chuckle.

"1700 is fine." He hung up.

"His timing is off," Warden said.

"Really? I think his timing's perfect. He contacted his two best agents before—"

"Before what?"

My face suffused with red, sudden shyness overtaking me. Warden lifted me into his arms. "Where were we headed a minute ago?"

"Second door on the left."

He carried me down the hall.

"Is this your bedroom?"

"No, but I thought of you lying on that blanket." I indicated the chocolate throw on the bed.

"I'm glad I'm not the only one imagining things." Warden set me down.

"And what did you imagine?"

"Well, I didn't realize you'd look like this, so reality turned out to be much better than any of my fantasies."

He unzipped my gown, slipped his hands inside, and pushed it to the floor. He inhaled.

"You have some new lingerie?" His voice was rough.

I almost smacked him, but the appreciation on his face stopped me.

"Did you keep a running inventory of my undergarments?" I moved closer, placing a hand near his thigh. He swallowed.

"I'm a man, and you're a knock-out. What did you expect?" He began to tug off his coat.

I stopped him.

"Undressing you is one of my goals. You wore clothes during our last romantic encounter, and I didn't like being at such a disadvantage."

After running kisses along the uninjured side of his jaw, I undid his bow tie and removed his jacket, tossing them both to the floor. As I unfastened a shirt button, I bent to let my lips linger on his skin, reveling in the feel against my mouth. Once his shirt was open, I ran my hands across his muscular chest, abs, and lower. Warden's breathing became ragged.

Undressing him took some time, but neither of us cared. We were alone at last with no chance of being interrupted.

I teased off a bra strap while Warden undid the clasp, and I let it drop. He tucked his thumbs on both sides of my hips and pushed down my much-admired underwear. Stepping out of them, I paused. My mind went back to the first time I saw Warden naked.

"Not going to turn around?" Warden teased.

"Never again."

We allowed ourselves time to check out every part of each other, bruises, scars, and all.

He reached for me, and I put my arms around his neck. We enjoyed some prolonged kisses, savoring the taste of each other. Impatience and desire burned white-hot within me as his hands caressed my body.

Warden brushed his lips against my ear and whispered, "Ready?"

Not waiting for an answer, he lifted me onto the bed, his mouth moving to my breasts and his hand running lightly up my inner thigh. Not wanting further delay, I pulled Warden up and into a deep kiss, and guided every glorious inch of him inside me.

"God, Davia," he groaned against my mouth. I ran my hands through his hair then gripped the base of his neck to deepen our kiss. Every stroke amplified our pleasure, fired by years of secret desire we could now fully express. The day's tumultuous events were driven away by the weight of Warden's body atop me and the sheer joy of being buried deep in each other.

Sometime later, much later, I snuggled against Warden's chest with one of my legs thrown over his. I thought about everything I'd been through since learning about the inheritance and the new perspective my time in Rancho Suprema had given me. Tomorrow I would tell him about the will's requirements and my adventures, but that could wait.

For now, I was where I wanted to be.

"How long are you staying?" I trailed a finger down his chest.

Warden raised himself on one arm.

"I don't know. How many rooms do you have?"

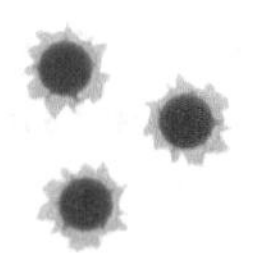

ACKNOWLEDGMENTS
(CONTAINS SPOILERS)

This book came out of a tense time in my life. A person I convicted as a prosecutor made death threats against me and was being released from prison.

To prepare, I worked with a trainer, Craig W., who was a former CIA operative. At the time, I lived in a pricey zip code and attended dressy social functions. While at events, I would get calls from Craig saying, "Tomorrow we learn counter-surveillance." Or sniper rifles. Or knife fighting. The list goes on. The incongruity made me smile, and I had to figure out how to mix up these two disparate worlds.

During the writing process, I received invaluable input from experts. Thanks to Warren, JB, Lou, Jim, and John, my badass buddies who helped me with technical knowledge and brought some of my characters and scenes to life. Thanks to Dr. Gerardo Garcia, Head of the Herpetology Department for the Chester Zoo, for advice on Golden Dart frogs.

Special thanks to Glenna Bloeman for her encouragement and guidance, Cherie Foxley for the cover art (Visit her at www.cheriefox.com), Robert Yehling and Karen McKellar for developmental editing, and Blissfull Studios for line editing. Thank you to all the beta readers, with a special shout-out to Brianna, Betty, Pam, Shannon, and Tammy.

Finally, to my parents, thanks for everything. I know you're cheering me on from the next world.

**Now that you've finished *Dior or Die*,
it would mean the world to me if you left
<u>AN HONEST REVIEW</u>
at Goodreads and/or Amazon**

Link to Amazon Review

Link to Goodreads Review

Questions to Assist with a Book Review

- Give potential readers a quick summary & note spoilers.
- How did this book make you feel?
- Did it evoke any strong emotions?
- Were there any plot twists you didn't see coming?
- Was it a page turner or a hard slog?
- Did you have a favorite character or characters?
- Who were they and why did you like them?
- Did the setting(s) help move the mood/plot forward?
- Were there any memorable scenes that stood out for you?
- Were the characters believable?
- Were you satisfied with the ending? Frustrated? Did you want more?
- This book is a must read for readers who like _____(type of book or character(s).

Questions for Book Clubs

- What did you like best about this book?
- What did you like the least?
- What characters did you like the best? The least?
- If you were making a movie of this book, who would you cast?
- What is a favorite quote from the book?
- What feelings did this book evoke for you?
- If you inherited money with the same conditions, what would you do?
- Which character would you like to meet? Why?
- If you could hear this story from another character's point of view, who would you choose?
- Did this book seem realistic?
- Were the characters believable? Did they remind you of anyone?

- If you wrote fanfic about this book, what kind of story would you tell?
- Who would you choose if you were Davia? Warden or Adair? Both? Neither?
- If you could ask the author one question, what would it be?
- What songs did this book make you think of?
- What would you like to learn about in future books?

Link to Downloadable PDF Questions for Book Clubs

Find out more about the upcoming Davia Glenn Book Two

Killing With Kindness"
at
https://www.lauraakers.com

Sign up for giveaways, read my blog,
& be the first to hear about other book news
Questions? Comments? Sheer boredom?
Email me directly at Laura@LauraAkers.com
I will get back to you!

Follow me on Social Media:
Twitter: @LauraAkers
Facebook: @LauraAkersAuthor
Instagram: @TheLauraAkers
TikTok: @thelauraakers
Clubhouse: @lauraakers
Goodreads: Laura Akers

ABOUT THE AUTHOR

Laura E. Akers is a former prosecuting attorney who handled high-profile murder, rape, domestic violence, and gang trials.
She is a Distinguished Toastmaster (DTM) and enjoys public speaking and providing workshops on self-confidence, likability, and jury selection.
Her interests include photography, Korean dramas, and spending time with her cats.

KILLING WITH KINDNESS
BY LAURA E. AKERS

Read on for the riveting first chapter of
Book Two in the Davia Glenn series
Releasing soon on Amazon and through
other booksellers worldwide.

CHAPTER ONE

It's zero-dark-thirty.

A heavy blanket covers the only door to a mud and brick house containing the two hostages we plan to rescue. Outside, we move seamlessly into position. We wait for James Warden, our team leader, to signal us to enter, engage the enemy, and hit our areas of responsibility.

The six of us are the most elite paramilitary team in existence, and I'm the only woman ever allowed. We wear tactical gear and night-vision goggles. In our hands are sub-machine guns.

Where's my weapon? Frantic, I drop to my knees to search beneath a shrub.

My teammates enter the building.

"Wait for me!" I chase after them.

Inside, our commander, Colonel Streeter, stands above the bullet-ridden bodies of the hostages. We take seats at tables that appear. Streeter points to a screen projecting photos of the hostages when they lived. They're in their thirties with friendly, open faces. He says, "They were captives of ISIS-K and did humanitarian work."

Seventy percent of rescues fail.

Our training leaves no time for regret. Lifting the dead, we hustle back out and down a ravine toward a valley where we will airlift out.

Warden and I are on point with Ned and Hodge carrying the hostages' bodies. K and Savant bring up the rear.

The familiar gray of a military helicopter speeds towards us as a thunderous hiss echoes. A rocket-propelled grenade whizzes past.

An explosion.

Smoke and fire engulf our extraction craft, and it plummets.

In an instant, hostiles surround us from the hills above, and bullets from their automatic weapons pepper the ground.

We drop to return fire. My missing gun materializes in my hands, and I aim and pull its trigger. The relentless, noisy barrage from both sides is as familiar as music.

Our daily target practice pays off as our attackers begin to fall.

We move toward where the twisted metal of the helicopter burns, eradicating any enemy survivors as we go. At last, the only sounds left are footfalls, ammunition clips jangling, and grunts as we work to extract the grim remains of the pilots from the wreckage.

"They're sending another bird, four clicks out," Warden's voice says in my earpiece.

Renewing our trek, I spot a group of militants in robes below us in a valley. Their leader is a woman dressed in an expensive black pantsuit and high heels paired with glistening gold earrings, moving like she's on a catwalk and not an unpaved road.

Why is she wearing that outfit in Afghanistan?

"Warden, there's a group of hostiles on that goat trail at 3 o'clock, and—"

An IED detonates.

The blast hits us, launching us skyward before we crash to the ground.

I lie dazed and disoriented, a haze of dust and smoke obscuring my view. Coughing, I force myself into a seated position. Warden is a few feet away, and I crawl to his side as dark liquid pours from his mouth.

"Warden!" I place my hands on his broad chest. Warm blood pours over them.

His eyes open, anger suffuses his face, and a feral growl emanates from deep in his throat.

"Davia, what are you doing here? You're not a part of this unit anymore."

My brow knits in confusion.

"What do you mean? This team is my life, my everything!"

The other men struggle to raise their bodies, pressing towards me with bloody wounds and missing limbs.

They're gravely injured, and I need to get them help.

"Yes, Davia. Why are you here?" they chant.

"I don't understand."

The group nears, reaching for me and I scrabble backward, tearing open the palms of my hands on the rock-strewn road.

The scene vanishes as I bolt upright.

My hands clutch luxurious silken sheets.

Bewildered, it takes a full minute of gazing blankly at my surroundings to realize I'm alone in bed in my 6,500 square foot home in the exclusive community of Rancho Suprema, California.

I gulp deep lungfuls of air to slow my hammering pulse.

It's just a dream, Davia. Just a dream. You got those hostages out alive, and no one got hurt or died.

Holding my queasy stomach, I throw back the covers and stumble to the bathroom, where I wet a washcloth to wipe my face and arms. The mirror reflects my colorless features and tangled mess of long, blonde hair. Pulling off my sweat-soaked t-shirt, I leave it on the counter and retrieve a clean replacement. After dressing, I run a wet brush through my disordered locks.

I'm alone to face both the aftermath of my days as an operative and the guilt for taking a year's leave of absence from my team.

If that convoluted flashback had occurred the night before, I would have sought comfort by waking Warden and cuddling into his solid form. Now, he's returned to Virginia and gone on a mission.

Still trying to make sense of the dream, I will myself to stop shaking.

It's after two a.m.

Get it together, Davia.

Unable to sleep, I retreat to the backyard and throw myself down on a padded chair by the pool. Pulling my knees up and hugging them close, I wish Warden were still here. During his ten-day visit, he made sure every room of my home held fond memories of him.

"I can't believe we waited three years for this to become a reality," *Warden said, rolling off me to catch his breath. He reached out a muscular* *arm to pull me tight against him.*

"World-record foreplay," I told him, prompting a deep chuckle.

Warden leaned over to kiss me, his green eyes dark.

"I can think of a few more world records I'd like to break," he said, voice *husky.*

"I'm up for it if you are." I reached for him.

Missing Warden brings up pain almost as incapacitating as my nightmare, and I force thoughts back to the present.

My property has spectacular daytime views, situated as it is on the crest of a valley. Tonight, clouds obscure the moon, and blackness shrouds the distant homes. All is quiet.

A series of quick flashes light a window in a house across from mine.

I stiffen and strain for a better view, but all is as dark and still as it was a moment before.

What did I see?

Playing back the images, I imagine calling 911.

Operator: 911. What's your emergency?

This is Davia Glenn. I want to report some flashes of light at a house *near mine, address unknown.*

Operator: Did you hear anything?

No.

Operator: It's probably someone watching TV or taking pictures.

Unless I disclose my secret past and how I can recognize suppressed gunfire, they'll conclude I'm a nutjob and lecture me about wasting their time.

If I'm honest, *I'm* not even one hundred percent sure what I saw.

Fighting off indecision, I race to the bedroom to pull on clothes.

Grabbing my .45, I hurry to the garage, fire up my Maserati, and speed to the road opposite my house. Security lights highlight my property to allow a quick read on position, and I count driveways until I'm at the correct address.

Do I miss a life of action so much I manufacture events?

Heavy iron entry gates stand open, revealing a cobblestone drive with elegant pathway lights marking its edges.

I hesitate, unsure what to do.

Just take a quick look around. If everything seems okay, I can leave.

As I begin to turn into the drive, a car with no lights races straight at me from out of the darkness, and I swerve. My headlights play through the cab and illuminate the driver's vague profile for an instant before a eucalyptus tree looms in my path. I slam on the brakes and bail out, gun in hand.

The vehicle screeches around a corner and is gone.

I crouch next to my car and listen, but chirping crickets are the only sound. Across an expansive lawn, flat stones decorate the one-story exterior of the unlit house.

Its front door stands wide open.

Okay, that's *not* normal.

With my mobile set to private, I call to report suspicious activity at the address displayed on one of the gate pillars and disconnect without giving my name. I set my internal clock to five minutes, planning to be gone before the police arrive.

Refusing to become a target by entering through the front, I run to the side of the residence. The backyard is fenced, but the gate I come to isn't locked. Ducking down, I open it and wait.

One-two-three.

When nothing happens, I slip through and scan my surroundings for any movement. Making my way past the still waters of an L-shaped pool with teak furniture and standing umbrellas at its edges, I come to a door. It opens with a slight click.

Now or never.

Keeping low, I enter. I dart through a laundry room and into the kitchen. Dim recessed lighting reflects on picture frames displayed on a counter. The photos feature a family of four, a couple with two children.

If the family is okay, I hope I don't get mistaken for a burglar.

I listen once more. A grandfather clock ticks steadily, its sound magnified in the stillness.

Tip-toeing out of the kitchen, I walk across a sizable living room with cathedral ceilings, around a grand piano, and towards a hall. The home holds expensive furnishings, with artwork and mirrors hung in strategic places. Praying my shoes won't squeak on the hallway's polished wood floors, I go toward the side facing my house.

The first open door reveals a bedroom filled with stuffed animals, a young girl's domain. No one is in the pink and white canopied bed, but the covers are disturbed.

The next bedroom has posters on the walls of sports teams, a scantily clad starlet, and a college pennant. A chair before a desk with a powered-on laptop lies on its back as if someone rushed away.

Ahead are two double doors, one open a crack.

I stay low and in the shadows.

What am I doing here again?

A faint, agonized cry emanates from the room and breaks the silence.

Crud.

How do I go in and not get shot?

Creeping to the door, I give it a slight push.

The scene widens, and a wall nightlight provides some visibility.

An adult lies at the foot of a bed surrounded by a dark pool of what is sure to be blood. Its familiar, coppery scent mixes with the lingering, acrid odor of gunfire.

Without hesitating, I enter, sweeping my weapon to check every visible point. Slamming myself against a wall, I peek around corners to assess the closet and bathroom.

Whoever did this is gone.

The prone body is a woman wearing a nightgown soaked with blood. Did I hear her dying gasp? She has three closely grouped bullet wounds to her upper torso. I bend to see if she's alive. Her body is still warm, but there's no pulse.

The hostage bodies of my dream merge with this ghastly scene before me, as if an endless nightmare has me in its grasp.

Sirens wail in the distance, and I refocus to calculate if there's time to get out and back to my car before someone arrives. To hell with any CSI concerns. I need to hustle.

As I'm about to exit the room, a whimper from the opposite side of the bed stops me.

Damn it.

I can't check the sound's source and get clear.

Unwilling to leave someone who might need help, I approach with my gun raised and look around the bed's corner. A dark-haired young man shelters a female child on the floor. His bloody torso covers her still form. Putting fingers to his neck, I conclude he's dead. Lifting him aside, I murmur, "I'm sorry. So, so sorry."

I place my ear close to the girl's mouth and hear shallow, stuttering breaths.

Taking out my cell phone, I redial 911.

"You're going to need an ambulance at 2645 Camino del Sol," I say. "A little girl has been shot, and two others are dead."

"What's your name?" the operator asks.

I inhale.

"This is Davia Glenn."